SOCCER
SKILLS
AND DRILLS

SOCCER SKILLS AND DRILLS

REVISED AND UPDATED

Gary Rosenthal

A FIRESIDE BOOK
Published by Simon & Schuster
New York London Toronto Sydney Tokyo Singapore

To Pat

FIRESIDE
Rockefeller Center
1230 Avenue of the Americas
New York, NY 10020

FIRESIDE and colophon are
registered trademarks of
Simon & Schuster Inc.

Library of Congress Cataloging-in-Publication Data
Rosenthal, Gary.
    Soccer skills and drills / Gary Rosenthal.—Rev. and updated.
        p.   cm.
    Includes index.
    ISBN 0-02-036435-0
    1. Soccer.   2. Soccer—Coaching.   I. Title.
    GV943.R663   1994   93-32462   CIP
        796.334'2—dc20

First Fireside Edition 1994

10 9 8 7 6 5 4 3 2 1

All photos by Bob Rose unless otherwise indicated.
Line drawings by Jim Thut.

Manufactured in the United States of America

Acknowledgments

Writing this kind of book is similar to coaching a winning soccer team. Both require the contributions of talent, skill, and common purpose of many people in order to achieve the desired results.

As a coach, I enjoyed success because the players on my teams gave so much of themselves in terms of skills, talent, intelligence, and the desire to win. Many, some of whom have gone on to coach at all levels—high school, college, and professional—taught me so much about the sport we all love. I thank all of my former players for their great contribution to their coach's soccer education.

Similarly, this completed book is the result of the generous contributions made by friends, colleagues, and organizations. I acknowledge them and thank them for their friendship, support, and contributions to the preparation of *Soccer Skills and Drills*.

My sincere appreciation goes to:

Hamilton Cain, my editor at Collier Books, for his enthusiastic support and creative guidance in preparing this book;

Bob Rose, my creative and talented friend, who freely gave his time and expertise to producing the excellent photographs of soccer skills;

Claire Colligan, Steve Mongelsing, Alan Rosenthal, and Ira Rosenthal, all of whom patiently endured hours of twisted positions in order to depict soccer skills for Bob Rose's camera;

Professors Brenda Bass and Ira Weiss, Chairperson of the Department of Health and Physical Education and Director of Athletics, respectively, at New York City Technical College of The City University of New York for their advice and support;

Dr. Lauren K. Gorman, M.D., for her professional talents and skills, which enabled me to understand the way "the real important game" should be played;

And, finally, to all my family and friends who, by just being themselves, made this project so much easier to do.

Contents

Contents

6   TACTICS AND SYSTEMS OF PLAY   135

Contents

HISTORY

IN THE BEGINNING

The elements of present-day soccer lie deeply rooted in antiquity. Nearly everyone, when speaking or hearing of soccer's origins, delights in the well-worn tale of ancient barbarians who allegedly contributed to the founding of the game by kicking around the skulls of their fallen adversaries.

There are drawings, paintings, and long descriptions of the Chinese playing a game that involved the kicking of round balls thousands of years before the birth of Christ. The Japanese, in their histories and art of ancient times, tell of ball-kicking games played on special holidays. These games are described as having rudimentary goals constructed of gaily colored ribbons and cloth. The Japanese acknowledge that the basis of these games was brought to Japan by the enterprising and far-ranging merchants and traders of China.

The Tarahumara Indians of Mexico play another type of ball-kicking game today that has been passed on from their earlier days to the present. The American Hopi Indians play yet another version of a ball-kicking game that has come from earlier generations. It is unlikely that the legendary Chinese traders visited the Tarahumara or Hopi Indians, but a kicking game with common elements existed in such isolated areas of the world.

For centuries, the Italians have played a game called "calcio," a rough-and-tumble sport in which large mobs of participants vigorously kick a ball (and one another) in pursuit of scoring goals. To this day, this spectacle in all its color, pageantry, and violence can be seen in Florence, in the Piazza della Signoria, on the feast day of Saint John the Baptist.

English history is replete with chronicles, art, histories, and even laws promulgated by kings and queens to control the rudimentary form of soccer that was played for one thousand years in Britain. It is from this point that soccer as we know it today evolved and that we can explore the factors contributing to its evolution.

It is important, however, to understand that the kicking games played in such diverse civilizations and countries are not the forerunners of modern soccer. While these games did contain elements of soccer, such as running, kicking a ball, and, in some cases, even rudimentary goals, they were games played for entertainment and simply on occasion. To indulge in all sorts of speculation as to which ancient civilization, through its kicking games, invented soccer, really takes our eye off the ball, which is as dangerous in searching for sources as it is in actually playing a soccer match.

ENGLISH ROOTS

Clearly, modern soccer is a sport that was devised by the British, refined by Scottish players and coaches, and began to take a form recognizable to us in the England of the 1860s. For nearly a thousand years before 1860, an undeveloped and unstructured game containing the rudiments of present-day soccer was played in England. Rudimentary soccer in the 1100s was a village affair—played within villages, between villages, and in the forests, fields, and countryside between villages. Often as many as five hundred men and boys on a side representing their village participated in a game. And the boundaries? Whatever distances were agreed on between participants. The goal lines could be one end of the village to the other, when the game was played within the village, or from village boundary line to village boundary line, when it was played between villages.

With as many as five hundred participants to a side, one ball, streets, alleys, and all sorts of structures on the playing area, and no rules governing play, one can imagine the damage done to players, property, and innocent bystanders.

From histories of these games, we learn that the most famous annual event was the Shrove Tuesday games, first played by London schoolboys in 1175. The Shrove Tuesday games were played for many years with violence, destruction, and blood marking the event.

The havoc created by the game led King Edward II, in 1314, to end Shrove Tuesday football by issuing a proclamation that said: ''Forasmuch as there is great noise in the city caused by hustling over large balls, from which many evils may arise, which God forbid, we command and forbid on behalf of the

King, on pain of imprisonment, such game to be used in the city in the future."

Richard II further objected to the game in 1389. Obviously Edward II's edict had not stopped the playing even with the threat of "pain of imprisonment." Richard's objection, however, was that playing football interfered with archery practice, which, given the state of weaponry at the time, was more important for maintaining his position than was the destructive game of football. Henry IV and Henry VIII reaffirmed Richard's law in the 1400s, which shows us that even so bloody an activity could capture the spirit of so many, causing men to turn away from or pay less attention to such vital matters as civil defense and the wishes of their rulers.

In the 1500s, the game was still being played, and in the same violent manner. In 1572, Elizabeth I banned football in London, while lords and writers of these times rallied to the queen's side against the playing of the game. The writers of Elizabeth's time give us a marvelous insight into the game. In these histories we find the words "bloody," "violence," and "fighting" and general rejection of the game as a recreational activity or pastime.

What rules there were in these early games were strictly local ones that made for all sorts of variation in play. The actual playing area could be of any size. Goals could be a town boundary line or a local landmark. Techniques of advancing the ball varied. While kicking was the generally accepted method, the hands were often used to carry or propel the ball. The length of play also varied, with some games lasting for as long as four hours. A defensive technique was aimed at mugging the player in possession of the ball and was the first technique learned.

From all evidence, the ball was actually pretty close to the one we use today. Rather than the rubber bladder of later times, an animal bladder was inflated and inserted into a round leather casing.

The wide variations in styles of play and the popularity of the game all served to highlight the need to put the game into a more universal form. But there was no central governing body, as there is today, and it fell to the uniquely English public schools to begin the transition from the mobs, the violence, and the streets to a tamer, more regulated and safer version of football.

The English public school is in reality what we Americans think of as a private school. These schools were attended, and in large part still are, by the English upper classes. The students were the sons of those who had position, education, and the money to enable them to attend these schools in preparation for university, business, or military life. The curriculum at these schools was difficult and the discipline was extremely stiff. Students and teachers were literally often at each other's throats because of the rigidity and demands of the system.

At a public school named Rugby, Dr. Thomas Arnold, the headmaster, began reforming the curricular and extracurricular activities. He believed that along with schoolwork, boys and young men needed directed physical outlets through which they could channel their thinking and energy. Dr. Arnold, we believe, was not interested in developing scholastic sports to the levels of importance that they hold today. He was mainly concerned with providing vigorous, hard play during free time so as to prevent the boys from thinking about the opposite sex or thinking frivolous, unimportant thoughts that were alien to Victorian thinking and behavior.

So it was that football began at the great English public schools, particularly at Rugby, Eton, Harrow, Charterhouse, and Winchester. The game had moved from the streets to the famous "playing fields of Eton" and other public schools. While the common man still embraced the game, it was at the public schools that the refinement toward today's game began.

The variations in terms of field and goal dimensions and regulation of play were great. At Eton, for example, the goalposts, or "goal sticks" as they called them, stood 11 feet apart and 7 feet high, with no crossbar. Each team changed goals at halftime, just as we do today. Eton restricted the use of hands on the ball but allowed the hands to be used to stop the ball, as ice hockey players are allowed to do in stopping the puck. But the hands could be used to hold, push, or even strike an opponent.

One of Eton's greatest contributions to the game, and one that many believe to be the forerunner of the modern offside rule, was the violation called "sneaking." The Etonian rule stated that "a player is considered to be 'sneaking' when only three, or less than three, of the opposite side are before him and the ball behind him, and in such a case, he may not kick the ball."

At Winchester, the goal was a straight line dug in the grass at each end of the field. The field was long and narrow: about 80 yards long and about 80 feet wide. There were no goalposts, simply a goal line 80 or so feet long.

The sidelines, or touchlines, were made of canvas stretched to a height of 7 feet. Just as in today's indoor soccer, a ball rebounding back onto the field from the canvas touchline could be played. Players would catch the ball and could run 3 yards before kicking it, while defenders were free to take it away from them. No dribbling of the ball was allowed—the ball could be advanced only through 3-yard runs and kicks.

A word about dribbling. Dribbling refers to controlling the soccer ball with the feet as the player moves on the field. Though dribbling was not part of the game at Rugby, it was part of the game at other schools. In some schools, a game was played in which nearly all the boys in the school were involved. The object was to gain possession of the ball and control it, by dribbling, for as long as possible. It is only natural that dribbling became one of the skilled methods of controlling and advancing the soccer ball.

Goalposts were used at Rugby. The goalposts were 11 feet apart and had a crossbar 10 feet above the ground. Kicking an opponent on or above the knee was illegal, although that rule still left room for all sorts of defensive tactics. It was at Rugby in 1823 that a student broke the rules of the game and ran with the ball, which led to the beginning and development of the game named in honor of the school, Rugby Football.

At Harrow, goals were 150 yards apart and the goalposts stood 12 feet high. Harrow added some interesting kinds of rules to its game: for example, if the game ended in a tie, the length of the field should be extended to 300 yards the next time the rematch was played.

Another delightful practice at Harrow was that a player who had caught the ball could scream out "three yards" before being tackled, as one is in rugby or American football. If he did so, he was entitled to a "free kick." If he was close enough to goal, he could also try to score by getting over the goal line in three consecutive jumps. It is clear that many of these practices would eventually reappear in games that led to rugby and American football.

Other rules originated at other schools. At Cheltenham, the throw-in was instituted to return a ball to play. The term "offside," applied to a player too far upfield, came into use there, too.

With so many variations in the game, the young men who wanted to play it when they went to the universities faced a great deal of confusion. Whose rules and interpretation of the game should they follow?

SOCCER GETS ORGANIZED

The first major attempt at codification of the rules was made in 1862. J. C. Thring drew up regulations believed to have been designed for matches at Cambridge University. His rules went under the title "The Simplest Game." While this code of rules was aimed at providing uniformity of play, it was still not the solution to the problem. Rather, it provided a foundation for building the game in a more rational, structured manner.

Under Mr. Thring's rules, a goal was scored when the ball was forced through the goal and under the bar, except when thrown. Hands could not be used to propel or carry the ball; they could be used only to stop the ball. Players could kick only the ball and not other players. Tripping was outlawed. When a ball was kicked out of bounds, it was to be put back into play by the player who kicked it out, and he had to kick it in a straight line toward the middle of the field. A ball that was kicked out of bounds over the goal line was to be kicked back into play from the goal line by a player of the defending team—a rule very similar to that of today. A player was "out of play" if he was ahead of the ball. And, lastly, a player could not be charged into when he was not in possession of the ball. Charging was actually a kind of blocking of the opponent in possession of the ball in an attempt to push him off the ball.

So there it was, the first big step to codification of the sport. Conspicuously missing were such things as field dimensions, goal sizes, and numbers of players to a side. But regardless of these temporary omissions, a clearer, more orderly game had evolved.

The year 1863 was the important year in the history of both soccer and rugby. It was at this time that the Football Association was formed at a meeting at the Freemasons' Tavern in London in November. A draft of new rules was presented by the elected secretary, E. C. Morley.

The rules that issued from this meeting included such noncontroversial ones as the field's maximum length—no more than 200 yards (no minimum width was offered)—and that goalposts should be 8 yards apart, with no mention of a crossbar.

The controversy that led to the great split between what were to become soccer and rugby came over the two other rules. Carrying or running with the ball was forbidden, as was what was termed "hacking," which is simply kicking an opponent in the shin or leg to stop his progress with the ball.

The Blackheath Football Club of London felt that hacking was an integral part of being a man and playing a man's game, and so they and others who felt the same way about hacking left the new organization. They continued their game, which included both carrying the ball and hacking and which eventually evolved into rugby.

Hacking, as a point of argument, was hot at the time of the split in 1863, but the practice fell into disrepute as injuries continued. In the late 1860s, hacking was removed as a defensive tactic from rugby; it is, of course, a foul play in soccer.

Soccer was now better regulated than it had been. Players at the various public schools were playing a basically similar game, subscribing to the rules laid down by the Football Association in 1863. Competitions were played at individual schools between dormitories or houses in which students lived. Teams would play one another, with the winners playing on to a final championship.

In 1870 C. W. Alcock, a soccer player from Harrow, became secretary of the Football Association. His experience with the intramural tournaments at Harrow and the other schools encouraged him to propose that a tournament be established by the association in which all members of the Football Association would be invited to compete. In 1871 the idea was accepted and became one of the most significant contributions to soccer throughout the world.

By this time, more refinement had come to the game through rules. The earlier maximum field length of 200 yards remained, but now a maximum width of 100 yards was laid down. The size of the goal, which would remain to this day, was set at 24 feet wide and 8 feet high, with a tape, rather than a crossbar, across the top of the uprights.

The throw-in rule came into effect, but allowed the ball to be thrown with only one hand, by the player who first got to the ball out of bounds. Later, around 1882, the rules would be changed to give the ball to the team that had not touched the ball last when it went out of bounds. At this time, the one-hand throw was replaced by the two-handed, over-the-head throw-in we know today. The rules also stated that both feet had to stay in contact with the ground while making the throw. At first, both feet had to be stationary on the touchline when the throw was made. Later changes allowed for part of both feet to be on or behind the touchline at the time of release, allowing for the long throws we see today.

The offside rule also had evolved and was very much part of the game, and it remained essentially unchanged until 1925. The offside rule of the 1880s was: "When a player has kicked the ball, anyone of the same side who is nearer to the opponent's goal line is out of play and may not touch the ball himself, nor in any way whatsoever prevent any other player from doing so until the ball has been played, unless there are at least three of his opponents between him and their goal line." This rule would be changed by reducing the number of opponents between the player and the goal to two.

The years 1873 and 1874 saw still further refinement of the game. Two umpires and a referee were provided to make sure the rules were adhered to. Each umpire surveyed half of the field; in 1895 the referee was given the responsibility of making all decisions concerning play. At that time the umpires were given flags, as they have today, but served only to move up and down the touchlines, acting simply as advisers to the referee on where the ball went out of touch or in what direction it should be played.

The free kick as punishment for handling the ball was introduced to the game in 1873. In 1874 the free kick, as a punishment, was extended to other fouls or violations of the rules. Players also could be sent off the field for serious violations of the rules. Goals were changed only at the half, rather than after each goal scored, and the wooden crossbar was universally adopted on goalposts.

Early soccer was played as an attacking, offensive-minded game. In the 1860s, a soccer team generally consisted of eleven players on a side, eight of whom were forwards and the remaining three defenders. At the beginning of the 1870s, a player was designated goalkeeper, and that player was able to use his hands to prevent a goal anywhere on the field. At the same time, the forward line had been cut from eight to seven, two men playing on each wing, with the remaining three in the middle of the field. Two halfbacks played behind the forwards and one more player patrolled the area behind the halfbacks and in front of the goalkeeper.

Around 1883, another forward was dropped from the forward line to become a center halfback. The player given this position was one who could be as strong in defending as he could be in attacking. This set the pattern for the center halfback role for years to come. The game was becoming progressively defensive minded and has continued to be so right up until today, much to the dismay of many soccer fans.

The founding of the Football Association in 1863 opened floodgates resulting in a wave of soccer enthusiasm that would sweep through England. The early years of the Football Association had by necessity been given over to the development, codification, and dissemination of a uniform set of rules. Although the version of soccer we know today had not yet emerged, teams from different places could at least play under the same set of rules.

It was through the Football Association and its member teams that in 1872 the corner kick became part of the game. Referees and umpires were given real control of the game, even to the point of being able to eject players for flagrant offenses, and free kicks were given for offside rule infringements, representing just a few examples of the progress being made.

However, the establishment in 1871 of the Football Association Challenge Cup, the first of its kind in the world, provided the impetus for the most sweeping changes. The Football Association Challenge Cup, now known throughout the world simply as the F.A. Cup, led to a sociological change in the game, the rapid development of professionalism, and the growth and development of rules and tactics. It also provided the model that would be adopted for competition in nations all around the world.

In 1872, at the first F.A. Cup game, soccer was being played mainly by teams made up of public school and university alumni. Alumni called themselves "old boys," and many of the teams of the 1870s had "old" as the prefix to their school name, to distinguish them from the school or university teams. Some of the famous teams of this era were the Old Etonians and Old Carthusians, alumni, respectively, from Eton and Charterhouse; the Wanderers, a team made up of alumni from several schools that would win the first F.A. Cup and five of the first six cup games; the Harrow Chequers; and the Royal Engineers, a team made up of officers.

The early years of cup play were dominated by these teams, playing in London or in the counties surrounding London. The first cup match had fifteen teams compete for the championship, with all but two from London.

The following season, the number of teams competing in cup play was twenty-eight. The F.A. Cup match was truly on its way, in terms of significance and the growing number of teams wanting to win the cup. The interest generated by the cup led to the great sociological change that profoundly influenced soccer in England and laid the groundwork for soccer to become the most popular game in the world. In the north and midlands of England, in Wales and Scotland, great numbers of soccer clubs started springing up. These clubs were related to churches, industrial mills, or businesses. The players on these teams were working-class men, which provided a much broader base on which to build the game's popularity. No longer would soccer remain the game of the "old boys" with the university and public school background. It was now fast becoming the working class's game.

By the end of the 1870s and the early 1880s, football associations were formed in locales other than London. Games were being played in all segments of the country, and it reached a point where most of the F.A. Cup entries were located in the industrial sections of the country, making regional elimination tournaments necessary to accommodate all.

The year 1882 saw the beginning of the end for the "old boy" teams. The Old Etonians beat the Blackburn Rovers, a team from the provinces, in what would be the last championship cup won by an "old boy" team.

The following year the Old Etonians lost to another provincial team, Blackburn Olympic, marking the first time that a team from outside of London had won the cup. The sudden appearance and rise of the Blackburn teams was important to soccer's development for two reasons. First, the balance of soccer power was evidently moving from London to the provinces. But of far more significance was the swing from the public school, amateur player to the working-class, professional soccer player who would captivate and shape the game forever.

SOCCER SPREADS
THROUGHOUT THE WORLD

The ingredients basic to the creation, evolution, and popular acceptance of soccer, first in England, then in the rest of the British Isles, proved to be as applicable, appealing, and acceptable to the rest of Europe, South America, and, ultimately, most nations of the world. Supporters could exult in victory and commiserate with one another in defeat, with the intervals between matches given over to endless, and to them stimulating, postmortems of games.

Britain was at the zenith of her colonial power at the time soccer captivated the British Isles. It is little wonder that the soccer contagion that swept through the British Isles would prove equally contagious to the rest of the world.

British citizens and expatriots were roaming or settling all over the world, establishing and building, managing and presiding over outside national interests. In support of these empire builders and the interests they represented, military personnel, businessmen, industrialists, clergymen, doctors, and ordinary workers and their families were needed. It might be said that wherever in the world the sun shone on Englishmen, soccer players and their fans could be found playing their own game.

Sailors, at the end of their long sea journeys, looked forward to playing matches against local teams wherever they docked. Local native populations started playing the game either through invitation or on their own, or they were invited to join those playing. As their talents and interests grew, they formed their own teams.

The inadvertent, but enthusiastic, exporting of soccer occurred with astonishing speed, in so many diverse places, except the United States and Canada, and the game experienced the same rapid surge in popularity as had been seen in England.

One of the most fascinating sidelights in the story of soccer's growth and acceptance has been the ability of each nation to take the English-Scottish soccer style of play and adapt it to its own particular national characteristics. Soccer has the unique capacity for allowing a team personality to emerge that translates into a style or system of play.

The Brazilians play a technically artistic style of soccer that rivals their music because there is an exciting and pulsating rhythm to their play. German teams play a well-disciplined and organized game with soundly executed tactics. Argentine teams play a physical yet technical game, whereas Americans, though less skilled at the moment, attempt to cover their lack of technical skill with hustle and the old college try, which is so much a part of many American sports. The Russians play with little subtlety, grinding methodically away at their opponent, using their well-conditioned players, in a constant flow, up and down the field.

Soccer's rapid rise to preeminence in the world of sport was and remains an amazing phenomenon. The fact that the sport of one nation could and continues to be eagerly embraced by nearly all the nations of the world is equally amazing. The appeal and attraction of soccer have been obvious to Europeans and South Americans for years. Happily, in the United States and Canada, both of which have long been holdouts in terms of large-scale enthusiasm for soccer, the qualities inherent in the game have begun to attract great numbers of soccer players and enthusiasts on all age levels, invirtually all regions of the two countries.

Much of soccer's rapid growth and popularity in the United States, especially in the 1970s, can be attributed to the fact that soccer can be played by nearly everyone, regardless of size, strength, age, or sex. How appealing to young athletes and their families to have an exciting sport, relatively free from injury, in which skill and stamina are required, as opposed to the violence and brutality of American football.

As for equipment and places to play soccer, the same factors influencing soccer's early growth around the world still apply. All that is absolutely needed is a ball and an area to play in. The need for shoes, uniforms, and other equipment grows in direct proportion to the seriousness given the game and funds available, regardless of the level the game is being played on.

These elements have helped to shape the future of soccer and make it possible for each nation to develop soccer according to its own national characteristics, but within a universally accepted code of play and regulation.

Be this as it may, and aside from the natural true competitive spirit of the game, one more factor lies at the root of the world's love of soccer. Dr. Edward O. Wilson, an eminent sociologist and biologist, has said of team sports that they are "an elemental struggle between tribal surrogates." Although Dr. Wilson's statement may be applied to all team sports, the nationalistic pride in one's country is especially true and far easier to recognize in the world of soccer. Every country provides opportunities for its teams to play other nations as part of its regular soccer offerings each season.

Dr. Wilson's observation is borne out whenever and wherever teams representing continents, nations, cities, or even political ideologies come together to play soccer. Players and their supportive fans view themselves as the designated defenders of their national, regional, or political honor. So much of this feeling of pride in one's team has contributed to soccer's phenomenal history.

REFINEMENTS
AND MODIFICATIONS OF THE RULES

Accompanying soccer's rapid spread, acceptance, and popularity throughout the world were the continuous and inevitable modifications in its rules and playing field configurations, and, of course, the changes in tactics to meet the modifications.

As in the evolution of most sports, popular and widespread participation, when combined with the ever increasing sophistication of players' skills and overall team tactics and the pace of a particular time or era, leads to reassessment of the game being played. From the players and spectators alike come demands to keep the game balanced competitively in the hope of keeping the level of excitement high.

Soccer of the 1870s was basically an attack-oriented game, with the attack based almost exclusively on the dribble. The best soccer players were the ones who could dribble, dribble, and dribble some more. A player in possession of the ball would dribble and control it until it was lost to a defender or disposed of in some other manner. The rest of the team milled about, not supporting the attack as today's players do but rather as on-the-field spectators awaiting their opportunity to put on a dribbling show should luck bring the ball to them. The game as played in this manner was hardly an example of team play or system.

It took the Scots to bring teamwork, through their short passing game, to soccer. The Scots realized early on that by passing the ball to a better-positioned unmarked teammate, progress could be made faster, more economically in terms of effort expanded, and with greater purpose. The Scottish passing game brought pace to the game and became the foundation for the rhythmic flow and continuity that is so much an integral part of soccer's appeal. It is in the utilization of the passing game that a team's or nation's style of play becomes apparent, as each team puts its own interpretation of the basic rhythm into action. Once the game had moved from a relatively plodding activity to a more team-oriented, flowing style of play, the need for modification became apparent and necessary. Changes in the game's format had to be made in order to keep pace with rapidly evolving playing styles.

Early in the 1880s, the Scottish Football Association put pressure on the Football Association for rule changes. In 1882 a conference was held in Manchester, England, between the four football associations of Britain, representing England, Ireland, Scotland, and Wales. From this meeting several important changes came about.

The first group of changes had to do with the ball, the field of play, and goalpost construction. A uniform, regulation size ball was to be used, thus ending the problems encountered by players because of varying ball sizes. Touchlines or sidelines had to be clearly delineated by appropriate markings, and, finally, crossbars were to be used atop the upright goalposts rather than the strips of cloth that were employed at many playing fields.

The balance of changes that became rules were conceived in actual play. The one-handed throw-in, baseball style, was abolished and replaced with the two-handed, over-the-head throw that could be made in any direction and taken by any player on the side awarded the throw-in. In a further effort at preserving life and limb, charging into an opponent from behind was abolished except if the opponent was deliberately obstructing or blocking one's access to the ball.

In 1873, the free kick was put into soccer to punish deliberate handling of the ball. In 1874 the free kick was further extended to penalize other violations of the rules. The original rules governing the free kick, although modified, are essentially the same today. When play was stopped because of a rule infraction, the offending team was penalized by awarding possession of the ball to the opponent, at the spot of the infraction. The opponent would return the ball to play by means of a kick, unhampered by a defender. The ball could be kicked in any direction to a teammate or even directly kicked into the goal. Naturally enough, this event came to be known as a direct free kick.

The direct free kick has come to be a free kick from which a goal can be scored directly against the offending team. The severity of this penalty reflects for the most part rule violations that threaten players with severe injury through kicking, striking, tripping, pushing, or charging into an opponent. It also punishes acts that blatantly interfere with the proper conduct of the game. These offenses are deliberate handling of the ball or handling of the ball by the goalkeeper outside the penalty area.

Later on, the indirect free kick came to soccer to penalize lesser violations of rules. The indirect free kick came to soccer to penalize lesser violations of rules. The indirect free kick is one from which a goal cannot be scored unless the ball has been played or touched by a player other than the kicker before it passes into the goal.

The penalty kick came to soccer in 1891 as a modification of the direct free kick. Originally, its purpose was to discourage intentional handling of the ball by defenders and then, quite naturally enough, to discourage violent fouls perpetrated by defenders in the goal area. The awarding of the penalty kick then, just as now, becomes a confrontation between the kicker and the goalkeeper, with just 12 yards separating the two.

To implement the penalty kick rule, an area had to be delineated so that all would know where skill had to prevail, since brute force would cost dearly.

An area 6 yards into the field was prescribed, thus establishing the goal area—the area in which the goalkeeper was permitted to handle the ball. Another line, 12 yards out from the goal line and running parallel to it, became the line from which the direct free kick at the goal was to be taken. Also drawn was a third line, 18 yards out from the goal line, behind which all players except the penalty shot kicker and the goalkeeper had to remain until the kick had been taken.

Some minor revisions were made in the original 1871 penalty shot rules and field configuration; but in 1902, the goal area and penalty area, as we know them today, came into being.

The original goalkeeper's box became the goal area and measured 6 × 20 yards. The rectangular penalty area extended 18 yards from the goal line into the field and was 44 yards wide. The spot from which the penalty shot would be taken was set at 12 yards from the center of the goal. No players other than the shooter and goalkeeper were permitted in the penalty area until the ball was played. The last change to come to the penalty area was the prescribing of an arc with a 10-yard radius from the penalty shot mark intersecting the 44-yard line, providing a restraining line for players until the kick is taken. This addition came in 1937.

The institution of the throw-in for returning to play a ball that had gone out of bounds over the touchlines never affected the kick-in return to play of a ball that had gone over the goal lines. The earliest soccer rules provided for returning a ball to play by kicking. These rules remained in effect for balls played over goal lines in the following way. If in going over the goal line the ball was last touched by an attacking player, the defenders would put the ball back into play with a goal kick. This kick was taken from anywhere in the goal area. Early on, it was recognized that if the ball went over the goal line, touched last by a defender, the attacking team should have its advantage returned to it.

In 1872, the corner kick was put into play by the Football Association. Simply stated, if the ball went over the goal line last touched by a defender, the attacking team would be awarded an indirect free kick at goal. The kick would be taken at the intersection of the goal line and touchline, on the side nearest to where the ball went out of play. It is important to note that the first corner kicks were indirect, meaning that a goal could be scored only after the ball had been played or touched by another player. Contrast that concept with today's play, in which skilled players are able to put the ball directly into the goal, thereby increasing the options and pressures on attackers and defenders alike. The change from an indirect kick to a direct one occurred in 1924, and has become a source of great thrills to soccer spectators.

The period following World War I was filled with evidences of soccer's energetic and dynamic growth. Professional teams were being organized in nearly every country. Football leagues were expanding through the addition of divisions to accommodate new teams, with the result being that soccer entered the realm of big business. Good, exciting teams attracted large paying audiences, making economics a factor in the game's development. Although the players individually did not reap economic benefits as the players of today do, the opportunity was there for the club to make money. As a result of this generation of income, good players could be purchased, stadiums and fields could be built, refurbished, or expanded, teams could travel; in general, it provided a fiscal base from which the club could operate.

The promotion and relegation system, instituted as the leagues expanded into divisions, first in England then in the rest of the world, added to the player's and his club's motivation. Simply stated, the bottom or two last place teams in a division were relegated or demoted to the division below. The two top teams in each division were promoted to the division above. Naturally enough, each team fought to be the best, but as usual, money became the important factor in building winning teams. In each country, teams in the top division tended to be the best teams. They were the best at the game and generally were best at the gate.

CHANGES IN TACTICS

The promotion and relegation system helped to make competition fierce and, as a motivational device, was given further bolstering through the point system. Points are still used in determining team standings within a division or league. Inadvertently and certainly inconsistent with the original intent of soccer's organizers and designers, relegation, promotion, and the point system led to new attitudes and strategies on the part of team managers toward evolving soccer tactics.

Up until the 1897–98 season the tactics of the game were predicated on scoring goals. Teams attacked en masse, leaving the defense of their own goal to the goalkeeper and two fullbacks, playing alongside one another, in the middle of the field. With division standing and the point system having become so prominent and important, tactics began to reflect the attitude that preventing goals, through strong defensive play, was the prime objective. It was obvious that if a team prevented its opponent from scoring, whether it scored or not, it could not lose a point. The team might not win the game, but certainly it could not lose; and 1 point for a draw was better than none.

One team manager espoused the prevailing theory and attitude best when he said that his team (and naturally the opposing team) had 1 point in hand at the kickoff, obviously true since the score at kickoff was 0–0. His tactics were to protect this point through heavy defensive concentration, looking to score only if, through the breaks of the game, an opportunity presented itself. If a team went into the lead, then it was to be an all-out defensive effort to protect the lead in order to capture the 2 points for a win, so vital to a team's standing in the division.

Sadly, much of this kind of defensive-oriented thinking remains in soccer even today. But the fact remains that defensive orientation has had much to do with soccer's evolution and coaching theory.

Once defensive soccer became the basis for soccer tactics, it wasn't long before players realized that the offside rule could literally become the main strategy by being employed legitimately as an integral part of defensive technique and tactics. The offside rule of the day, in fact until 1925, stipulated that a player was onside only if, when the ball was played, he had at least three men between him and the opposing goal line. If there were fewer than three defensive men between the ball and the goal, a player in advance of the ball was offside. This resulted in a loss of possession and a free kick being awarded to the defense.

Exploiting this rule was a relatively simple thing to do. As the team in possession of the ball began moving upfield, building its attack, one of the three defensive players would sneak upfield past the otherwise occupied forwards, leaving only two defenders—the goalkeeper and a fullback. Any unsuspecting forward caught in advance of the ball when the ball was played was offside. The offside trap had been born.

Credit for developing and refining the technique of the offside trap is generally given to Bill McCracken and Frank Hudspeth of Newcastle United and Montgomery and Marley of Notts County. All were fullbacks who, by virtue of their strategic positions on the field, their view of the action taking place in front of them, and their crafty and wiley talents, were able to stop an attack with a well-timed, sneaky move upfield out of the defense.

The effectiveness, in terms of stopping attacks, of the offside trap inevitably led to its implementation throughout the Football League. With all teams employing the offside trap, games became disasters. Forwards would not attack for fear of being caught offside. This, when coupled with the defensive tactics of the day, simply stopped the game. Games would be played at midfield with little or no penetration goalward, resulting in the cutting off of the flow of the game by incessant whistles blown to stop play for offside violation.

To the spectator, soccer had become a dull, lackluster, slow affair. Forwards wallowed in a sea of defenders, with the ever-present offside trap further repressing individual dribbling, passing, and other attacking skills. No longer were forwards running off the ball, looking for passes to lead them toward the opponent's goal. Rather, they milled about midfield, divested of their attacking roles, wasted, as forwards at least, by being used as defenders.

Of course, goals were scored, but the game had deteriorated to a point where defense and offside traps were choking soccer and making a travesty of the game. Spectators were being turned off as well. The game had come full circle from the spirited exuberance of the early attacking game to the deadly, earnest quest for points and the sacrifice of attack in order to prevent goals from being scored.

It was soon realized that if something was not done to change this dreadful situation, soccer would continue to lose its appeal. The four British football associations, which at the time also governed the International Board for soccer rulemaking, gathered to consider solutions to the problem. Many suggestions evolved from their meeting, and several were experimented with in the summer of 1925. Most suggestions were aimed at limiting the area in which an attacking player could be deemed offside. Oddly enough, currently in the North American Soccer League, a player beyond the 35-yard line cannot be ruled offside, regardless of the number of men between him and the goal. The Football Association experimented with various-sized offside areas but found none satisfactory.

What was decided in 1925, however, and remains in effect today, was to reduce from three to two the number of players necessary to put a player onside. This simple reduction in the number of players needed to be onside put attack back into the game and breathed new life into soccer.

The change in the offside law immediately reopened the defense. Goals were being scored in abundance. Great scorers, particularly center forwards, were back in the game, scoring at record pace.

With the defenses opened it soon became apparent that the fullbacks, playing in the middle of the field, clearly were unable to handle the attackers' penetration down the wings and through the middle. The center forward would move upfield in the middle while the wings work the ball up the sideline. When a fullback would commit to the outside threat and the defense had been split, the wing would cross the ball to the center forward, who was relatively free to receive the pass and attack the goal.

Something had to be done to stop the high-scoring center forwards who were simply ravaging old-style defenses. Credit for developing the tactics to stop the center forward scoring threat goes to Herbert Chapman, manager of the North London soccer team Arsenal, and a clever inside forward named Charlie Buchan, who had come to Arsenal from Sunderland in the 1925–26 season.

Early in this season, Arsenal had been beaten and humiliated by Newcastle in a 7–0 rout. Newcastle's center forward, Hughie Gallagher, literally had shredded Arsenal's defenses. As a result, Buchan suggested to Chapman that Arsenal's center halfback be employed strictly as a defender with the sole purpose of defending against the opposing center forward. Up until this time, the center halfback played some defense but his main function was to support attacks, distribute the ball, and provide a link between attackers and defenders. After the Newcastle defeat, it was obvious to Buchan and Chapman that they could no longer afford the luxury of an attacking center halfback.

Guarding an opponent closely, or "marking" as it is called in soccer, on a man-to-man basis, was not yet a regular part of soccer's defensive tactics. The fullbacks were generally expected to cover the opponents' inside forwards and center forward. The wing halfbacks played wider on the field in order to cover the outsides on the right and left. The center halfback had a loosely defined defensive responsibility and a more defined attacking role; but, in the main, he had the freedom to roam the field, defending if necessary but more often than not up on the attack.

Buchan's plan provided that the center halfback become strictly a defender, positioned between the fullbacks, with his principal function that of stopping the opposing center forward. The fullbacks could then play wider, closer to the touchlines, and the wing halfbacks were to take over the middle-of-the-field responsibilities. An inside forward would come back off the forward line to take over the linking position between defenders and attackers, formerly the role of the center halfback.

Chapman agreed to Buchan's plan and tried it in Arsenal's next match, against West Horn. Arsenal won the game 4–0 using the new tactics, and the third-back game came into existence. Chapman, always innovative, was so delighted with the outcome that he began searching for players who could fit into the positions created by the new tactics and meet the demands of the system.

Chapman brought Alex James to Arsenal, a player perfectly suited to fill the midfield inside forward position. James's formidable skills were also perfect for performing the linking role between the defenders and attackers so necessary to Arsenal's style of play. Herbie Roberts, selected by Chapman because of his outstanding defensive skills, came to Arsenal from Oswestry Town. Roberts became known as "Policeman" Roberts because of the way he stopped opposing center forwards. Roberts became the model center half-back, or "stopper" as he was called; all the other teams began searching for a player of his caliber.

With Roberts policing the center forward and controlling the middle of the field, the fullbacks moved further outside to control and mark the wings. When Chapman brought David Jack to Arsenal in 1928, he had found a player capable of performing the linking role as well as Alex James. Jack was also positioned behind the forward line; the two inside forwards could thus provide greater depth to the attack.

Remaining on the forward line were the wings and center forward—upfield, poised, ready to attack the goal. James and Jack played behind them, patrolling the area between the halfbacks and forwards, receiving passes out of the defense and distributing the ball upfield, and then joining the attack themselves. The wing halfbacks in the Arsenal system of play were now able to cope with the opposing inside forwards.

Arsenal's style of play was exciting because they had built their team in a way that would allow them to absorb pressure on the defense with solid coverage but at the same time, through Jack and James and their outstanding forwards, counterattack quickly. Indeed, many of their goals came on break-aways.

The alignment employed by Arsenal was named the W-M formation because of the on-paper configuration of the players. As would be expected, other British teams tried to emulate Arsenal's system of play, but most lacked the kind of personnel that Chapman had put together. While most were capable of organizing the defensive component and did succeed in stopping attacks, they lacked the talented inside forwards and wings who could carry off the counterattack. The teams with less gifted personnel had simply put the emphasis on defensive aspects of the three-back game and were unable to adopt Arsenal's more positive attacking aspects of play. It is true, however, that the third-back game was developed primarily as a defensive tactic. It was this defensive attitude and the desire to prevent goals from being scored that became the trademark of teams employing the three-back system. Once again, British football was leading the way to defensive soccer.

Arsenal's great success with the third-back game in the 1930s set the tone for British tactics and style of play for years to come. The rest of the soccer-playing world did not as yet embrace the defensive orientation the British had given the game.

Continental and South American teams still played the more free-wheeling, passing game, with many teams still featuring the attacking center half-back. Attacking, fluid soccer presented more opportunities for tactical development than defensive soccer and also provided spectators with more entertaining matches.

But the pressure to win, earn points, and attract fans and their money by staying at the top of league standings was growing. This pressure led to developing team tactics, in most cases to preent being scored upon rather than to score. The 1 point that could be earned for a draw apparently had more appeal than risking all to win. Arsenal's successes in Great Britain had proven that it was possible to devise tactics, in this case, stopping the scoring center forward, that would work toward specific outcomes.

British teams, anxious to emulate Arsenal's winning ways, in most cases were able to come up with only the defensive aspect of the game, losing the essence of the system because of inadequate midfield and forward personnel. Clearly, coaches and managers must build and fit the tactics to the players, and not the players to the tactics, which is so often the case.

The next major tactical breakthrough came from Italy. Italy had long resisted the third-back game, but in the early 1940s, the same pressures to win games and points and stop the opponent from scoring prevailed and laid the groundwork for the development of Italy's infamous, all-out defensive tactics.

The Italians had adapted and modified a defensive tactic invented by the Swiss called the verrou, or bolt. The verrou, or bolt, got its name from the bolt in a door or gate lock, which slides from left to right to lock the door. Indeed, this was what the man playing the ''bolt'' position was supposed to do: close the door on any openings in the defense.

What the Swiss had done was to drop a forward into midfield to participate mainly in defense, leaving the remaining four forwards up front. Two midfielders, defensively oriented, would provide the link between the forwards and the last line of defense, composed of the left and right fullbacks and the normal center halfback.

Behind the defense, one player, generally a fullback, was left free. It was his strictly defensive responsibility to close any openings that should appear in the defense. He ranged back and forth behind the defense to wherever the attack was coming from, providing additional cover and support to his defenders.

The Italians, copying the Swiss innovation, called their tactical system *catenaccio* or the "big chain." The deep defender played behind the Italian defense, free of specific defensive assignment. The Italians call this position *libero*, or "free back," while the English-speaking world dubbed this position the "sweeper," obviously referring to the *libero's* duty of sweeping away anything coming through its defense.

The Italian innovation was played in the following manner. The *libero*, or sweeper, worked behind a line of four defenders, each of whom marked his opponent in a tight man-to-man arrangement, shadowing the opponent wherever he went. The *libero* roamed freely, moving to plug any gaps that should develop in the defense.

Parked in front of the four defenders and *libero* are three midfield players whose main function also is to play defense. One or two attackers remain upfield should a counterattack develop. Obviously, *catenaccio* is strictly a defensive system with attacks coming from fast-breaking counterattacks rather than through a concerted buildup of attack.

Understandably, Italian league games have been low-scoring affairs. With both teams given over to defense, games become rather dull for spectators except on those rare occasions when a team has the personnel to turn the fast break and attack frequently out of their defensive set. Inter-Milan, in the 1960s, had the personnel to do this and enjoyed great success in international and league play.

It is interesting to note that Italy's adherence to *catenaccio* in international matches, and in the World Cup in particular, has been unsuccessful, causing Italian teams humiliating defeats at the hands of less skilled teams.

From Brazil came another major tactical concept called 4–2–4. Brazil's approach to soccer tactics was never a defensive one. Brazil attacked their opponents, content to outscore them rather than prevent the opponents from scoring.

The evolution to the 4–2–4 came after Brazil had completed a tour of Europe in 1956 and had absorbed some bad losses. England had beaten them by a score of 4–2, and England had missed two penalty shots. It was simply a case of Brazil's attack orientation taking precedence over their defensive play. Brazilian defenders could not cover opponents properly.

In preparing for the 1958 World Cup, Brazil came up with the 4–2–4 tactic to use in shaping up their defenses. The plan began by providing each defender with a support player to assist in the coverage. Four defenders were set in a line in front of the goal. Two of these four played in the middle of the field while the other two played wide, as conventional fullbacks do. Should pressure develop in the middle of the field, the two centerbacks would be there to support each other. Meanwhile, should one of the outside defenders need support in coverage, the stopper back was there to help. This was a remarkably simple approach to the coverage problem, resulting in double coverage whenever needed for each deep defender.

The two midfield players were of exceptional quality, especially able to link the four deep defenders with the four attackers. Their ability, endurance, and spirit were the key to this system because these two could attack or defend brilliantly as play demanded. The forward line also was exceptional at attack and keeping the ball from opponents. After all, four forwards, all of world class—Pele, Garrincha, Vava, and Zagalo—would have made any team attack oriented.

After Brazil's great success in the 1958 World Cup, coaches and managers everywhere tried to use the 4–2–4 system. Even here in America on the college levels, coaches were falling all over themselves extolling the 4–2–4 play. But the system could only be played with midfield players of the quality of Brazil's. Lesser players in the middle made 4–2–4 a deadly trap for coaches who didn't have the personnel to make it work.

In the 1962 World Cup, Brazil modified its 4–2–4 system by dropping Zagalo, a talented forward, into a midfield position. Pele had been severely injured and could not play. Without Pele keeping the pressure on the opponent's defenses, too much pressure would be put on the two midfield players. To meet this pressure, Brazil chose Zagalo, a skilled forward, to strengthen the two-man midfield line. it is interesting that when most teams would have chosen a defender for his role, Brazil went to a forward. Still it was Zagalo's skills as a forward that made this tactic work. His great physical stamina and temendous playing skills made it possible for him to defend, move into the attack, participate in the attack, and return to help cover when his part in the attack was over.

The 4–2–4 and the 4–3–3, by their very nature, design, and implementation, provided the groundwork for the development of total team soccer. Players simply were not confined to a specific role. Brazilian fullbacks, long noted for their participation in attack, provided the example of how it could be done. Zagalo had shown how good skilled players could perform several functions in a game. From 4–2–4 and 4–3–3 were to come many of the important tactical advances of the 1960s, 1970s, and 1980s.

Others quickly adapted the 4–3–3 to their own purposes and did it in terms of their own personnel. Alf Ramsey, England's team manager, built the

1966 World Cup championship team on the 4–3–3 tactic, with appropriate modification to suit his players.

Ramsey's 4–3–3 did not use conventional wingers. Ramsey, in evaluating his team, felt that he lacked the individual strength on the wings but could generate that strength through the use of other players who could fill the void. Ramsey had as fullbacks George Cohen and Ray Wilson, two fast backs who were able to move upfield quickly, overlap the midfielders, and turn up as outsides when the situation was right.

When Cohen and Wilson were occupied and unable to get to the outside, Martin Peters, a midfielder, or Alan Ball, a striker, would burst onto the wing and attack, much in the maner of Brazil's Zagalo. And Nobby Stiles, playing a sweeper's role in front of the back four, was assigned the job of marking the opposition's best forward. Modification of the 4–3–3 was made possible through intelligent use of players' talents, using these talents to advantage in covering weaknesses.

The sweepers' position was also given new meaning by the immensely talented Franz Beckenbauer of West Germany. Beckenbauer transformed the defense-oriented sweeper position into an attacking role.

Beckenbauer had played as an attacking sweeper for his club, Bayern München, for years. From his position deep in the defense, he moved like a phantom, hidden behind his line of defenders and free of a specific defensive assignment. Beckenbauer put into practice his theory that when he felt he was able, at the propitious moment, he could slip up unmarked into the midfield buildup for the attack, distribute the ball to his forwards, and even go up farther and attack the goal itself.

While Beckenbauer's feats were well known in West Germany, they really came to world attention when he joined the West German national team coached by Helmut Schoen. Schoen believed that rigid tactics should not be imposed on players, since they tend to divest the players of their own individuality, talents, and instincts. Although Schoen's teams had their own particular style, individuality was encouraged.

For Beckenbauer, this approach to tactics was ideal. He played his defensive role as sweeper but was free to build the attack and participate in it. Three deep backs played in front of or even behind Beckenbauer. These backs marked specific attackers. Three midfielders played farther upfield, linking attack and defense, and three forwards remained upfield to attack. Beckenbauer would roam free between the midfielders and last three deep backs, sweeping up defensively where necessary but always searching for a way to contribute to the attack.

Soccer tactics are very much a part of soccer's history, development, and success as the world's greatest team sport. Each new tactical variation causes a response, which brings further development. Today, the call is for total soccer, soccer in which players perform all aspects of the game. As players improve, tactics change to meet new demands. It is in the evolutionary process that soccer's future will be determined.

2

WORLD CUP SOCCER

Every four years, amid great excitement and pageantry, the World Cup tournament is played. This competition, more formally known as the World Championship—FIFA World Cup, has become the most captivating, celebrated, and prestigious international tournament played in the world of sports. It is in this great tournament that each soccer-playing nation puts on display its best in soccer players, soccer thinking, and, in turn, soccer tactics. The players who are selected to represent their country and to carry their national colors onto the field become the focus and embodiment of intense national pride.

In its fifty-year history, including a twelve-year hiatus (1938–1950), the number of entries in the tournament has grown from thirteen in 1930 to one hundred and six in 1978. Adding to the tremendous interest in the World Cup and running parallel to soccer's rapid post–World War II growth was the great technological advances made in television. Television brought the 1978 World Cup final rounds to every corner of the world, with viewers estimated to be around the 500,000 million mark, surpassing even the Olympic Games as a viewing attraction.

While nationalism plays an important motivating role in the attraction of World Cup soccer, soccer enthusiasts find more meaningful outcomes stemming from the tournament. When the qualifying teams gather to play the final rounds, they present to the world the best of soccer at that particular time. Newly developed theories and tactics are put into play. Variations on basic themes are seen and then analyzed, adapted, rejected, or simply appreciated. The team tactics in World Cup competition, especially those of the winners, become the styles of play most often copied, refined, and discussed in the years between World Cup competition.

The World Cup sponsoring organization, Fédération Internationale de Football Association (FIFA), is also the controlling body of world soccer. In 1980, 140 nations were members of FIFA.

At the first FIFA Congress, held in Paris in 1904, one of the clauses in the original charter stipulated that FIFA alone had the right to sponsor and organize a soccer world championship. It was farsighted on the part of the original members to consider the possibility of such a tournament, since the Olympic Games, with soccer very much a part of them, appeared to have satisfied the growing need for an international tournament. While international competition did go on and flourish between individual nations, the Olympic Games were the only vehicle at the time that brought to one site large numbers of international teams for a large-scale tournament. This lasted until the conclusion of World War I.

The end of the war saw the rapid development of professionalism in soccer in virtually every country. The Olympic ideal of amateur athletic competition for the sake of sport alone was systematically being torn apart in the soccer competition. A nation's best soccer players were no longer amateurs; they were clearly professionals, openly acclaimed as such in their home countries.

By adhering to strict Olympic rules, banning the participation of professional athletes, a nation's best soccer players could no longer compete in the Olympic Games. The Olympic Games could not be used as a vehicle for soccer's greatest, albeit professional, players.

It became clear that a world tournament was needed, one structured quite apart from the Olympic Games, to provide the opportunity for the best international teams to meet. At the FIFA Congress of 1928, a resolution was adopted by a vote of 25–5 to organize a world championship soccer tournament, commencing in 1930 and to be played every four years thereafter.

The prime movers in the design and development of thw World Cup tournament were Jules Rimet, president of FIFA from 1921 to 1954, and Henri Delauney, general secretary of the French Football Association. Rimet and Delauney recognized both the need and the value of creating a tournament for the best soccer players in the world. Through their determination and leadership, the first World Cup tournament came into being, with each successive tournament providing new thrills and excitement. In 1946 the trophy given to the tournament winners was officially named in honor of Jules Rimet. Under FIFA regulation, a team winning the world championship three times would retain permanent possession of the Jules Rimet Cup, as did Brazil in 1970. After Brazil's retirement of the Jules Rimet Cup, a new trophy was designed and named the FIFA World Cup. Brazil's capture of the first cup led to a revision in the rules, in that the new cup will always remain the possession of ΓΙΓΛ, with a small version of it to be the permanent possession of the world championship team.

3

EQUIPPING FOR SOCCER

One of the more appealing aspects of soccer to both players and sports budget administrators alike is the attractiveness and relatively inexpensive costs involved in outfitting soccer players.

The very nature of the sport dictates uniform needs and design. The soccer uniform is simple, attractive, and functional. Each player needs little more than a shirt, shorts, stockings, and shoes. The only necessary protective gear are a pair of shin pads. When costs for the uniform package are added up, it is plain to see that equipping a soccer team is compartively inexpensive when compared to other team sports.

Inexpensive, however, should not be confused with cheap. While it is possible to save money by sacrificing in some way in the purchase of shirts, shorts, or stockings, nothing should be sacrificed in the purchase of good soccer shoes, which are the most crucial and basic items in a soccer player's equipment.

Fortunately, modern soccer equipment—players' personal gear, balls, and field equipment—is readily available and abundant on the American and Canadian markets. This has not always been the case. It has been only in the past fifteen to twenty years that soccer equipment has become available in so varied and wide a market as it is today. With the rapid growth in participation in soccer, sporting goods manufacturers, both in the United States and abroad, quickly respond to the burgeoning market. This aggressive marketing response resulted in providing the kind of variety in equipment and price levels that had prevailed for so long in most other sports fields.

It is now possible, thanks to our free enterprise system, for players, teams, and other soccer equipment purchasing administrators to indulge personal tastes, shop competitively, and, even more important, exercise options in

The soccer player's uniform was basically the same from the 1920s to the 1950s. Although the shorts were baggy, they allowed the player freedom of movement. Photo by Ed Polansky, courtesy of Long Island University.

terms of which items of equipment should receive priority over others within the framework of budgetary limitations.

For example, many college, high school, and amateur teams which are almost always faced with limited budgets, build the overall equipment segment of their budgets by beginning with the best they can afford in shoes. Since good soccer shoes are essential to good performance and safe play, it is far more prudent to spend more money on shoes than on shirts or shorts, neither of which have any real bearing on performance and safety.

As late as 1960, there were very few choices to be made in the purchase of soccer equipment. To outfit a team in the manner of dress worn by the teams of the world meant having to purchase uniforms, shoes, and other equipment that was manufactured abroad. Naturally, uniforms, shoes, and equipment that had to be imported to North America were expensive, and outlets for the purchase of this equipment were few and far between. Very few American manufacturers of sporting goods carried a line of soccer equipment. Those that did merely copied the uniform styles worn by teams abroad. And the uniform styles were fairly consistent.

The well-dressed soccer players of the world wore basically the same uniform from the 1920s through the 1950s. Of course, uniform colors varied, but the cut and style were widely consistent, with few variations in the basic fashion. The soccer shirt was generally made of cotton (synthetic cloths were a later development), with the most interesting aspect of the shirt being an open placket strung with a lace, similar to a shoelace, that enabled the player to tie the shirt closed. Soccer shorts were always baggy and extended down the leg to at least mid-thigh. While these long, baggy shorts gave players a certain comical appearance, their design obviously was meant to provide the player freedom of movement and, I suspect, a modicum of modesty. Soccer stockings, designed and worn to encase the lower leg and the thick, heavy shin pad, had stirrup bottoms. This meant that the player had to wear a pair of sweat socks under the soccer stockings. But, given the style of shoes worn in those days, the extra socks worn very often provided the additional necessary cushioning of the feet.

As is still the case, soccer shoes were the most important pieces of equipment worn by the player. The term "football boot," still used by British players when referring to soccer shoes, was a most apt description for the footwear being worn to play soccer. It must be remembered that very few man-made synthetic substances were available until the 1960s. Consequently, soccer shoes were made entirely of leather.

Most players in the early 1950s wore soccer boots imported from England. These boots were constructed of unlined leather, had metal toe plates in the toes, and had cleats made of small leather disks fastened to the sole of the boot by small cobbler's nails. As one might expect, the leather cleats wore down quickly and, even worse, would come away from the shoe during play. The cleats that stayed on the boot had an insidious way of having the nails work up through the bottom of the shoe into the sole of the foot. In the mid-1950s some improvement came in the cleat arrangement on the soccer shoes. The sole of the shoe was provided with individual cleats that screwed into threaded receptacles, much the same as American football shoes. However, the uppers of the shoes still came to the ankle and the toes retained the metal reinforcement.

Two typical soccer uniforms of the 1950s. The player on the left is wearing the old-style soccer boot, and the player on the right is wearing the more modern, screw-in cleat type shoe. Photo courtesy of Long Island University.

Since the 1960s the widespread development of man-made fabrics and materials has proved a boon to sporting goods manufacturers. Uniforms and equipment for all sports can be made of less expensive but more durable materials that require infinitely less care than natural materials. Just as in other sports, soccer uniforms and equipment have benefitted from modern technology. The result is that modern soccer gear is attractive, comfortable, easy to care for, practical, and safe. So great has been the upgrading and styling of modern soccer uniforms that we can see soccer styles in shirts and shorts copied and adapted for general leisure wear.

THE SOCCER SHIRT

Soccer shirts are generally made of a synthetic knit fiber, such as nylon or Durene, or the natural fiber cotton. The material used in the soccer shirt is dictated by weather conditions and price range. The style of shirt selected is based on personal preference.

Short-sleeved shirts are generally worn in warm climates, whereas long-sleeved shirts are preferable for teams playing in cold weather. Where budgets are a determining factor, teams purchase long-sleeved shirts, rolling the sleeves up on warm days and down in the cold. Colors and design of the shirt conform to team or school colors. Besides color and pattern selection, neck style presents the only other option in shirt design. Neck styles range from V-neck and crew-neck shirts to the more elaborate collared shirts preferred by some teams.

The number worn on the back of the shirt must conform to league regulation. Numbers, team names, and emblems are either sewn onto the shirt or, in many cases, pressed on or transferred to the shirt by heat-application methods.

Most teams have two sets of shirts. The dominant color is generally worn when playing at home and the other color worn when playing away.

SOCCER SHORTS

Today's soccer shorts are generally made of nylon or a cotton twill, these materials being both lightweight and durable. The key to a good fit in soccer shorts is that the shorts be loose enough in the thigh area to allow freedom of movement when running or kicking. The waistband should be elastic, tight enough to hold the shorts up comfortably but not so tight as to restrict movement or breathing.

The color of the shorts is either the same as the shirt or the team's second contrasting color. Many teams, in order to save money, wear the same color shorts regardless of whether the home or away jersey is being worn. This eliminates the need for buying two different sets of shorts or one set for each color.

SOCCER STOCKINGS

The best kind of soccer stockings are called soccer hose. Soccer hose have a full foot bottom like regular socks and are long enough to be pulled up to the knee and folded down after being secured. A strip of gauze or inch-wide elastic secures the stocking just above the calf muscle and just below the knee. Care should be taken not to tie the gauze or elastic too tightly since that would cut the circulation to the lower leg and result in leg cramps.

Sock colors should conform to the basic uniform colors. Once again it should be noted that cost-conscious teams can buy one set of colored stockings rather than two sets. It is only the soccer shirt that must be changed for home and away matches.

SHIN PADS

Shin pads are the only protective equipment worn by soccer players and they are inserted between the shin and the stocking. Shin pads are designed to protect the player from the inevitable scrapes, bruises, and cuts that result from being kicked in the shin area. Modern shin pads are lightweight and thin. When worn correctly in conjunction with soccer hose, they will in no way hinder kicking, running, or ball control.

SHOES

Shoes are the soccer player's most important items of equipment and serve two important functions. The first is to provide the player with traction, stability, and foot support while running, changing direction, stopping abruptly, and jumping. Naturally, this function has a great deal to do with a player's personal safety as well as performance. The second function is their rather obvious use as the basic working tools for the player, providing the varied kicking and control surfaces that repeatedly come into contact with the ball.

Soccer shoes are subjected to great strains on their construction by the vigorous use they get during play, and it is for that reason that soccer shoes must be given the greatest amount of consideration when being purchased and why quality should never be compromised.

Good soccer shoes are made of full grain, calf, or split leather. The insides of good leather uppers are lined with a "breathable" material that allows perspiration to evaporate. The toes of the shoe are soft and flexible and free of any internal exposed stitching. The area around the ankle is lightly padded and cut just below the ankle bone protuberance. The heel of the shoe is

The multistudded soccer shoe. Photo courtesy of Patrick Shoes.

The studded soccer shoe. Photo courtesy of Patrick Shoes.

A soccer shoe with small studs and traction surfaces is best for playing on artificial surfaces. Photo courtesy of Patrick Shoes.

lightly reinforced with support for the Achilles tendon and padded for protection and comfort. The tongue of the shoe is also lightly padded to prevent the laces from abrading or cutting into the instep. Most good leather shoes constructed in this manner are lightweight and durable. Regardless of the sole design of the shoe, the leather uppers remain virtually the same.

The soles of modern shoes are made of molded polyurethane or rubber, bonded to the leather uppers for permanence. In contrast to the soccer shoe of the past, modern molding techniques have provided shoe manufacturers sole design options to meet demands made by specific and varied playing surfaces and playing conditions. Regardless of choice of soles, the leather-topped shoe with the molded sole is currently the best shoe available.

The most popular shoe, and certainly the most versatile—that is, it can be used under most playing conditions—is the multistudded, molded-sole shoe. This shoe has anywhere from fourteen to eighteen studs molded onto the sole. It certainly meets the needs of the majority of players in the youth league, scholastic, or collegiate level, where games are played primarily on grass fields. Where budgetary restrictions prevent players from having shoes for all occasions, this shoe is the best.

The studded shoe, which has either six studs molded into the sole or six cleats that screw into the sole of the shoe, is best for soft fields or muddy conditions. These studs or cleats are slightly longer and thicker than the studs on the multistudded shoes, thus enabling the player to get better traction by deeper penetration into soft and muddy ground.

In order to meet the demands presented by artificial surfaces that are prevalent in professional outdoor soccer and are standard in indoor soccer, molded soles have been developed that combine small studs with traction surfaces. Artificial surfaces are hard and often slicker than grass, making outdoor-type shoes unsuitable.

Once shoes have been selected, the most important concern is that the player's shoes fit properly. Good leather shoes tend to stretch with use, particularly the use given them in soccer. Most players, therefore, tend to get shoes one-half size smaller than their normal street-shoe size. As the shoes break in, they will stretch to the proper size and conform to the player's foot.

One method used by many players to get a proper fit and to speed up the breaking-in process is to put on the shoes, lace them, and soak them for a few minutes in warm water. The soaking softens the leather, allowing it to stretch slightly and conform to the player's foot. The shoes are then worn for an hour or so while they are drying. Good leather shoes will not be harmed by this soaking treatment.

During and after the breaking-in process, soccer shoes should be cleaned and polished after each use. Cleaning and polishing will keep the leather supple, ensuring the player's comfort and extending the life of the shoes.

The "well-dressed" goalkeeper will wear long pants for play on synthetic surfaces to protect against leg burns. Photo of goalkeeper David Brcic courtesy of the New York Cosmos.

GOALKEEPING EQUIPMENT

The basic uniform for the goalkeeper is very similar to that of field players. The goalkeeper's shoes, stockings, and shorts are usually the same as worn by teammates. But, since the goalkeeper has special duties and operates in a manner different from field players, he or she uses special equipment.

The goalkeeper's shirt or jersey must be a different color from the other players' to eliminate confusion about who is handling the ball in the penalty area. Goalkeepers almost always wear long sleeves to protect their arms when diving for the ball and to help keep them warm in colder weather.

The most important item of the goalkeeper's equipment is gloves. Goalkeeper's gloves can be made of cotton, wool, or leather, with strips of nubbed rubber attached to them. The strips of nubbed rubber are similar to the rubber faces glued onto the striking surfaces of Ping-Pong rackets. The strips provide the necessary friction to handle the ball surely. Goalkeeper's gloves are a must on wet or damp fields or in rainy weather, when both the goalkeeper's hands and the ball are slick with moisture. In extremely cold weather, gloves will help keep the goalkeeper's hands warm and help prevent numb-

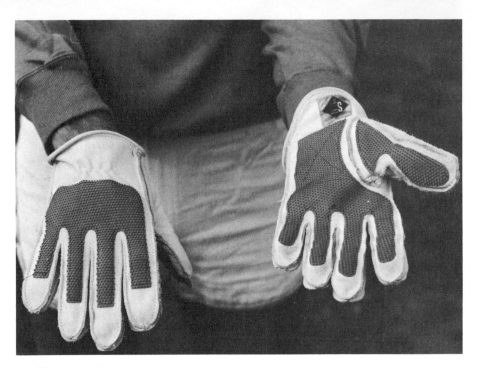

Goalkeeper's gloves.

ness in the fingers. More and more goalkeepers, however, are wearing gloves under all conditions.

While goalkeeper's gloves take a little time to get used to, they eventually give the keeper surer control in catching, deflecting, or clearing the ball. Their use should be encouraged on all levels of play.

One last item that should be a part of every goalkeeper's equipment is a peaked cap. An ordinary baseball or golf cap will suffice for those times when sun and glare interfere with the goalkeeper's vision. Players should wear a hat during practice so that when it is needed during a match it will not be a distraction.

THE SOCCER BALL

Central to the game of soccer, naturally enough, is the ball. There is now a variety of choices to be made in selecting a soccer ball. Soccer balls are made of leather, synthetic substances, or rubber and, to many people's great surprise, can be purchased in different sizes, with each size geared to meet the special needs of the participants using it.

The early soccer ball was made of eight leather panels, with an inflatable rubber bladder laced inside of it. The eight panels were stitched into a nearly round shape. With extended play, the leather panels would stretch, causing the ball to "balloon" out of shape. To combat this stretching, ball manufacturers went to a sixteen-panel ball, theorizing that smaller panels would stretch less. Their idea was a good one, but it was soon realized that even smaller panels stitched well would stretch even less. The result of the manufacturers' experimentation has given us the thirty-two leather panel black-and-white ball that is the most popular in North America today. Modern stitching and waterproofing methods make today's soccer ball last longer and play better under all conditions.

To purchase anything less than a reputable manufacturer's top soccer ball is to invite trouble that can result from inferior stitching and waterproofing. Cheaply made balls, which look quite good when new, simply are not constructed well enough to withstand sustained use. After hard kicking or if they get wet, they will get heavy and out of shape.

A good ball must be cared for just like any good piece of leather equipment. After use the ball should be cleaned with leather or ball cleaner. When not in use, the ball should be partially deflated so that the air pressure within doesn't exert undue stretching on the panels and stitching.

Soccer balls come in five different sizes. Size Five (5) has a circumference of 27 to 28 inches and a weight of 14 to 16 ounces. This is the ball used by adults and older children and is the official size for high school, college, and professional play.

Size Four (4) has a circumference of 25 to 26 inches and a weight of 11½ to 13½ ounces. This ball is generally used for schoolchildren aged eight to eleven.

Size Three (3) has a circumference of 23½ to 24½ inches and a weight of from 10½ to 12 ounces. This ball is used for small children from three to eight years old and is very often the official size used by midget leagues.

Sizes Two (2) and One (1) are the sizes used for decoration or are purchased by a proud father, mother, aunt, or uncle for an infant they hope will someday play soccer.

Every good soccer player I have known has his or her own soccer ball at home. To be good at soccer, practice with the team is not enough. By having a good ball of one's own, every player can practice ball control skills whenever the urge to do so comes on.

4

INDIVIDUAL SKILLS

To achieve success in soccer, an athlete must learn to execute the basic skills of the sport. The individual skills of kicking, passing, dribbling, trapping (controlling the ball), heading, tackling, and throwing-in are fundamentals necessary to good playing performance. Each skill must be learned well, practiced, and polished to be brought to the high level of execution demanded by the intense pressure of game conditions.

The main objective in practicing and refining soccer skills is to make the response to the ball or the situation an automatic one. By using conditioned responses to the demands of the game, the soccer player can constructively get on with his or her role in the game, without the hesitation caused by not knowing what to do.

The way to achieve the desired conditioned skill responses is by practicing the following skills, working from the simple to the more complex, mastering one step before going on to the next, under a variety of conditions.

KICKING

Controlled kicking is the essence of good soccer play. In the course of growing up most people have kicked various objects—footballs, playground balls, pebbles and small stones, and tin cans. This kind of kicking is far different from that in soccer because it is generally done without real purpose, skills, or accuracy.

It is important to understand that there is little difference in technique between passing the ball to a teammate and shooting on goal. All field position players must learn to kick the ball properly. Action is so rapid and responses must be so quick that good kicking techniques demand that the player kick well in all situations and in any way that does the job best. Basic kicking technique is the same for all field positions. Good kicking demands accuracy and control, techniques that can only be mastered through long hours of well-directed practice. Only then can the player expect to go on to the finer, more sophisticated aspects of the game.

It is important to understand the relationships between the foot striking the ball and the result of this contact. These principles, listed below, hold true regardless of the part of the foot used to contact the ball.

1. To keep the ball low or move it along the ground, the foot contacts the ball at the midline or slightly above it. This applies no lift to the ball. See illustration 2-1.

2. To lift the ball from the ground, the foot strikes the ball below the midline. See illustration 2-2.

3. To make the ball curve while in flight or to put "English" on it, the ball must be met to the left or right of the vertical midline. See illustration 2-3. This is not recommended until the basics have been mastered.

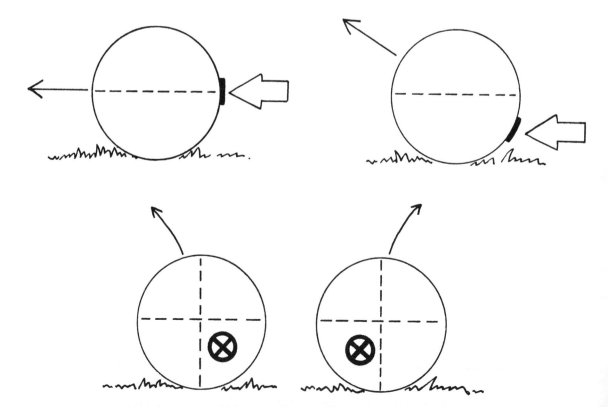

4. Most power behind the kick comes from a full swing of the kicking leg, the knee over the ball and contact made between the foot and the ball at the lowest point in the foot's swing. See illustration 5-4.
5. The rate of speed with which the foot contacts the ball will determine velocity and distance.
6. The follow-through of the kick is in the direction of the intended line of flight. Observe caution in using a big follow-through in areas crowded with other players.
7. The relatively flat surface areas of the foot provide the best kicking surfaces. The instep, inside, and outside of the foot seem made for striking a ball well. The toes do not provide a good contact surface because the rounded shape of the toe portion of the shoe and the shape of the ball are incompatible for accurate, powerful contact; and injuries to the toes are likely when power is applied to the kick.
8. The ability to kick with either foot is a prerequisite to good soccer play. Practice using both feet.

The instep kick.

The inside-of-the-foot kick.

The outside-of-the-foot kick.

The follow-through on the inside-of-the-foot kick is low and in the intended direction of the kick.

Kicking with the Inside of the Foot

Passing and shooting with the inside of the foot is a good place to begin learning kicking technique because:

1. This skill allows quick success; therefore, it is self-motivating.
2. Practice is safe and there is little possibility of leg strain or injury.
3. Gradual conditioning and strengthening of the legs take place.
4. Both legs can be used with little or no problems if an adjustment is made for the weaker leg and foot.
5. This skill may be easily applied in practice drills that are meaningful and fun.
6. This skill is the basis for developing controlled passing and shooting skills, dribbling techniques, and general ball control skill.

The inside of the foot between the big toe and the heel, and along the shoe to the ankle, provides a flat, hard, kicking surface. The surface is relatively big and allows for easy contact between the foot and the ball. There is little chance of missing the ball; therefore, the ball can be easily aimed at a target. Success is probable, even for the newest soccer player.

The player approaches the ball looking for his target. As he prepares to kick, he keeps his eyes focused only on the ball. The kicking leg is turned outward to allow the inside of the foot to make full contact with the ball. The sole of the shoe travels about an inch above the ground, and the ball is struck at the midline. This ensures an accurate roll along the ground in the intended direction. The nonkicking foot is placed alongside the ball, close enough so that the kicker does not have to reach for the ball but far enough away to allow a free swing of the kicking leg. The follow-through is low and in the intended direction of the kick.

At first, the inside of the foot kick is practiced as a pushing of the ball to emphasize control and accuracy. As the player develops confidence and control, the push should be turned into a well-placed solid jab at the ball. This will increase the impetus applied to the ball. The jabbing motion also allows the player to get rid of the ball quickly in actual game situations. Both legs must be used in practicing this skill. Control and confidence will both come quickly.

The Instep Kick

The instep kick is the heavy artillery in the soccer player's arsenal. When properly executed, it blasts at the opponent's goal or can provide the accurate, booming long kick out of the defense to a teammate well downfield. Its velocity and distance can be awesome when good contact is made and proper kicking principles are applied.

The beginning player, who wants instant power and distance and is eager to achieve both, tends to substitute the toes for the instep. This results in inaccuracy and, even worse, invites toe injury from hard contact with the ball. The player should be assured that when good form and techniques have been mastered, power, distance, and accuracy will soon follow.

The striking area of the foot contacting the ball is the instep. The instep runs just below the shoelaces. Here the bones of the foot form a relatively flat, broad, and hard kicking surface.

In this kick, the player chooses the target as he approaches the ball in a full running stride, at an angle to the intended line of flight. The angle is determined by which foot the player intends using. If the right foot is being used, then the angle of approach is from the left. The angle of approach allows the kicker to employ full hip rotation in swinging the kicking leg to add empetus to the ball. The full running stride and the angle of approach allow the kicker to swing the leg back in a wide arc and give more power to the kick. The nonkicking leg should be placed firmly alongside the ball, just far enough away to allow for a free leg swing.

At contact, the player must keep his eyes on the ball. The head must be kept down because raising it will cause poor contact and loss of power and direction. The kicking foot swings through the ball at the lowest point of the

44

For an instep kick, the player approaches the ball in a full running stride, at an angle to the intended line of flight.

The nonkicking leg should be placed firmly alongside the ball, just far enough away to allow for a free leg swing.

To lift the ball, contact is made below the ball's midline, and the follow-through is directed toward the intended line of flight.

arc, making contact with the ball at the midline. On contact, the knee is straightened vigorously, adding power. The toes are pointed down, the heel is well up, and the ankle is rigid at contact. This ensures a solid contact, giving power, distance, and accuracy. The follow-through is in the direction of the intended line of flight.

To lift the ball, contact is made below the ball's midline. This time, the nonkicking leg is placed to the side of and slightly behind the ball. The full leg swing of the kicking foot remains the same. However, because the nonkicking leg is slightly behind the ball, the kicking foot will contact the ball a little later in the swing or actually at the start of the upswing. The toes are pointed down to get under the ball and the ankle is kept rigid to support the contact. The follow-through is directed toward the intended line of flight. The head is down, as in all kicking.

A word of caution. If on the approach, the nonkicking foot is placed in advance of the ball, the kicking foot will make contact on the downswing, causing the ball to be pinched between the ground and the foot. Not only will the ball not travel far but, also important, injury to the ankle is likely.

Kicking with the Outside of the Foot

The outside-of-the-foot pass is effective for getting the ball quickly and accurately to a teammate on your right or left, or for passing around an opponent. It is difficult to get great power behind this kick, but surprise and accuracy make it valuable. When combined with a feint or two, it can confuse an oncoming defender.

Contact with the ball is made by the surface (outside) of the shoe on the area extending from the little toe to the heel.

The player approaches the ball while looking for his next move. The nonkicking leg is kept wide to the left or right of the ball, leaving enough room for the kicking leg to get between it and the ball. At the point of contact, both feet are on the side of the ball opposite the intended line of flight. The body's weight is borne by the nonkicking leg.

The kicking leg jabs crisply at the ball. There is a slight follow-through in the direction of the kick. The head is down at contact and the eyes are on the ball.

In going around a defender, the player waits for the opponent to come at him, feints once or twice, pushes the ball to the side, places his body between the defender and the ball, and regains control of the ball with the inside of

For the outside-of-the-foot kick, the kicking leg jabs crisply at the ball. The nonkicking leg bears the body's weight.

the same foot as he goes around the defender. The outside of the foot pass is easily learned and practiced. Success comes quickly and both feet are easily used with immediate good results.

The Heel

The heel can effectively be used to pass the ball back to a teammate coming up from behind. This is easy with a still ball, but it becomes tricky and dangerous when the player attempts to step over a fast rolling ball to get his heel into kicking position. If he steps on the ball accidentally, he is open to leg or ankle injury. Beginning players should exercise great care in using the heel pass.

To make the pass, the nonkicking leg is slightly in front of a stationary ball. For a forward-moving ball, the nonkicking foot is farther forward to compensate for the roll and pace of the ball. The kicking leg then passes directly over the ball, touches the ground in front of the ball briefly, and then is brought back sharply at the ball, the heel making contact with the ball.

The heel kick is tricky and deceptive. The trailing teammate, as the defender, has to be alert for this pass, since it may fool him as well. Use the heel pass only in a situation where there is no possibility of turning around for a safer, more accurate, and visual type pass.

The Volley

A volley refers to playing the ball with the foot while it is in the air. Timing is the most important aspect in volleying. The object is to get the foot to the ball at the right instant so that control can be maintained or new direction imparted. This can be learned only through intensive practice.

Beginners must get as much solid foot on the ball as possible. In order to achieve this, the ball must be watched all the way onto the foot. This reduces

The inside-of-the-foot kick is the best type for the volley because it provides the kicker with the greatest contact surface.

the difficulty of meeting the ball solidly and will lessen the possibility of making weak, off-center, and erratic contact with the ball.

The inside of the foot is best for the volley because it provides the kicker with the greatest contact surface. The player should make contact with the ball as close to the ground as possible. The inside of the foot should be at a right angle to the incoming line of flight of the ball. The nonkicking leg supports the weight of the body and the eyes are on the ball.

The impetus is supplied by the knee and the upper leg, which, on contact with the ball, sweep up and away. The ankle is held rigid to provide the striking power for the foot.

The inside of the foot provides a safe way of clearing long passes out of the defense. If the ball comes at the player fast and if his timing gives the rigid inside of the foot good, solid contact, the ball will clear a long way upfield. The player will have to exert less effort to gain distance on a ball coming in hard than with a slower ball. Either leg can be used, and a player should practice with both legs.

The instep may also be used in volleying. The instep volley is capable of delivering far more power to the volley than the inside of the foot, but it is more difficult to execute.

The difficulty arises because the instep provides less of a striking surface to meet the ball. Therefore, both the timing of the speed of the approaching ball and the placement of the instep on the ball become critical. However, when coordination is achieved, the power generated by the full swing of the leg combined with the solid placement of the instep with the ball is awesome.

In performing the instep volley, the toes are pointed down and the heel is brought up as far as possible. The ankle must be rigid. If the ankle is not rigid while the toes are pointed down, a "V" will form between the foot and the shin, causing the ball to be lifted nearly straight into the air and cover little distance. The follow-through should be in the direction of the intended line of flight. As always, the eyes must follow the ball onto the foot and the head should be down.

On a waist-high to knee-high pass from the right or left, the player can use the instep volley to clear the ball or to even shoot on goal. In this instance, the player is facing the incoming ball. As the ball approaches, the player leans back, putting the weight on the nonkicking leg, and throws his kicking foot well back and parallel to the ground. At the proper instant, much like a batter in baseball, he whips the instep across the incoming pass. This results in a powerful kick that goes off at right angles to the approach of the ball. This is a difficult but spectacular play. It will only come after much practice on timing and coordination.

Lifting or Chipping the Ball

The lift or chip is a ball control skill used to get the ball over an opponent's leg or even over an opponent's body. Its uses are many, particularly when trying to handle the ball in tight quarters with legs and feet all around. It even can be used to score an easy goal over the fallen body of a goalkeeper.

To achieve the lift or chip, the upper part of the shoe above the toes and along the laces makes the contact with the ball and the kicking foot and toes

To lift or chip the ball, the upper part of the shoe, above the toes and along the laces, makes contact with the ball.

are slid under the ball. The foot then lifts the ball from the ground. By leaning the body back and lifting the foot faster, the chip can be made to cover more distance.

The Toe

It is an axiom in soccer that the toe is never used to kick a ball with force, since safety, accuracy, control, and consistency cannot always be controlled. But when extra inches are needed to nudge a ball away from an opponent, or to flick out quickly to deflect a pass, that is the time to use the toes. Practice is really not necessary. Using the toe is a natural reaction that will occur at the proper time, in the proper instance, and in the proper manner.

Kicking Hints

1. To be a complete soccer player, you must be able to use either foot.
2. Devote at least fifteen minutes a day to using the weak foot exclusively in practice. Only through concentrated practice can you develop the use of both feet.
3. Get into the habit of searching for your receiver or where you want to direct the ball as you approach the ball. At contact, the eyes should be on the ball.
4. After kicking the ball, move to useful positions on the field. Don't stand and watch where the ball is going.

Weather and Kicking

Soccer is played in all kinds of weather. Naturally, adjustments to weather conditions have to be made. Fortunately, the adjustments are not made in technique but rather in the application of the technique to what the player actually wants to do with the ball.

The two biggest weather factors that the soccer player will have to contend with are wind and rain and their effects on the ball.

Wind can have a strong effect on the flight of the ball. If the wind is blowing hard at the kicker, any attempts to get the ball into the air will result in short high passes because the wind will hold the ball up. This is important especially to goal kickers and goalkeepers, who very often try to put the ball as far upfield and away from their goal as possible. The same is true for a corner kicker, who has to put the ball into the field in front of the goal but has to go against the wind.

Obviously, this is not the way to play into the wind. The idea of playing into a wind is to keep the ball as close to the ground as possible. Passes, kicks, and long clearances should all be geared to movement along the ground so that the wind will not be able to get under the ball and stop its flight. The adjustment should be made to the passing game and more work should be done through shorter passes than on a normal, windless day.

If the wind is blowing from left to right or from right to left across the field, the same adjustments have to be borne in mind. Any ball kicked high in the air will be pushed off target by the wind. Therefore, the game plan should be adjusted to cope with the wind's play of the ball. This is best accomplished by keeping the ball along the ground, where the wind will be less likely to affect the flight of the ball.

Defenders and goalkeepers must be aware of the wind's direction. If the wind is to the attackers' backs, the defense and goalkeeper should be alert to the added distance that the kicks will have.

It is to the advantage of every team to use the recommended corner posts and flags not only as markers but also as devices to show the direction of the wind.

Practice should be held on windy days as well as calm days to help the players develop a firsthand understanding of the effects of wind on the ball.

Rain presents several problems. The ball, if not plastic impregnated, usually will absorb water as the game progresses and get heavier and harder to pass. One solution is to try to use as many balls as possible on a rainy day and keep interchanging them. The best solution is to use plastic-impregnated balls, since they retain their normal weight over the game and help to keep the kicking and heading as close to normal as possible.

The biggest problem results from wet fields, slippery footing, and the resulting effect on the ball's performance. Little can be done about slippery footing except to have the players warm up thoroughly to help guard against pulled and strained muscles. Cuts and directional changes should not be made as sharply as on a dry field, and the players should get out on the field early to get a feel of the running conditions.

The biggest change on a rainy day and a wet field is the way the ball reacts. On a wet field, the ball has a tendency to slide rather than bounce. This means that if a player is coming up to play a ball that under normal conditions he would play on a bounce, he should look for a slide toward him rather than a bounce. In these cases, it is better to use the inside of the foot to bring the ball under control, since that provides the greatest foot-blocking area.

Goalkeepers will have to be ready to go down for shots that they would normally field on a bounce. The ball will be wet and this will add to their problems of handling it.

Since there is always the possibility of having to play in the rain, teams should practice in the rain. If warm-ups are thorough and the players are dressed properly, a short meaningful ball control practice can be held so that the players will get the feel of handling the ball under adverse conditions.

Following this kind of practice, a hot shower and good brisk towel drying will prevent colds or illness.

The whole point of this kind of practice is to simulate the actual game playing conditions that will not always be good, especially as the season progresses into the late fall and winter.

PASSING

Tactical soccer depends on controlled passing. Although styles of play may vary from team to team, or from game to game, all systems of play are successful or unsuccessful, according to how well the players pass the ball to one another. This teamwork results in the ball control and movement on the field known as soccer tactics.

To achieve the desired passing relationships, heading and foot passing must be mastered. The ball must be passed to a teammate at the right moment and in such a way that he can use the ball immediately to execute his next move. Anything less than this goal results in sloppy, hit-or-miss soccer playing.

The passer's prime responsibility is to get the ball to the receiver as quickly and accurately as possible. For this to occur, the passer must anticipate the receiver's moves and also understand the total team's efforts to get men free and into good receiving position. Practices and scrimmages are geared toward achieving these goals. When the players understand what the team is trying to accomplish, the passing game will start to become effective.

The biggest difficulty beginning players have is taking their eyes off the ball while in control of it so that they can see their teammates' efforts and moves to get free of defenders. The way to beat this problem is through hard practice in all individual skills involved with controlling and passing the ball. Players must develop a feel or sense of the ball whie they are in control of it. The only way to accomplish this is through daily passing and ball control drills.

Most passing drills are best practiced by players in combinations of first twos and then threes. Passing drills begin slowly, the players walking through the drills, passing the ball to one another as they progress up and down the field. After they get off the pass, they move to a position in advance of the

Giorgio Chinaglia, legendary forward for the New York Cosmos. Photo courtesy of the New York Cosmos.

partner now in control of the ball, ready for a return pass. In this way, players begin to develop a sense of touch in applying power to the ball for each varied kind of pass. They will soon learn to lead the ball to a teammate so that they do not impede the flow of the ball or the other player. After a while, the passes become controlled and effortless. As speed is increased in this type of drill, a pass-run-receive rhythm—the heart of all passing combinations—will be established.

When players have become more adept at two-player passing combinations, three-player combinations can be started. These drills should also start slowly. The players will quickly notice new options of passing. They are now able to pass forward, to the sides, and to the rear. At times, a player in possession of the ball can no longer go forward. A teammate trailing the player in possession of the ball can become the best receiver at that moment.

Passing drills can become a game when the coach combines them with relay races and other kinds of competition. All sorts of competitions can be devised, making the learning and practicing of the skill more fun and infinitely more valuable because of the built-in competition.

When players are able to handle passing drills with speed, accuracy, and skill, they are ready to move on to two-player drills against defenders. Here the players work on getting passes off quickly and accurately to guarded receivers, then moving to a new, constructive position on the field. The receivers work on receiving and controlling the ball, protecting their possession, and getting organized for their next move. All of this practice lies at the heart of developing the basic elements of team play. As proficiency increases, players should move to three-against-three drills, bearing in mind and putting into practice the same basic objectives.

Just as it is the passer's responsibility to move the ball quickly and accurately to a teammate, so it is the receiver's responsibility to find a good field position in order to receive, control, and handle the ball. The old soccer adage of passing to open spaces is really not realistic.

The objective of team tactical play in soccer, regardless of the system of play used, is to create open spaces on the field in which receivers can successfully be reached with good passes that they can use constructively.

For example, there are open spaces all over the midfield where receivers can run to receive passes. These spaces exist because they are of little importance in terms of scoring or being scored upon. It is, of course, important to control the ball at midfield, since that is where most attacks begin to build and where regaining control of the ball far from the goal eases the pressure on the defense. But closing all of the open areas at midfield by the defense often creates open spaces closer to the goal for the attacking team.

A good defense tries to allow no open spaces near the goal. Conversely, a good offense has to create the open spaces from which the goal can be attained.

The team's tactics will be designed to provide these spaces, but the actual execution of the play is directly dependent on the passing and ball control talents of the individual attackers. By moving the ball well, by passing and moving to another position, by giving and returning crisp, multidirectional passes, and by seeking out space while not in possession of the ball, space in front of the goal area can be created.

A fundamental example of creating space is seen in illustration 5-16. A is in control of the ball and passes to B, who is coming up along A's right side. A then goes behind B upfield and toward the corner alongside the sideline. As the defenders close on B, B passes ahead to A, who is making his run toward the corner. B then goes to his left and A controls the ball and crosses in front of the goal, where B, C, and D are coming in for the shot.

The passer must anticipate his teammate's moves and get the pass to the correct spot quickly and in such a way that the receiver will be able to perform the next step immediately. It is important to remember that once the pass is made, the receiver must move to a new field position that will allow still another alternative for the player now in possession of the ball.

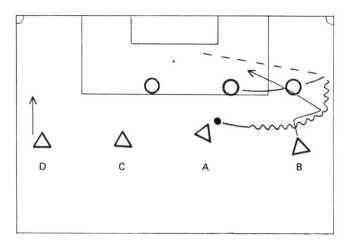

An example of creating space.

DRIBBLING

Dribbling refers to controlling and maintaining possession of the ball while moving in any direction or around opponents. As in basketball, a player dribbles to avoid defenders as he moves into a position from which he can pass the ball or shoot more effectively. Every player must dribble well regardless of field position.

However, when the dribble is done improperly or at the wrong time or is carried on for too long a time, it can slow the team's attack and defensive clearances, provide time for opponents to recover, provide opportunities for turnovers, and, in general, interfere with fluid, fast-moving soccer.

Many coaches and players become upset at their inability to teach or gain a high level of dribbling skills with beginners. Highly skilled dribbling takes years to develop and patient, regular practice is needed to learn the skill well. But if the basic skills and objectives are observed in learning dribbling techniques, the beginning player will soon show growth. Practice will give the player more sophisticated options to get past a defender, but these options must wait until the basics are mastered.

Dribbling is a highly personal skill that, when combined with feints, passing skills, and good technique, becomes an important part of the individual player's repertoire of skills. But if the learning of the skill is rushed, the basic principles and objectives concerning the use of the dribble will be lost. Understanding and reinforcement of the basic skills and objectives of dribbling will help the player proceed at the proper learning rate.

Franz Beckenbauer, former midfielder for the New York Cosmos. Photo courtesy of the New York Cosmos.

The Basic Principles and Objectives

1. The dribbler must keep the ball close to himself to ensure possession. If the ball is kicked too hard, it will be within reach of a defender. To change direction or exercise control in close quarters, the player in possession must keep the ball within his stride so that he can retain control and keep the ball out of danger.

2. The dribbler must be well balanced so that he can move in any direction.

3. The dribbler must have good control over the ball's speed and movement so that he will be able to stop, go, or change direction at the instant the defender commits himself.

4. The player must learn to control the ball without constantly looking at it. In this way, he will be able to see what the defense is up to and also where his teammates are in terms of creating his next move.

When dribbling, the player must keep himself close to the ball to ensure possession.

5. The player must learn to dribble at various speeds, accelerate and slow down, in order to stay away from a repetitive, easily diagnosed style.

6. For straightaway runs and changes of direction, the player should run as naturally as possible. The dribble must become part of the player's natural running style so as not to show his movements.

To master dribbling, the player must use every opportunity to practice the skill. This means that in practice time must be set aside specifically for dribbling skills, and conditioning drills should also contain dribbling. Players should not carry soccer balls to the practice field; they should dribble them there, and if the dribbling is made more difficult by changes of surface, so much the better.

The emphasis on dribbling practice is designed to help the player develop a feel for the ball on his foot. This will pay off in the player's ability to know how much power to put into the ball for speed, for directional changes, and for moves around defenders, and will also increase passing and receiving control. As touch and feel increase, skill will grow, since what the player is really doing is controlling the soccer ball as he or she wants to control it.

Dribbling with the Inside of the Feet

The insides of the feet provide—as in basic passing—a relatively strong, smooth surface for contacting and controlling the ball.

Place the ball between the feet. Use the inside of the foot to nudge the ball forward. Nudge it with one foot on a line forward and slightly in line with the other foot. Follow the ball and nudge it with the other foot. Keep the ball going straight. You can practice by going along a sideline; with each nudge of each foot bring the ball back to the line. Try to develop the right amount of touch in each foot to move the ball forward, but close to you, in order to maintain control. Alternate the feet, getting the feel in both feet. Walk until you feel that you have feel and control of the ball, then change directions—all still under control. Increase speed slowly, maintaining the pace until you feel control at increasing speeds.

To avoid boredom at first, the coach can use relay races between players, stressing control and directional changes, not speed.

When dribbling with the inside of the foot, nudge the ball with one foot on a line forward and slightly in line with the other foot. Follow the ball and nudge it with the other foot.

Dribbling with the Outside of the Feet

Place the ball ahead of your toes and between your feet. Using the outside surface of the foot, nudge the ball off in the intended direction. The surface above the toes and along the outside of the foot makes contact with the ball. This walking-running stride gives a slightly pigeon-toed appearance to the player's movement.

Alternately use each foot to propel the ball. Begin as always by walking, following a sideline and concentrating on developing touch and feel for controlled ball movement.

Increase speed as ball control develops. The player will quickly notice that this method of dribbling provides the most natural running style while dribbling. As speed technique and touch develop, the player will find that quick jabs of the foot, if applied well below the midline of the ball, will apply a bit of backspin to the ball. This backspin will neutralize some of the impetus applied to the ball as running speed is acquired. When real speeds are achieved by the player, this backspin will be invaluable to controlled, high-speed dribbling.

It is not necessary or desirable to touch the ball in each stride. Touching the ball too often slows progress or can put the ball out of control. What is important is to be able to touch the ball, change its direction, pass it, or stop it whenever the player wants to do so.

Combinations

To develop improved dribbling skill, the player has to be able to alternate striking surfaces of the foot as he moves along. For example, if a player is moving forward and he wants to move to the right, he can move the ball in the desired direction by using either the inside of the left foot or the outside of the right foot. In most cases, the outside of the right foot would be the best surface to use since the directional change would require a simple flick of the foot.

Begin development of dribbling combinations as a walking drill, consciously alternating feet and striking surfaces, inside and out. This may appear to be difficult at first, but as touch and feel develop, the players will soon begin to feel greater control over the ball and will pick up greater mobility.

Getting Around Opponents

After players have begun to acquire touch and can more confidently move at good speed and change direction with the ball under control, they are ready to learn how to get around defenders.

When dribbling with the outside of the foot, the player nudges the ball off in the intended direction with the outside of the foot and the surface above the toes.

It is common practice for players and coaches to spend hours dribbling around traffic cones, sticks in the ground, or even live teammates who have been instructed not to move.

Though this kind of practice is valuable for learning controlled dribbling and for mastering the basic directional changes, it is not real practice in the sense of meeting the demands of game situations. The fact that a player can capably dribble around a nonchallenging adversary does not mean that he will be able to elude a challenging defender—which is, after all, the purpose of dribbling. The player must practice against mobile defenders who are just as eager to gain possession of the ball as the dribbler is to bypass them.

One-on-one drills are especially helpful when players want to practice basic skills and build speed, control, and confidence.

The best practice for learning how to beat an opponent is to practice one-on-one in a prescribed area. At first the defender should defend with passive mobility, not making the challenge too difficult. Rather, the defender should make the player in control of the ball feint, change direction, protect the ball, and move around the defender. Players should take turns at defending and at dribbling. One-on-one drills, properly supervised, will give players the opportunity to practice basic skills and discover alternatives that are possible, while building speed, control, and confidence.

One of the basic aids to successfully avoiding an opponent is the use of the feint. Most beginning soccer players have learned to feint, or "fake someone out," as part of growing up playing children's games. In the tag games that children play the world over, they have learned that to escape a pursuer, the pursued must feint, or fake, in different directions, making the pursuer go one way or the other before turning a burst of speed in the opposite

A basic feint is made by moving the head, shoulders, or body in one direction, giving the appearance of wanting to go that way and causing the defender to move toward the threatened route.

direction. The same situation exists in soccer. No defender will allow an opponent in possession of the ball to dribble by if he can avoid it. Generally, the defender will not go for the ball until he is sure where the ball is going. By the same token, the player in possession of the ball must use feints to put the defender into a position where he can get by the defender. Here is where the feint must be employed.

The object of the feint is to get the defender to commit to one side so that the player in control of the ball can go by to the side opposite the commitment. There are many ways to do this, with or without the ball.

The basic feint does not "offer" the ball to the opponent. The player in control of the ball waits for the defender to move into possible tackling distance. The feint is accomplished by moving the head, shoulders, or body in one direction, giving the appearance of wanting to go that way. A good feint will cause the defender to move toward the threatened route. At the

The player in control of the ball can often "tease" his opponent into a committed route by pretending to offer the ball to him, then placing the sole of his shoe on the ball to stop it and drawing his foot (and the ball) back to him.

instant of the defender's commitment, the dribbler pushes the ball in the opposite direction and moves by the defender, with his body acting as a screen between the defender and the ball.

A tendency that must be avoided in this simple feint-and-go move is that the player will want to feint and move in the direction honoring his better kicking foot. The intelligent opponent will be looking for this tendency—so it should be avoided. Therefore, these skills must be performed with either foot and in all directions. Often a combination of feints must be used to get the defender to commit. The dribbler could feint his head and shoulders right, left, and then right again, and take off to the left. Of course, he must be ready to go instantly whenever the defender commits as a result of the feint.

The defender can also use the feint to make the dribbler go where he wants him to go. This makes it even more necessary for the dribbler to remain balanced and in control so that he can work his move to get free. Balance, speed, and ball control are the essence of good dribbling. If the defender makes an aggressive move for the ball, the dribbler must be in such control that he can reach the ball quickly, move it out of danger, and turn the opponent's aggressive challenge to his own purposes.

As dribbling control and confidence develop, the player can "offer" the ball to the opponent, teasing him into commitment, or may roll the ball forward (to all appearances a dribble) toward the defender. As the defender reacts, the player in control places the sole of his shoe on the ball to stop it. By drawing his foot back while in contact with the ball, the ball will come back to him. By pushing the ball forward to one side or the other, he can pass the overcommitted defender.

A variation of this can often be accomplished by drawing the foot back, allowing the ball to roll up the shoe to the instep. Now the ball can be lofted over an opponent's outstretched and committed foot.

"Offering the ball" is a feint that emphasizes ball control as well as speed. The purpose of this feint with the ball is to make the defender either lunge forward for the ball or lean backward on his heels waiting for the ball to come to him.

If the ball is pushed quickly at the defender, with a sincere, hard forward feint and offer of the ball, the defender will lunge at the ball or go back on his heels to recover. At either of these points, the ball is pushed around the defender and the dribbler follows with a burst of speed.

Practice this move by rolling the ball back and forth under the shoe sole. Drill with both feet so that this move can be done efficiently and equally well to both sides. This will keep defenders from concentrating on defending against one side only.

All kinds of possibilities concerning ball control arise when players use and work with the ball in practice. Touch and control are invaluable in the close-quarters dribbling situations that arise in every soccer match.

A player in control of the ball can go around an opponent by using a change of pace or a variation in speed. This is a quite natural means of avoiding an opponent, whether in control of the ball or not. As the defender approaches, the dribbler maintains his steady, controlled pace while he sizes up the opponent's threat. As the defender commits himself to the ball and the player in possession, the dribbler passes the ball to one side of the opponent, puts on a burst of speed, and goes around the defender. Here the essence is speed, not the dribbling move. The dribbling move is simply a strong push of the ball out of the defender's path, but the burst of speed sets the dribbler free.

This is also a valuable technique in beating an opponent approaching from the side. The dribbler moving at controlled speed waits until the defender is in position to attempt taking the ball from him. He then pushes the ball forward and puts on speed. This will usually give the dribbler a few steps on the defender, since only the player in possession knows when he will accelerate and what he has in mind.

For these reasons, players must not run flat out every time they are in possession of the ball. A player running at top speed cannot easily change direction or surprise the defender. The change of pace can be effective only in going from one speed to a faster speed. Going from nearly top speed to top speed is not quite deceptive enough. All-out speed in dribbling is best reserved for those bursts necessary for getting through a small opening quickly or for taking quick advantage of a last opportunity.

A player in control of the ball can go around a defender by first maintaining his pace until the opponent commits himself to the ball's direction and that of the player in possession.

He then can dribble the ball past the opponent while putting on a burst of speed.

*To go around a player effectively, the dribbler should screen his opponent;
that is, place her body between the ball and the defender.*

Another good technique is to fake a pass or shot. This is especially valuable
when a teammate is on the left or right. The player in control of the ball
swings his foot over the ball—as if to pass—then returns to dribble if the
defender moves in that direction, or pushes the ball in one direction and then
stops it with the same foot and moves off in the opposite direction. The dribbler can also bring the kicking foot back vigorously, as if a powerful kick
were coming, and then bring the foot to a stop, behind the ball.

All of these feints must appear to be the real thing—to make the feint
count, the opponent must think you will go through with the move.

To go around a player effectively, the dribbler should try to position himself in such a way that his body is between the ball and the defender. This
is called screening the opponent. The ideal situation occurs when a defender
is behind the player in possession of the ball. The dribbler has the ball in
front of him, well out of reach of the defender.

To accomplish this ideal positioning while in possession of the ball, feints
and quick moves must be employed. A head or shoulder feint or a push of the

ball to one side or the other, with a quick pivot in the intended position, can set the dribbler free, with the opponent effectively screened out by the player's body and the ball.

Constant practice and development of coordination will give the player more and more options. When an opponent sees a variety of moves performed, the defender has to respect each move or feint, which in turn gives a distinct advantage to the dribbler.

Dribbling Drills

Dribbling drills are best put into two categories. The first deals with learning the skills, the second with practicing and refining them by applying them to gamelike situations.

Control can be gained by dribbling on the sidelines, within the penalty area, up and down the field, and in circles. These individual dribbling skills should be practiced every day, with the stress put on developing touch, control, and a variety of moves.

Game simulation is necessary to implement the learned skills in a more meaningful way. Players should be kept within their skill abilities, increasing either the pace or difficulty of the practice as skill develops. The following are some recommended practice aids.

Relay races. These allow players to dribble and practice ball control against other players. Races should stress control and ball handling. Speed will develop as control develops. From simple straight-ahead races, the players should progress to races that include going around obstacles emphasizing control first and speed second, as the players develop.

One on one. Individual players pair off against each other. One player is the defender; the other, in possession of the ball, attempts to get by the defender. The space to work in should be limited and the defender instructed to give passive resistance until skill develops. Each player should play at offense or defense for five or six times and then switch roles.

This kind of practice gives ample opportunity for the dribbler to try all sorts of feints and moves to get by the defender.

Six-on-a-side games. Played in small areas with no goalkeepers, these games help develop dribbling techniques, as well as passing and defending skills. The players have to dribble and get rid of the ball quickly or go around a defender rather than lose the ball to the defenders.

TRAPPING THE SOCCER BALL

Trapping refers to bringing under control a ball that is approaching the player either along the ground or in the air. With the rapid exchange of ball possession in modern soccer, it is essential to develop trapping ability in order to succeed in the sport.

The ideal trap in soccer is one that brings the ball under control quickly and in such a way that the player will be able to perform easily the next desired move. As the level of soccer playing increases, defense ability and demands for good ball control made on the individual player will also increase.

Control is the key to trapping and must be stressed to the beginning player. The ball must be brought under sure control so that the next move can flow smoothly from the trap.

Principles of Trapping

To provide beginners with a basic understanding of trapping principles, it is helpful to start with the familiar example of the baseball player fielding a fast-approaching line drive. The baseball player moves into position quickly to face the oncoming ball and to get as much of his body as he can in front of the oncoming ball. As the hands make contact with the ball, the arms are simultaneously· drawn back toward the body. This arm action provides a cushion for the ball to ride toward the body, thus softening the impact. In this way, the ball is brought under control with little danger of striking a hard surface and bounding away. This action also helps prevent injury. To relate this to soccer:

1. The player must move as quickly as he can to the spot where he intends to trap the ball. It is essential that he get as much of himself as possible between the ball and the direction it is heading. The body will help stop the ball should the trap not come off as well as planned. Speed is important, since others will also be going for the ball.

2. As the player moves into position, he must decide what part of his body will do the trapping and how, so that he will be ready to make his next move. Practice and experience will make the choices easier, and any adjustments to changes in the ball's approach will be handled more automatically.

Julio Cesar Romero, star midfielder for the New York Cosmos, trapping, or bringing the ball under control and out of the defense. Photo courtesy of the New York Cosmos.

3. The player's eyes must be on the approaching ball. In this way he will be able to "read" the ball's flight path, always subject to variation because of spin, wind, bounce, and weather conditions.

4. At the moment of contact, that part of the body performing the trap must be relaxed and allowed to give in the direction from which the ball is approaching. If the trapping part of the body were held rigid on contact, the ball would strike hard and bound away uncontrolled.

5. The objective of trapping is to provide control of the ball in such a way that the player himself will be able to use the ball for his next move.

These principles apply to all kinds of traps, regardless of the part of the body being used.

Trapping with the Sole of the Foot

This is the best trapping technique to begin with because it is relatively easy to learn.

As the ball approaches the player, the trapping foot is elevated a few inches off the ground. The height varies, but the idea is to keep the foot high enough so that the ball can get under the sole but not so high that the ball will pass to the heel. The toes are drawn upward, thus forming an angle between the sole of the foot and the ground. The body crouches forward slightly but the weight is borne by the nontrapping foot and leg. The trapping knee is bent so that it will be able to move.

As the ball makes contact with the sole of the shoe, the leg is relaxed and the foot is drawn back to absorb the force of the ball. When the ball is stopped, a slight pull backward of the sole of the foot on the top surface of the ball will ensure control.

Caution must be exercised to avoid putting weight on the trapping foot, since that could result in stepping on the ball, causing the player to lose balance and possible injury to the ankle or the foot.

Trapping with the Inside of the Foot

This is a natural variation of the technique used to kick a ball with the inside of the foot. Either foot can be used quickly and successfully. When properly executed, the trapping leg will be in good position to pass the ball or for the player to dribble the ball in another direction.

As the ball approaches the player, the body leans in the direction of the oncoming ball and turns slightly toward the trapping leg. The nontrapping leg is in advance of the trapping foot. The trapping leg is raised slightly backward with the inside of the foot at a right angle to the ball's approach, thus forming the angle for trapping between the ground and the inside of the foot. At the point of contact, the leg, ankle, and foot are relaxed and drawn back to absorb the force of the ball. At this point, the player brings the inside of the foot to the front and the ball is in position to be played.

Trapping with the Outside of the Foot

This technique is generally used by a player who wishes to control the ball and move off quickly in a new direction. This is a trap that must be, by its very nature, executed quickly and smoothly in order for the player to accomplish his objective.

When trapping with the sole of the foot, the toes are drawn upward, forming an angle between the sole of the foot and the ground.

When trapping with the inside of the foot, as the ball approaches the trapping leg is raised slightly back-ward with the inside of the foot at a right angle to the ball's approach. The nontrapping leg is ahead of the trapping foot.

At the point of contact in trapping with the inside of the foot, the player brings the inside of the foot to the front and the ball is in position to be played.

As the ball approaches, the player extends his trapping leg toward the ball with the foot turned outward. This creates a long, nearly straight line from the hip through the toes. The trapping angle is formed between the ground and the outside of the foot. In most instances, the trapping leg will be ahead of the nontrapping leg, or, in cases where the player wants to move in the same direction the ball is coming from, the trapping leg will cross over the nontrapping leg. Upon contact, the trapping leg, foot, and ankle are relaxed and drawn back slightly in the same direction the ball was going. As the ball is stopped, the player sweeps his leg forward, thus putting the ball into posi-tion to be dribbled with the outside of the foot.

As the ball is stopped when trapping with the outside of the foot, the player sweeps his leg forward, putting the ball into position to be dribbled with the outside of the foot.

When trapping a ball from the air with the foot, the trapping foot is raised beneath the dropping ball.

The ball is "caught" on the instep of the foot and in one motion downward the ball is brought to the ground.

Controlling a Ball in the Air

Balls coming at players at varying heights off the ground can be effectively controlled by using the inside of the foot, the outside of the foot, the thigh, or the chest. Once again, as in all trapping techniques, the principles of relaxation and withdrawal of the trapping part must be observed. The player must move quickly to the trapping position and use the part of the body most effective for the best trap according to the height of the approaching ball. The objective is to control the ball in such a way that the player will be able to make the next move easily. Most of these traps will result in having the ball land at the feet, thereby facilitating subsequent action.

Bringing the Ball Down from the Air with the Foot

This technique is particularly useful in bringing under control a ball that is falling from a great height. It is not difficult to do and a player can work

Using the same technique and principles, a player can trap with either the inside or the outside of the foot to control a falling ball.

on this at practice with a partner or on his own by tossing the ball into the air and bringing it down under control.

The player moves to his position under the falling ball. The trapping foot is raised beneath the dropping ball with the instep facing up. The leg is bent at the knee to enable the instep to face upward. At the point of contact, the leg and foot are lowered, with the ball "caught" on the instep of the foot. The ankle is relaxed on contact to help soften the impact. In one motion downward the ball is brought to the ground. The instep is withdrawn from under the ball and the ball is in position to be played.

Using the same technique and principles, the player can use the inside and the outside of the foot to control a falling ball. Position and game pressure will often dictate which surface of the foot should be used, but as long as the basic principles are observed, the results will be the same.

When trapping with the thigh, the player turns his body sideways to the ball's approach.

On impact when trapping with the thigh, t[he] thigh is relaxed and withdrawn, which softe[ns] the impact and allows the ball to drop to t[he] ground, ready to be played by the same trappi[ng] foot.

Trapping with the Thigh

In controlling a ball approaching the player at a good speed and at a height between the knee and the hips, the inside of the thigh can be used as a good trapping surface.

The player moves into position to play the ball, turning his body sideways to the ball's approach. He raises his thigh to right angles with his body, with the full inside of the thigh facing the oncoming ball. On contact, the

In the case of a falling ball, on occasion the top of the thigh can be used to control the ball.

The ball is allowed to fall on the top of the thigh, which is drawn down at impact to cushion the force.

thigh is relaxed and withdrawn in the direction of the ball's line of flight. This softens the impact and allows the ball to drop to the ground ready to be played by the same trapping foot.

On occasion, particularly in the case of a falling ball, the top of the thigh can be used to control the ball. The ball is allowed to drop on the top of the thigh, which at impact is drawn down to cushion the force. However, the round surface of the thigh combined with the hardness when the knee is flexed make it a difficult surface to use unless the player is exceptionally good at it. Much better results will be gained by using the other traps described for bringing a ball under control from out of the air.

Trapping with the Chest

Trapping with the chest is a very effective means of bringing a ball under control. The beginning player may feel some trepidation at placing his chest in front of a fast-approaching shot, but this is because of inexperience. The skill should be taught slowly and with very little force behind the ball. It is best to begin by tossing the ball at the player's chest rather than shooting at him. If there is any difficulty in overcoming fear, switch to a lighter ball, such as a volleyball, to help develop confidence and technique. Once this has been learned, it is safe and desirable to use a soccer ball. Once the technique is mastered, hard shots will not hurt the player.

The contact area is the area from the sternum to up under the neck. The stomach should not be used. The player must be able to vary his body height on approaching chest shots to get the described surface on the ball. High shots can be taken on the chest, but the player has to jump for them. Great care should be taken as to how far down the player will go for low shots. Anything low might be better taken by the legs. This is much safer.

The arms must be kept clear of the chest when trapping. Any contact with any part of the arm will result in loss of the ball and a direct kick penalty. Beginning players have the tendency to want to catch the ball with the hands as it approaches the chest. To avoid this, practice chest trapping with the player holding some small objects (such as pebbles) in his hands to remind him not to reach for the ball.

The player moves quickly into line with the oncoming ball. It is important that this positioning is done quickly because the chest should face squarely in the direction from which the ball is approaching. Upon contact, the chest is relaxed and drawn back to soften the impact. Drawing the chest back at contact places the body in a forward lean, which causes the ball to be directed toward the ground.

When trapping with the chest, the arms must be kept clear since any contact with the arms will result in loss of the ball and a direct kick penalty.

The chest should face squarely in the direction from which the ball is approaching when trapping. On contact the chest is drawn back, forcing the body into a forward lean and causing the ball to be directed toward the ground.

Caution: If the chest is not relaxed at contact, the following could result: an uncontrolled rebound with little chance of possession, and possible chest injury from impact.

As in most soccer skills, there should be a direct relationship between trapping the soccer ball and the next move attempted by the player. Bringing the ball under control quickly and effectively is a major demand. Whenever possible, in practicing any other skill, also take the opportunity to employ ball control. Only in this way can you hope to keep this vital aspect of the game sharp.

HEADING THE BALL

Although it is true that soccer is played mainly with the ball on the ground, and that kicking is the principal way of getting the ball from one place to another, heading also is an integral part of the game. No play in soccer can compare to the spectacular thrill of seeing a forward rise out of a crowd in front of the goal and head one in. Nothing gives as much lift to a harried defense as seeing a defender leap into the air and head a hard, well-placed shot out of his defensive zone. These are but two examples of when heading really counts, and they are indicative of the need for the beginning player to master the technique.

It must be understood from the outset that heading is by no means a natural way of propelling a ball. Therefore, it is imperative that the beginning player and his coach exercise patience and care in the development of heading skills.

The greatest single problem the beginning player must master is overcoming the natural tendency to close the eyes as the ball approaches the head. To cope with this natural reaction the player must be brought to confidence slowly. The basic problem with players having difficulty in mastering the techniques of heading is a fear of the approaching ball. The skill itself is not difficult, but years of ducking objects coming at the head and natural eye reflexes can prove to be formidable obstacles indeed to quick mastery of heading techniques.

With players exhibiting these kinds of learning problems, beginning heading techniques should be taught with a volleyball or a partially deflated soccer ball. This will allow for softer contact with the head, thus allowing a gradual buildup of self-confidence, a gradual removal of fear, and a technically correct application of the skill when the player is ready and confident enough for the regulation soccer ball.

Basic Principles of Heading

The basic principles of heading must be understood prior to first attempts at heading a ball. They relate to both good technique as well as safe, injury-free performance.

1. The ball must be struck by the head rather than the head being struck by the ball. This allows the player directional control over the ball while preventing injury.

Pele about to head a ball. Photo copyright © 1975 by Tim Considine. Photo courtesy of the New York Cosmos.

When heading the ball, the eyes must stay open and look at the ball in flight all the way onto the head.

The head, neck, trunk, legs, and feet must be used in coordination when heading to give impetus and direction to the ball.

2. The eyes must be trained to stay open and look at the ball in flight all the way onto the head. This is another necessary principle for directional control and safety.
3. The part of the head coming in contact with the ball is the forehead, between the eyebrows and the hairline. This surface is hard, relatively flat, and least likely to be injured by striking the ball.
4. The actual striking of the ball by the head must be achieved through coordination with the feet, legs, trunk, and neck in order to give impetus and direction to the ball.

When heading the ball, the eyes follow the flight of the ball onto the head. As the ball approaches, the player leans back slightly.

At contact, the head is thrust at the ball.

The power of the legs, trunk, and neck is behind the thrust of the head.

Playing Head Balls with Both Feet on the Ground

The feet and legs are most important in forming the power base from which the player will head the ball. Whether the player has one leg in front of the other, similar to a boxer's stance, or whether he is squarely facing the flight of the ball with both legs parallel is relatively unimportant. In a game situation he will have hustled into his heading position and must head the ball from this solid base. Therefore, he must learn to quickly set himself with both legs in position in order to strike swiftly and accurately. The eyes follow the flight of the ball onto the head. As the ball approaches, the player leans back slightly, cocking his head, neck, and trunk. At the point of contact, the head is thrust at the ball with the power of the legs, trunk, and neck behind it. The follow-through is in the direction of the intended line of flight.

The follow-through in heading is in the direction of the intended line of flight.

Taking Head Balls While off the Ground

The technique for playing head balls while in the air is virtually the same as playing head balls on the ground. However, it becomes apparent that the feet-legs power base has been removed. In order to give the ball real impetus without the power base, the player must develop and use a much stronger trunk and neck thrust. This stronger thrust is developed through calisthenics and long patient hours of heading practice while the player is off the ground.

Good timing, which is essential to effective heading while in the air, is difficult to attain. The player must coordinate his jump into the air with the arrival of the ball. The only way that this critical timing can be learned is through training and drills, at first alone and then against defenders in varieties of situations.

To change the direction of an incoming ball, the player uses all the techniques of heading except one.

On contact with the ball, the trunk, nec and head are turned and the forehea strikes the ball in the intended directior left or right.

Since a player going up in the air for a head ball will be challenged by his opponent, it is important that the player be able to leap high in the air. There he can borrow the technique of a basketball player going for a lay-up shot. Wherever possible, a short run is the player's advantage. A one-foot takeoff is most desirable, with a rocking motion from the heel to the toe of the take-off foot, a vigorous upward thrust of the other knee, and a strong upward thrust of the arms—all contribute to greater height in the jump. The player must practice taking off from both legs because he will not always be able to choose his favorite takeoff leg during the quick action in the game situation.

Changing Direction with the Head

To change the direction of an incoming ball, the player uses all the techniques of heading described previously. The variation in technique comes in at the point of contact with the ball. The trunk, neck, and head are turned at the point of contact, with the forehead striking the ball in the intended direction, right or left. The forehead is still the point of contact. That never changes, but the trunk, neck, and head approach in the intended direction.

To head a ball downward, the forehead must strike from directly behind the ball and above the midline of the ball. The head must be actually over the ball so that the ball is struck at a lower point in its descent. The chin is tucked to the neck at contact and the trunk goes forward toward the ground. With practice a player will be able to take a ball from the air with his head and set it down at his feet for his use.

To head a ball up and away, the player strikes from beneath the ball with a vigorous jump off the ground. Power is supplied to this head shot by the upward thrust of the legs that contribute to the jump. This kind of heading is particularly useful for clearing the ball out of the defense, well upfield.

Deflecting a ball with the head is another valuable move. The objective here is to allow the forehead to become a deflecting surface rather than a striking surface. What is desired is a slight directional change of the ball's flight without taking away from the speed with which the ball is approaching. This is accomplished by allowing the ball to graze the forehead and glance away in the altered direction. This is especially valuable when attacking the goal and the goalkeeper is expecting a hard, fully struck head shot on goal. The goalkeeper comes out to play this hard shot, which he expects to come in directly at him, but the forward allows the ball to deflect off his head and into the corner.

It should be remembered that in heading the neck muscles must be rigid to support the deflecting surface of the forehead. Only balls coming from the player's side should be played in this manner. That is the only way to get

To head a ball downward, the chin should be tucked to the neck at contact and the trunk moved forward toward the ground.

To head a ball up and away, the player strikes from beneath the ball with a vigorous jump off the ground.

deflection. In all other approaching shots the head should strike the ball. This is the only technique in which the ball should be allowed to strike the head, but only with a glancing blow.

A word of caution in regard to heading. For beginning players the rule should be to never attempt to head a ball that is approaching below the chest line. By attempting to drop the head to heading position lower than the chest, the player runs the risk of being kicked in the head as an opponent is correctly playing a ball at that height with his foot. The rules of soccer define this kind of heading as a dangerous play that results in loss of possession of the ball and a free kick for the opponent.

THE THROW-IN

The throw-in provides the only opportunity for field players to handle the ball with their hands. Most soccer training and teaching necessarily concerns ball movement and ball control with everything but the hands. It is a mistake, however, for this aspect of the game to be neglected. The throw-in must be approached by the beginning player with the same degree of importance attached to it as any other soccer skill. There is no excuse for losing possession of the ball in a game because of a technically incorrect throw-in, although this is perhaps the most common infraction in soccer as played in the United States by beginning players.

The throw-in is one of the few techniques in sports that has its form totally prescribed by the rules. To violate form is to violate the rules, and that results in the turnover of the ball to the opponents. There is no room for argument or preferences as in most other skills. The rules must be followed to the letter.

The rules require that:

1. Both hands must be on the ball while delivering it for the throw-in.
2. The ball must be released from over the thrower's head with a follow-through. This ensures that a throw occurs rather than a dropping of the ball onto the field of play.
3. The thrower must be facing the field.
4. Both feet must be no closer to the field than the sideline but may not step into the field until the throw is released.
5. Both feet must remain in contact with the ground until the ball has left the thrower's hands.
6. The thrower may not play the ball until it has been touched by any other player on the field.

These are the rules. All that is required is learning the correct form within this legal framework that will allow for a controlled throw-in. Control in the throw-in refers to accuracy and desired distance.

Technique

The player assumes a comfortable stance with the legs about shoulderwidth apart. The feet are parallel, or one is in front of the other, depending entirely on personal preference and comfort. For beginners it is best to stay some inches outside of the touchline, to avoid stepping over the line.

The fingers are well spread apart on both sides of the ball, which ensures the good grip necessary for control. The ball is held at the chest as the player looks at the field to determine his receiver. When he is ready to throw, the knees begin to flex forward in the direction of the throw. The trunk leans back, and the arms raise the ball over the head and down toward the neck. Distance to be covered will indicate how much backward body bend is needed, but in all cases the ball must be brought back over the head. This action cocks the body and prepares it for the throw.

The throwing action begins with the knees straightening and the body following the knees in a forward movement. The arms follow the body whip and the hands come through and flick the ball off. The greater the distance required, the greater the body whip must be. The follow-through is in the direction of the throw, with the toes bearing the weight. Both feet must remain on the ground.

Beginning players should learn the skill from a standing position with no run-up. This will help them learn the technique without concentrating on the approach to the line. It will also aid in building up strength and coordination in the body for the long throw.

Using the Run-up

Greater distance can be accomplished by adding a short run-up to the throw-in technique. (The momentum from the run can be effectively harnessed to go into the throw.) However, it must be remembered that both feet must remain in contact with the ground at delivery. The run-up must be controlled so that violations do not occur.

The run-up should begin from about 5 yards from the touchline. The player should aim to throw from well away from the line. In the run-up technique most players have the tendency to throw with one foot in front of the other. This is natural and perfectly legal. The front foot is planted

When the player is ready to throw in, the knees begin to flex, the trunk leans back, and the arms raise the ball over the head and down toward the neck.

The follow-through of the throw-in is in the direction of the throw, with the toes bearing the weight. Both feet must remain on the ground.

The run-up for the throw-in should begin about 5 yards from the touch-line.

For the throw, the front foot is planted closest to the line.

The follow-through will be stronger using the run-up in a throw-in. Therefore, the body has to be stopped by the toes to prevent the player from falling forward onto the field.

closest to the line and the back foot is drawn up quickly parallel to the front foot at the time of delivery. The drawing up of the back foot is nothing more than a sliding motion along the ground to ensure contact at delivery. Since the follow-through will be stronger because of the added momentum, the body has to be stopped by the toes to prevent the player from falling forward onto the field before the ball is delivered.

Utilizing the Throw-in for Advantage

The player must realize that the throw-in is not merely a device for putting the ball back into play. The throw-in is a valuable tool in initiating attacks, provided the player uses it in an intelligent way. Throwing to a free man who has slipped his defender is one of many ways to initiate attacks.

The throw-in is also valuable in relieving pressure when the opponent is down deep in your territory and has lost the ball on out of bounds. The thrower can then throw long upfield or even directly to his goalkeeper, thereby relieving the pressure of attack on his defense. It is obvious that if in either of these examples the ball is lost through an improper throw, the harm to the team can be considerable.

Basic Throw-in Ideas

The throw-in can be made in any direction on the playing field. The player should not overlook the possibilities of throwing back in the direction of his own goal, provided that a man is free and ready for the throw. This includes throwing to the goalkeeper if the situation is right. Defenders have a tendency to overlook the possibilities of a "backward" throw. Conversely, when defending against throw-ins, be alert to this threat; it follows that a team that understands all of its alternatives will be adequately prepared for the opponent's alternatives.

If the throw-in is to be made to a teammate who is in motion, the thrower must give him a lead pass, which will allow the receiver to continue in the direction he is going without breaking stride or going back for the ball.

Receivers must make every effort to keep defenders from getting the ball. The receiver can do this by keeping his body between the defender and the thrower. This screening is very effective in getting the pass. However, the receiver must pay attention to the defender since he will be on him as quickly as the ball reaches him.

Another technique of getting free to receive the pass is to get set, let the defender move into position, and then fake and take off in another direction. You will then have a step or two on the defender, and if the pass is right and the lead is good enough, you will be on your way with the defender trailing.

The closest man to where the ball went out of bounds should quickly move to take the throw-in. His teammates should also be moving quickly into receiving positions. The throw should be taken as quickly as possible since speed can catch the opponent in poor defensive positions. For this reason, all players on the field must be able to perform the throw-in accurately and intelligently and are expected to do so.

There are situations where a "specialist" may be used. There may be a player on the squad who for some reason can throw the ball a great distance. He might be especially valuable in making the throw-in from the side of the field, when his throw-in distance will be able to put the ball in front of the opponent's goal. In this case his throw-in can have the same effect as a corner kick.

When defending against throw-ins, it is important to understand that these same options can be employed by the opponent. Speed in covering possible receivers is important. It is just as important to note that if the attacking team waits for someone special to take the throw-in, chances are the player is able to deliver the long, dangerous throw-in. Learn to read the situation and then defend against it.

Special Conditioning Considerations for the Throw-in

It is understood that good soccer performance depends on top physical condition. However, the throw-in demands certain extras that will ultimately assist the player in carrying out this skill with the strength and fitness that it requires.

The body whip is essential in getting strength and distance behind the overhead throw-in. Building up the muscles for this unnatural throwing motion is best accomplished through the use of medicine balls. After warming up thoroughly with the usual conditioning calisthenics and drills, time should be taken in each practice for medicine ball work.

Players begin by doing situps with the medicine ball held at arm's length behind the head. They are actually performing the same movements that they perform when they take the throw-in, except that they are lying on their backs. This situp drill with the weight of the medicine ball offering resistance will strengthen the arms, trunk, and back muscles. These muscles are the ones that give the power to the throw-in.

Following these situps, a player can stand and actually throw in using the correct techniques but substituting the medicine ball for the soccer ball. This will aid in building strength.

These medicine ball drills, when added to the normal conditioning routines, will pay off in stronger, more confident throws and greatly lessen the chances of strains or pulls. Do these drills whenever possible in season and out of season.

When practicing other skills in pairs, and when throwing the ball to a partner is more desirable than kicking a ball at him, such as in beginning heading practice, the opportunity to further utilize throw-in techniques is present. Use this as often as possible.

In practice-game situations, the coach should correct throw-in violations as they occur and on the spot, regardless of the purpose of the drill.

TACKLING

The rapid changeover from attack to defense makes it necessary for all players, regardless of designated field position, to be able to play defense. A forward who has lost possession of the ball is as responsible for defensive tactics at that point as are the fullbacks for stopping an attack. The old theories of offensive functions and defensive functions according to positions are long gone.

The offensive-defensive concepts of modern soccer must be expressed in terms of "whole team concepts." This means that when any player on the team has possession of the ball, the entire team is on offense. When any player on the other team has the ball, the whole team is on defense. Strong, efficient, and successful team defense begins with strong and determined individual work. No defensive system can be effective if not all individuals are capable of carrying out their responsibilities.

Individual defense is based on well-learned and accomplished skills, concentration, courage, and pride. Knowledge of the skill and the ability to carry it off well go a long way in the courage-development area. Pride is important to the player because it stimulates a motivation to defend well. This feeling of pride is based on matchups of the player's defensive skills against the attacker's offensive skills.

Good field position is crucial to defending against an opponent with or without the ball. Challenging an opponent along the sidelines, for example, presents a different set of alternatives than tackling in midfield. The defensive player obviously has ,the sidelines as an ally and can use them to force the player in possession into unwanted moves. The player in possession must move away from the sideline if the defender has cut off this route. Knowing this, the defender can take advantage of the situation and be ready to make the stop between the sideline and the alternate route.

Midfield defense is more difficult since there is maneuvering room and the attacker has more options. But there the defensive player can rely on help from his teammates to back him up should his moves prove unsuccessful. Having these kinds of field problems pointed out during scrimmages and games will quickly make alternatives apparent to all players.

The defender has four major objectives when playing defense against an opponent.

1. Prevent the receiver from receiving a pass. This can be accomplished by playing between the man in possession of the ball and the receiver. The key factor here is to be able to watch both the ball and the possible receiver. This comes from game condition experiences.
2. Intercept the ball, if it is passed to the man you are guarding. The interception must be done with good timing because if the defender misses the interception, the play will pass him by.
3. Make the player in control of the ball take a different route than he planned, or make him get rid of the ball. This is successful if the dribbler feels he must get rid of the ball and the rest of the defense is covering well. This causes turnovers from poorly executed passes.
4. Take the ball away from a man in possession through a good, strong, well-executed tackle.

Although shutting off the possibilities of receiving passes and interceptions are the most desirable defensive tactics, a player should realize that, most often, good defensive play is concerned with actually taking the ball away from the man in possession.

This is called tackling. The objectives of tackling are to stop the player in control of the ball from doing what he wants to with the ball, and to take the ball away from him.

It is important that tackling be taught patiently because beginners have a tendency to go at it too hard, without the control necessary to prevent injuries. All players should wear shin pads when practicing tackling, and, if the field conditions allow their use, should be encouraged to practice this skill in sneakers for further safety.

It is difficult and also meaningless to contrive tackling drills that are not part of actual game conditions. In practice tackling drills, teammates have a tendency to "take it easy" on each other and the whole point of tackling is lost. The players should learn the skill, be shown the skill, and then be allowed to practice it in as close to game conditions as possible. This is usually best done through six-on-a-side games in small areas where all vital skills are best learned and the motivating action is present.

Tackling. Photo courtesy of the New York Cosmos.

Teaching proper tackling technique begins with reviewing and understanding the options that the player in control of the ball has and how he intends to beat his opponent. Dribbling techniques that have been taught and learned well are designed to throw the defender into an off-balance position so that the dribbler can go around his opponent.

Now reverse thinking has to be considered. The defender wants to put the attacking dribbler into a position of unbalance or force him into a commitment with the ball that will enable the defender to stop his progress and possibly gain possession himself.

The defender moves himself into a balanced position, one that will allow him to strike quickly for the ball at the right instant. Just as the man in possession of the ball will use feints to get the defender out of balance, so should the defender. Very often, the better faker will win this battle. The defender is trying to get the dribbler to make his move. The defender hasn't got the ball to feint with but he can use head, body, and trunk feints, which are very effective in these situations. The biggest thing the defender has to worry about when he feints is that he keep in balance so that he does not "feint himself out." Concentration is important in this individual defensive play. The defender must concentrate on the man and not the feints. He must be patient and wait for the right instant to strike. The right instant is that moment when the man in possession plays the ball with a legitimate—not a fake—move.

Tackling Head On with the Dribbler in Full Possession of the Ball

The tackle is attempted by the defender at the instant the dribbler moves to play the ball. The inside of either foot is used, since this provides the greatest and surest trapping area. The foot should be drawn up to the ankle and held rigid. This rigidity provides the firm area that will withstand the impact of the tackle against the ball and will also prevent injury from strain that could occur if the ankle were kept relaxed. The body weight is put over the ball with the nontrapping leg on the side of and behind the ball. Crouch the body forward to help avoid being pushed off balance and therefore off the ball. The shoulder should come into legal contact with the opponent. The trapping leg swings in quickly and forcefully, jamming the ball between the dribbler's leg and the trapper's leg. The pressure on the ball should be steady and maintained for the next move.

The tackler (in white) moves in against the dribbler to trap the ball.

The tackler's body is in a crouch forward to help avoid being pushed off balance.

The tackler's trapping leg swings in quickly and forcefully. *The ball is then trapped between the dribbler's leg and the trapper's leg.*

At this point, phase one of the successful tackle has been accomplished. The opponent has been stopped from playing the ball. Now to wrest control from the opponent, the following can be attempted:

1. Put a shoulder in to the charge to get the opponent off balance and going backward away from the ball.
2. Slip the foot under the ball and lift it up quickly. This will cause the ball to roll or be lifted over the opponent's foot. Then a screen with the body between the ball and the intended direction will help in the getaway.
3. A combination of a forceful leg push with the shoulder charge can force the ball free either to the right or left or even through the opponent's legs.
4. If after the initial stoppage and while the ball is jammed between the player's feet the tackler feels a weakening of force being applied to

the ball, he should quickly exploit that weakness by either playing harder at it or by using one of the described maneuvers for freeing the ball.

Problems to Avoid in Tackling

1. Going in gingerly for the ball. The attempt to get the ball must be forceful and quick. A weak "poke" or jab for the ball leaves the player off balance and open to injury.
2. Lunging at the ball. A lunge is one of the best things a defender can do if he wants to allow the dribbler to go around him. Never lunge. The play should be a well-planned strike at the ball from a balanced position.
3. No shoulder behind the charge. This leads to a weak tackle and usually means that weight and balance will not be supportive of the tackle. This will result in a half-hearted attempt to get the ball. In such a weak tackle, where body weight is not being applied, controlled, steady, and strong pressure is not behind the tackle, and in most cases the tackler will have committed himself in a given direction. This will allow a good dribbler to go around him.

Tackling from the Side or from Behind

All of the techniques of tackling from the front are applicable to tackling from the rear or from the side. The variation comes in the approach to the tackle and then timing the tackle for success. It is here that speed is essential. With beginning players it is safe to assume that the man in possession of the ball will not be faster than the defender coming up from the side or from behind.

The object in this tackle is for the defender to get as close to the ball as possible. The nontackling leg—depending on which side the approach is being made from—should be in front of the ball before the attempt at tackling is made. This will allow the tackler to plant the nontackling leg and use it as a pivot to swing the rest of his body around and bring himself squarely into the path of the dribbler. This pivot should take place with enough room to give the defender a chance to stop. If the pivot is done too soon and without compensation for the dribbler's speed, a collision could occur that would result in a free kick for the attacking team and a worse situation for the defenders. The body pivot must be executed quickly so that the momentum of the body will be carried through the pivot, and will then be nearly equal to

When tackling from the side, the defender (in white) plants his nontackling leg (in this case, his left) to use as a pivot to swing his body around into the path of the dribbler.

the momentum of the dribbler when the shoulder contact occurs. To have less than maximum momentum behind the pivot would result in the tackler being knocked to the ground.

When the tackler has succeeded in getting into this position in front of the dribbler, all tackling principles are observed.

The important thing for the tackler to remember is that he should not extend his leg into the dribbler. He should be in the balanced position and he should strike when he is sure. With the leg extended, the body weight will not be in position to stop the tackler from being knocked over. Reaching in for the ball is an overcommitment on the part of the tackler and is an obstacle that a good dribbler can easily cope with.

Using the Heel to Tackle

This is an advanced tackling technique that can be used only by skilled players in special situations. The tackle is best performed when the players are running shoulder to shoulder in the same direction. It is best used when the dribbler is using the same leg to dribble as the side that the tackler is on.

To execute this tackle, the tackler times his stride with that of the dribbler. At the right instant, the tackler moves his inside leg into the path of the ball, and blocks the ball with his heel. This heel-blocking motion will cause the ball to reverse its direction. At this point the tackler must pivot sharply and reverse his run to go in the direction of the ball. The pivot should be made to the inside so that the tackler's body will effectively screen out of the play the player having lost possession.

Tackling, like all soccer skills, can and must be learned by everyone on the field. Size is not a factor in good tackling. What is a factor, however, is the determination of the player and his willingness to go in to get the ball. This is the "secret" to good tackling.

When tackling with the heel, the tackler (in white) moves his inside leg into the path of the ball, blocking the ball with his heel and causing the ball to reverse direction.

Former Rochester goalie Claude Campos. Photo by George Tiedemann, courtesy of the New York Cosmos.

5

GOALKEEPING

To be a goalkeeper is to be different. While teammates are struggling to learn foot and head skills, the goalkeeper is concentrating on building his eye-hand coordination skills. While teammates are concentrating on developing their passing, ball control, and tackling skills, the goalkeeper concentrates on learning angles and how to get into the best positions to make saves. While others are practicing interplay between positions, the goalkeeper works alone in polishing the skills that only he can perform in his kind of isolation. Of course, at times the goalkeeper is a team player too, but, when going for the ball for a save, he is on his own. If the ball gets by him and into the goal, all eyes are on him and not on the defender, who may have made the mistake that set up the score.

The goalkeeper's position requires a composite of skills and talents that are reflected in other sports. He has to combine the sure hands of a shortstop, the agility of a gymnast, and the jumping ability of a basketball player with the courage and determination of a linebacker. Many American youngsters possess these talents and basic attributes and can use them to become good goalkeepers. The years of childhood spent learning the skills used in the most common American sports can be prerequisites for good goalkeeping.

But this is still not enough to make a good goalkeeper. The prospective goalkeeper has to learn the "art" of goaltending. This involves getting into the proper position in order to cut down the angle the shooter has on the goal. The goalkeeper must know how to go after the ball and the best techniques for handling it safely and controlling it. He must know what to do when he can't catch the ball and, just as important, how to initiate his team's attack once he has gained control of the ball.

The goalkeeper's task is to protect a goal that is 24 feet wide and 8 feet high, or cover an area of 192 square feet. This can be accomplished only through an understanding of angle theory and learning how and where to position himself in order to use his position as a defensive aid.

CATCHING THE BALL

The most effective play by the goalkeeper is to catch the ball. Once the goalkeeper has possession of the ball, the attack is over. His team then begins its offensive.

No matter what the height of the approaching ball, whether it be on the ground or in the air, certain basic principles apply to catching the ball.

1. The ball must be watched all the way into the hands. This is essential since many factors could be at work that could change the ball's line of flight, such as deliberate spin put on the ball to make it curve or wind blowing the ball off its line of flight. The goalkeeper must keep his eyes on the ball and not on the attacking players. This requires both concentration and courage.
2. The goalkeeper should always use both hands in attempting to catch the ball. This is the surest way of maintaining possession of the ball.
3. As the ball is caught, there should be a drawing back of the arms toward the body to allow a cushioning of the impact. The ball then should be drawn into the midsection and protected as quickly as possible.
4. The goalkeeper should attempt to put as much of his body as possible behind the catch, in case the ball should slip through his hands.
5. He must protect himself at all times when making a save by getting control of the ball and then getting out of the way of the oncoming players.

Catching the High Ball

The high shot, pass, or cross in front of the goal forces the goalkeeper to jump into the air to gain possession of the ball. The goalkeeper should move quickly to the possession that he judges to be the best from which to make his jump. Moving to the spot and coordinating that movement with the jump will add to the height he attains. The best takeoff is the one that is

The goalkeeper should always use two hands in attempting to catch the ball.

When the goalkeeper catches the ball, he should draw his arms back toward the body to cushion the impact.

The goalkeeper should attempt to put as much of his body as possible behind the catch. This illustration shows poor goalkeeping technique. The goalie did not put enough of his body behind his arms and the ball has slipped through his hands. Photo courtesy of the New York Cosmos.

the same as the basketball layup shot. The goalkeeper leaves the ground with a one-foot takeoff and brings the other foot up, bent at the knee, to protect him from the crowd that will be forming around him.

The goalkeeper's eyes are on the ball all the way as he moves into position and into the air for the ball. The arms are brought up with the fingers well spread out and facing in the direction from which the ball is coming. The catch should be made in front of the head so that the ball can be cushioned by the arms to soften the impact without the goalkeeper straining backward. Once impetus has been stopped, the ball should be drawn to the stomach area and protected by the body and arms. This is essential since the goalkeeper usually comes down with the ball in a crowd.

The best takeoff when catching a high ball is the same as the basketball layup shot. The goalkeeper leaves the ground with a one-foot takeoff and brings the other foot up, bent at the knee.

When catching a ball in the chest area, the arms should move back toward the body once the ball is caught and the body should bend over the ball to help protect possession.

To catch a ball below the chest area, hold the arms with the elbows against the sides and with the hands forming a basket.

Catching the Ball in the Body Area

To catch a ball that is coming into the upper chest area, the goalkeeper should move into a position in which he gets as much of his body as possible in front of the ball. The arms are held up in front of the body with the elbows close to the sides. This allows little chance for the ball to slip through. The hands are up at ball height with the fingers spread and facing the on-coming ball. As the ball is caught the arms move back toward the body to cushion the impact and the body bends over the ball to help protect possession.

For a ball that is approaching lower than the chest, at stomach height, the arms can be held with the elbows against the sides and with the hands form-

To field balls that are lower than the stomach but still off the ground, the goalkeeper stands erect and bends from the waist, keeping the legs as straight as possible.

ing a basket. As the ball comes into the hands, it is cradled between the arms, which are wrapped around the ball and the lower chest. Another way to catch in this area is to have one arm above and one arm below the ball.

To field balls that are lower than the stomach but still off the ground, the goalkeeper should move into a position in front of the oncoming ball. He stands erect and bends from the waist, keeping the legs as straight as possible. His arms form a basket for the ball, and the hands are pointed down with the fingers spread to form a guide for the ball to follow in toward the body. As the ball is caught, it is brought into the stomach area and protected by the arms and body.

FIELDING GROUND SHOTS

Fielding ground shots can be difficult because the ball is traveling over rough ground that may cause the ball to change path. In fielding this kind of shot, the goalkeeper must take care not to commit himself too soon. He must move to the spot that is between the ball and the goal quickly, but must concentrate on the path the ball is traveling. These kinds of saves require as much body behind the ball as possible so that no "holes" are formed through which the ball can slip. An added complication to fielding low shots is the foot traffic that develops from attacking forwards and the goalkeeper's own defense. The goalkeeper has to not only make the save but must get out of the way of the players around him.

Once the goalkeeper has reached a position where he is between the ball and the goal, he should turn his feet at right angles to the oncoming ball. The body faces squarely the approach of the ball. He then kneels down on one knee for the ball with his arms down and his palms facing the oncoming ball. The fingers are well spread. This position allows for the greatest amount of body between the ball and the goal. The elbows are held close to the body and the catch is actually made by the hands in front of the bending knee and the shoe of the other foot. This ensures cutting off any "hole" that the ball can go through. The ball is then tucked into the body for protection and the goalkeeper is able to get up and out of the path of the oncoming players.

DIVING

The goalkeeper's ready position for diving should be one that allows him to move quickly. His weight should be on the balls of his feet with a good balance that will allow him to go forward or backward or to the right or left, as the situation demands.

The mechanics of the dive are the same for either side. The objective of the dive is to get the hand or fist into the path of the ball either to catch the ball or to fist it away from the goal.

The low dive must be aimed to get the hand and fist into position to protect the lower corners of the goal. The arm on the side from which the ball is approaching should be thrust at the ball with the body hopefully following. The side of the body should be low and parallel to the ground. The legs drive the body into this position with a strong thrust.

The goalkeeper's ready position for diving—
weight on the balls of the feet with a good
balance that will allow him to go forward, backward, or to the right or left.

In the dive, the arm on the side from which the
ball is approaching should be thrust at the ball
with the body following. The side of the body
should be low and parallel to the ground.

The low arm will present the greatest amount of reach to the ball. As the stop is made, the opposite arm should be brought up to wrap around the ball. Then both arms pull the ball into the body, which is then curled around the ball for protection. Once the goalkeeper has full possession, he should get to his feet quickly.

Diving for the Ball at the Forward's Feet

A forward in possession of the ball, dribbling in at goal through the penalty area, presents probably the most difficult problem to the goalkeeper. The goalkeeper should remember that the forward will come in at the goal in such a way that his favorite kicking foot will be the one that takes the show. This means that he will also most likely be coming in on an angle to the goal that will favor his better foot.

This illustration shows good diving form—getting as much body as possible in front of the ball. Photo courtesy of the New York Cosmos.

The goalkeeper's dual objective in this kind of situation is to get the forward into a field position that makes the shot as difficult as possible, and to get himself into position to smother the shot, once it has been taken.

To get the forward into the least desirable shooting position, the goalkeeper moves out toward the dribbler, taking the best angle for shooting away from the forward. This can be accomplished through feints and movements toward the dribbler. If the goalkeeper has been alert and has discovered which foot the forward prefers to shoot with, he should move into such a position as to force the shot from the weaker foot. As the goalkeeper learns his position, he will discover how to get the attacker out of position through fakes that will be upsetting to the forward, who has to contend with these moves as well as control the ball and make a good shot.

When this has been done, it is time for the goalkeeper to attempt to dive at and smother the ball. The objective in going down for the ball should be to get as much body as possible in front of the ball. The body goes down on

Once the goalkeeper has the ball in his possession after a dive, he should pull the ball into his midsection, draw his knees up, and tuck his head in to protect both the ball and himself.

the side with the head and hands on the side that the shot will be coming from. The trunk and the legs should be stretched long, thus providing a wall between the ball and the goal should the ball get by the hands.

Once the goalkeeper has the ball in his possession, he should pull it into his midsection, roll over toward the forward, draw his knees up, and tuck his head in to protect the ball and himself. Once the danger is passed, he gets quickly to his feet to begin the attack.

The danger involved in diving for the ball usually occurs if the goalkeeper commits himself too soon and gets to the ground too far away to make contact with the ball. In this case, a good forward will be able to either lift the ball into the net over the fallen goalkeeper or dribble around the fallen goalkeeper and on into the goal. This is why the goalkeeper must feint and maneuver the forward into doing what he wants him to do rather than allow the forward to set him up for his score.

Beginning goalkeepers, either because of the excitement of the action or through inexperience, will have the tendency to rush the forward and dive headlong at his feet. This kind of dive will be unsuccessful because the wide blocking surface of the body has been lost and the forward will be able to shoot over or around the much smaller blocking surface. This is also an extremely hazardous move and one that very likely can get the goalkeeper kicked in the head or face. Avoid this kind of dive. By learning position play and by learning how to feint forwards into poor shooting, reckless diving can be eliminated from the goalkeeper's methods for stopping shots.

TIPPING THE BALL OVER THE CROSSBAR OR AROUND THE UPRIGHT

There are some occasions when it is not desirable for the goalkeeper to catch the ball. For example, when playing a high shot or cross close to the goalmouth, with opposing forwards charging in to head the ball, it would be best not to catch the ball. The vulnerability of the goalkeeper in the air close to the goal makes it all too easy for the charging forwards to bump him into the goal with the ball, resulting in a goal.

It is in situations like this, where the threat of a score is great and when catching the ball could mean trouble, that the goalkeeper should tip the ball over the crossbar or around one of the uprights.

The goalkeeper moves to the position from which he will go up for the ball. He goes up in the same way that he would for a high shot in front of

Tipping the ball over the crossbar.   *Tipping the ball around the upright.*

the goal. Instead of catching the ball, he gets his palms and fingers under the ball. As the ball makes contact with the hands, the wrists flick up and in the direction of the goal. The idea is to get the ball safely up and over the crossbar. The lift that is applied under the ball is meant to give the ball the height necessary to clear the crossbar, and the flick that is applied is to ensure the power to get the ball away and out of the field of play.

Two hands should be used whenever possible, but on many occasions only one hand will be practical. The technique is the same. Of course, one hand makes the shot more difficult to handle, but the use of the fingers and palm and a good lift combined with the flick over the bar can be very effective.

121

PUNCHING THE BALL

On high crosses that are not close to the goal and for which the goalkeeper must come out, there is always the possibility that he will not be able to catch the ball. In this situation the goalkeeper will be too far from the goal line to tip the ball over the goal. Since forwards will be moving into position to play the ball, the goalkeeper's objective is to get the ball out of the danger area as quickly and as far away from the goal as possible. In this instance he punches the ball.

Generally, the goalkeeper will be moving forward and, therefore, has the momentum of his run behind the punch. Whenever possible, the goalkeeper should use both fists because they present the largest and flattest striking surface. The goalkeeper goes into the air and, with both fists close together, punches the ball away with both arms providing the punching power. As soon as the punch is made, the goalkeeper must move quickly into his next position in order to be ready to play any returns that may come back at him.

As in tipping the ball, it is not always possible to get both hands in on the ball. Generally, when using one hand to punch out high passes or crosses, the goalkeeper will use the hand and arm opposite the direction of the oncoming ball. In this way he is able to put more of his body in front of the ball and get more power into the punch, with greater certainty of making a good connection with the ball.

Tipping and punching the ball are good goalkeeping techniques for special situations. It should be understood that neither of these guarantee possession of the ball. Catching the ball does guarantee control of the ball and stops the pressure of the defending team. Goalkeepers must remember this and avoid the tendency to punch every shot instead of catching whatever they can.

INITIATING THE ATTACK

The goalkeeper in possession of the ball is the initiator of the attack. Once he has possession of the ball his entire team is on the offensive and should be moving to positions of attack on the field. What the goalkeeper does at this stage of the game is crucial to the kinds of pressure and attacks his team can mount against the opponents.

The goalkeeper's responsibility is to get the ball to a teammate in good field position as quickly and as accurately as possible. He must therefore be able to pass, throw, or kick the ball as accurately as any of his teammates.

To punch the ball the goalkeeper should use both fists.

The goalkeeper goes into the air and, with both fists close together, he punches the ball away with both arms providing the punching power.

KICKING AND PASSING RESPONSIBILITIES

The goalkeeper should be good at basic kicking and passing techniques. He will be called on to take goal kicks that require him to kick, with good distance and accuracy, a standing ball from the ground to a teammate upfield. On occasion, he will be required to get a quick pass to a teammate standing outside the area when his upfield possibilities are covered. He is also expected to be able to punt the ball with great distance and accuracy out of the goal area. Punting is not the best way of getting the ball out of the area since the ball is usually kicked high and far, thus enabling defenders as well as teammates to get under it. It is also not as accurate as the throw for clearing the ball from the goal and so should be used sparingly.

The goalkeeper, once in possession of the ball, drops it to punt upfield.

Throwing the Ball

Throwing the ball is the most accurate and safest way for a goalkeeper to get the ball to a teammate. When throwing a short distance, the goalkeeper can use an underhand, bowling sort of motion to deliver the ball. The underhand delivery gives the ball to the teammate on the ground, where he will most likely be able to move the ball quickly. The goalkeeper should make the roll quickly so that the defenders will not have time to set up against the play.

To get the ball to a more distant teammate, the goalkeeper should use an overhand throw similar to the kind used in baseball or in basketball. By utilizing a good strong follow-through, the goalkeeper can get great distance into his throw.

Clearing the ball should be done quickly. The longer the goalkeeper takes in setting up for the throw, the more time the defenders will have to guard

A punt should be kicked high and far out of the goal area.

To pass a ball to a teammate a short distance away, the goalkeeper can use an underhand, bowling sort of motion to deliver the ball.

their men. It is for this reason that the short, quick underhand throw is generally most desirable for clearance. It is most important for all players to understand that once the goalkeeper has possession of the ball, they are all on the attack and should be moving to offensive positions. This must be stressed in practice and in all game situations.

For teammates far upfield, the goalkeeper should use an overhand throw.

A good, strong follow-through in an
overhand throw will provide great
distance.

CUTTING DOWN SHOOTING ANGLES

Nothing is more frustrating to an attacking team than to have their passes through the area in front of the goal intercepted by an alert, properly positioned goalkeeper. Anticipation of the opposition's movements and proper positioning for maximum effectiveness and security are directly related to high-quality goalkeeping performance.

Anticipation of the opposing team's movement comes from experience in the goal area. As the goalkeeper develops a working knowledge of his defense men's abilities—strengths and weaknesses—and as he develops an awareness of what the attacking team is trying to do, he will know the necessary anticipatory movements.

The time that the goalkeeper spends uninvolved in game action must be used for studying his opponents. Long periods of time can go by in which the goalkeeper is not directly involved in his main task of defending the goal. But this time is not "relax time." It is scouting time—learning which foot the opposing player prefers to use, where the opponents prefer to attack from, how his defense is handling the opponents, how the opponents work for shots, and who they want to do the shooting. This kind of information is invaluable to the goalkeeper.

The goalkeeper's main objective is to move to a position that presents him with the greatest possibilities for making a save and presents the opponent with the smallest possible target. In order to achieve this, the goalkeeper must get off the goal line and into the path most likely to be exploited by the opposing forward. Standing on the goal line, in the center of the goal, offers the largest scoring opportunity to the forward. As the goalkeeper advances toward the forward in possession of the ball, the target area becomes smaller.

The simplest way of illustrating this point to beginning goalkeepers is to use a live demonstration of the concept. Place the goalkeeper in the center of the goal on the goal line. Put a forward on the penalty shot spot. The goalkeeper will immediately see the high scoring possibilities on either side of him. A good shooter can easily put the ball by him, on either side and close to the uprights of the goal. The goalkeeper should then advance, one stride at a time, paying attention to the narrowing angle as he gets closer to the forward. He will soon learn that the closer he gets to the forward, the narrower the shooting angle and the lower the chance of scoring. This concept is crucial to the development of proper positioning for the goalkeeper.

In narrowing the angle against forwards coming in from the side of the goal, the goalkeeper operates under the same angle principle. He moves off the goal line in the direction from which the forward is approaching. The goal-

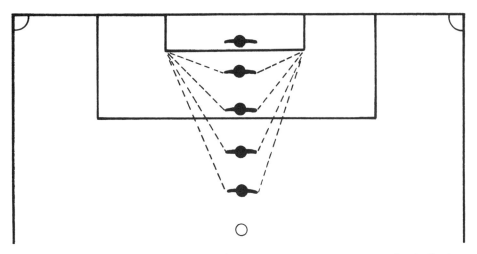

As the goalkeeper advances toward the forward in possession of the ball, the target area becomes smaller.

keeper should move to a position that will allow him to protect the area behind him toward the far goalpost. It will always be easier to contend with a shot that approaches the near goalpost because then the goalkeeper would have the play in front of him, which makes it easier to watch the ball all the way, and because it is easier to move forward to make a save than it is to move sideways or backward to cover a shot from behind. Therefore, the goalkeeper should not get too close to the near post since that would leave too much exposed target area for a shot to be scored in behind him. Experience and practice defending against oblique angle shots will assist the goalkeeper in getting into the proper position to handle these shots.

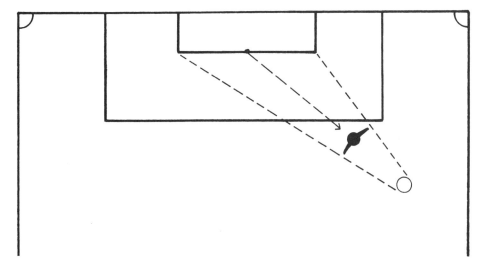

To narrow the angle against forwards coming in from the side of the goal, the goalkeeper moves off the goal line in the direction from which the forward is approaching.

Some words of caution are necessary at this point, especially for beginning goalkeepers. Moving toward the man in possession of the ball offers the shooter the smallest possible target, but the advance must be done in a balanced, controlled manner rather than in a reckless, haphazard way. If the goalkeeper advances too far out of the goal too quickly, the man in possession of the ball gains important options. The forward can:

1. Pass to a teammate in a good scoring position made available by the goalkeeper's commitment to the ball.
2. Dribble around the oncoming goalkeeper.
3. Lift the ball over the oncoming goalkeeper. The farther the goalkeeper comes out, the easier this becomes.

The goalkeeper's movements within his area of responsibility are directly related to his understanding of his defense's style of play and the talents of his teammates. By practicing together, they will learn how to function as a unit. The defense men will learn how the goalkeeper reacts and how he moves to back their challenges to opposing forwards. The goalkeeper will learn how to position himself to take full advantage of his teammates' role in forcing the attackers into difficult shooting angles as well as out of their intended strategy. This can be achieved only by practice together and a real understanding of the relationships necessary for a strong, unified defense.

GOALKEEPING DRILLS

Medicine Ball Catch

This drill is used to help strengthen the arms, wrists, and hands. It is performed in pairs using a standard medicine ball. The players face each other and pass the ball back and forth using two-hand chest passes, two-hand over-the-head passes, and one-hand baseball-type throws. Players should begin this drill with 10 yards between them and gradually work up to a 20-yard distance. This drill should be performed for five minutes each day.

Catch-Save Drill

The goalkeeper takes his normal position in the middle of the goal, about 2 yards off the goal line. A partner then throws the ball at the goalkeeper at varying heights and at varying speeds. The objective of this drill is to make the goalkeeper move to the ball and make the catch. The goalkeeper should concentrate on first making the catch and then quickly returning the ball to the thrower.

Catch-Save Pressure Drill

The objective of this drill is to put pressure on the goalkeeper to make the catch and recover in time to make the next save. Have five to eight players, each with a ball, line up facing the goalkeeper. In order, starting from the goalkeeper's left, the first player throws the ball at the goalkeeper, who must make the save, return the ball to the same thrower, and get set for the next throw from the next player on the throwing line. This goes on right down the line until all players in the line have thrown at the goalkeeper. This drill should be repeated until the goalkeeper has made forty or fifty saves.

This drill may also be performed by the players on the serving line kicking the ball at the goalkeeper. This is also an aid to the kicker since they will be urged to keep the ball on target. If kicking is used, the shots should be taken from the 18-yard line.

Grounder Drill

Grounder drills are organized in the same manner as the catching drills. The only difference is that the balls thrown or kicked at the goalkeeper are thrown or kicked along the ground. The goalkeeper must make the save, get to his feet quickly and return the ball to the thrower or server, and then get ready for the next attempt on goal.

Save and Clear Drill

This drill is a direct outgrowth of the catch-save drill, adding the realistic element of clearing the ball from the goal area. Using any of the aforementioned drills, the goalkeeper must first make the save and then throw the ball to teammates moving downfield away from the goal. The receiver may be the player who threw or kicked the ball to the goalkeeper, who now has moved off the throwing and kicking line into a receiving position. The stress for the goalkeeper is to make the save, get to his feet quickly, look for the receiver, and get the ball to him. Generally, the best way would be by passing the ball, but this is also a good opportunity to practice kicking clearances from in front of the goal.

Challenge-Save Drill

The challenge-save drill is designed to give the goalkeeper practice in making saves while being challenged by an opposing player. This is a most realistic way to practice this position play and is comparable to the practicing of dribbling and tackling in the one-on-one situation. The drill can be performed in many ways. One group of five to ten players lines up in single file facing the goal on the 18-yard line on the extreme left side of the penalty area. A player who can cross the ball well into the goalmouth should be placed on the right side of the penalty area. He should have four to eight balls with him. The player crosses the ball into the goalmouth area. As he kicks the ball, a forward from the left side of the penalty area moves in to play the ball and challenge the goalkeeper. If the ball is high, the attacker attempts to head it; if it is low, he uses his foot. At all times the attackers should be instructed to play the ball and not the goalkeeper. The goalkeeper must gain possession of the ball and then clear it to the kicker. The attacking player then returns to the end of the line he came from. Using this same basic formation, the shooting line and the kicker can be moved to various positions on the field to allow for crosses and challenges coming from all sides of the field. This same kind of drill can be used to the benefit of the goalkeeper and other defensive players, as well as to the attacking team, by practicing offensive corner kicks.

Ground-Save Reaction Drill

Very often the goalkeeper will stop a shot on goal, but because of the power behind the shot or because he was unable to gain control of the ball, he will be forced to make a second save from a ground position. The goalkeeper must be trained to react and move for the ball when he is off his feet in order to prevent goals. The first way to practice making these kinds of saves is to have the goalkeeper kneel on the ground facing a thrower. The goalkeeper may not move until the ball is thrown just out of his reach to the right or left or over his head. He then moves for the ball in the best way that he can. He may dive right or left or stand up for the throw. The important factor in this drill is that the goalkeeper may not move until the ball is thrown. This ensures that he will have to react quickly to get to the ball.

A second method of training this kind of ground-save reaction is best practiced in groups of three: the goalkeeper, an anchor man, and a thrower.

The goalkeeper stretches out along the ground on his right ride facing the thrower. The anchor man holds the goalkeeper's feet down in contact with ground in such a way that he cannot move. The thrower then throws the ball to the goalkeeper forcing him to stretch for the ball, raise his body sideways from the ball, and curl his body toward his feet in order to make the save. This should be done in rapid succession for five minutes on the right side and then for five minutes on the left side. The goalkeeper then moves to his stomach with his head facing directly at the thrower. The anchor man puts his weight on the goalkeeper's lower leg to keep him down. The thrower now tosses the ball directly at the goalkeeper above his head, forcing him to lift his body from the ground to make the catch. Other throws should be made to the right and left of the goalkeeper's head forcing him to move and stretch his trunk and arms in order to gain possession of the ball. Once the player is thoroughly warmed up, the balls should be thrown at the goalkeeper in rapid succession.

6

TACTICS AND SYSTEMS OF PLAY

POSITION PLAY

In order to intelligently grasp modern soccer tactics, the beginning player must first understand the role and function of each position on the team. An understanding of position and functions and demands gives the perspective necessary to each team member to see how each role relates to the functions and responsibilties of teammates. Positional demands are largely the same, regardless of the overall strategy or tactics used by the team. It should be apparent that any player not able to carry out basic positional functions, for any reason, detracts from and weakens any tactical system employed.

Therefore, it becomes the responsibility of each individual player to bring four basic prerequisites to the tactical plans of the team. The coach, on the other hand, must see that these prerequisites are maintained and given the atmosphere in which they can continue to grow.

The prerequisites each player must bring in order to achieve individual and team success are:

1. Desire. This implies determination, motivation, and the willingness to strive to be a better than average soccer player. The player must be willing to work hard at learning the basic skills necessary for good performance and at developing an understanding of how these skills enable him to perform his positional function.

2. Individual skills. The player must practice individual skills, constantly striving to bring these skills to a high performance level. All field

players, regardless of specfied position, must be able to perform all the required skills of passing, dribbling, ball control, heading, and tackling. All of these skills relate to overall total team soccer, whether the team is on the attack or defending its goal. Without these skills, no system of play can be effective.

3. Physical conditioning. Conditioning might well be another name for soccer. Without superb physical conditioning, skills (no matter how well performed) will suffer and deteriorate as fatigue sets in and muscles are no longer able to respond to the game's physical demands. An out-of-condition player cannot be expected to perform well and soon becomes a liability to the team.

4. Soccer intelligence. Soccer intelligence implies an understanding of the strategies, intricacies, and alternatives available in the team's over-all tactical plans. The coach as teacher is responsible for giving the players a rationale for the team's playing style, but the player is responsible for learning, retaining, and putting into play the system employed. This involves a good understanding of team positional functions, team objectives, both offensively and defensively, reacting to the opponent's style of play, adjustment to the demands of the game as they emerge, and, finally, seeking and implementing the alternatives necessary for coping with and overcoming the inevitable changes in the basic game plan caused by the opponent's tactics.

Functions by Position

Up until the late 1960s, positions on the soccer field had individual names that described where the player was on the field. Major teams even assigned a specific number to each position to enable fans to see exactly where the center forward (number nine) was at any time, thus giving a major clue as to what he was up to when away from his central field position.

As late as the early sixties, soccer teams and their tactics used a system of play that read as follows: Five forwards, three halfbacks, two fullbacks, and one goalkeeper. Each player was named and numbered according to his placement on the field.

The center of the forward line was naturally enough called the "center forward" (number nine). Flanking the center forward were the inside right (number eight) and the inside left (number ten). Playing outside these two, patrolling the sidelines, were the outside right (number seven) and the outside left (number eleven). These players were also called wings—right wing or left wing.

The halfbacks were also named according to position. The name "halfback" described the position midway or halfway back between the forwards and the deeper defenders. From his center of the halfback line, the center halfback (number five) was to control play in the middle of the field. Flanking the center halfback was the right halfback (number four) and the left halfback (number six). They were also referred to as wing halfbacks.

Lying back yet deeper and representing the last line of resistance to attack before the goalkeeper were the two fullbacks. They divided the width of the field in half, thus becoming known as the left fullback (number three) and the right fullback (number two).

The goalkeeper was and generally is still designated as number one.

In more recent years, changes in tactics and strategies have modified the basic five-forward, three-halfback, two-fullback system of play. To accomplish more attack or defense, players have been moved about to serve specific purposes. One of the best examples of this may be seen when, in an attempt to strengthen the defense, many teams go to a three-fullback system of play. A domino effect then occurs. If the center halfback is moved back to create a three-fullback line, an opening occurs in the halfback line that could compromise midfield halfback functions. A simple way to regain this lost strength is to drop a forward from the five-player forward line, thus creating a four-forward, three-halfback, three-fullback alignment.

As these developmental changes took place, terminology changed too. Today, we speak of forwards not as graphically as before in terms of position, but rather as a general group called strikers. Halfbacks are referred to as midfielders or linkmen, the term coming from the midfielder's role linking the strikers to the defenders. Fullbacks are now called defenders, with no right or left designation, since there are as many as four being used, depending on the tactical system of defense being employed.

While it is true that terminology has changed, it must be remembered that changes in tactics were the cause. In the search for greater defensive strength, more productive offensive power, and overall team control of the ball and the resultant control of the game, players were shifted to other roles. Names were coined for these new roles.

To understand how modern positional play and how total team offense and defense emerged, it is best to go back to the five-forward, three-halfback, two-fullback system of play to look at the roles each position played in the total team strategy. In this way, the individual player's role can be viewed in terms of the skills necessary to that particular position and how that position relates to total team concept.

Although the names of positions have changed, modern players are forced by the flow of the game to operate in a great many situations in traditional roles. Outside strikers, for example, still operate on the sidelines in order to spread the defense, with interior strikers moving goalward, as did traditional center and inside forwards.

The Center Forward

The center forward, by virtue of his forward central field position, is generally the high-scoring member of the team. At least he gets the opportunity to be the high scorer. The center forward must be able to shoot well with both feet. Scoring opportunities come quickly and the center forward must be able to get the shot off swiftly and accurately, often under crowded conditions around the goalmouth. His scoring opportunity will usually come without the luxury of being able to set the ball up in any way. He must play it at once and not always in the way that he would prefer.

Similar demands are made on the center forward in the heading department. He must be able to jump well and be rugged enough to go up in the air for the ball in a crowd. His head shot on goal must be powerful and accurate.

Because of the threat a good center forward represents to the defense, he is usually "blessed" with close man-to-man coverage any time he moves for the ball. It is here that the center forward must be as skillful a strategist as he is a ball handler. When he is tightly marked (covered), he has the opportunity to move into another part of the field taking part of the defense with him in order to cover his threat. An alert center forward will soon know how well he is being covered by the number of passes attempted to him and the number completed. If he were to stay in the center field position, he would in effect be contributing to the defense by allowing defensive concentration at midfield and a cutting off of the easiest route to the goal. It is at this time that the center forward should leave his scoring and attacking role and become the decoy who takes the defenders out of the middle, thus leaving the midfield to a teammate cutting into the vacated position.

The center forward's central position also demands that he be a strong, accurate passer. Every time he gets the ball, the defense will move to get him. When the defense concentrates on him, one of the center forward's teammates will be taking advantage of the situation and probably will cut into a new space. At this point, the center forward can hit one of his teammates with a pass that takes advantage of the coverage on him.

Generally, the center forward will stay upfield around the midfield line when his team is on defense. This position allows him to move for the ball when his defense clears it from their portion of the field. This does not mean that if he or one of the attackers loses possession of the ball, he is absolved of responsibility in helping to get the ball back or in slowing up the opponent's attack while his defense gathers. On the contrary, the center forward must be able to tackle the man with the ball in a sure and efficient manner or, at the very least, slow the opponent down.

The Inside Forwards

The inside forward must be adept at all phases of soccer skills. His main task is the development and finishing off of attacks on the opponent's goal. Therefore, he must be an excellent passer and shooter and a clever strategist. He must be able to read the defense well in order to be able to interchange positions with the other forwards and move to open spaces created by the center forward and the wings.

His second task is to control the midfield area. He attempts to do this in two ways. First, he tries to break up the opponent's attempts to organize attacks in the midfield area, and, second, he sets up his own team's offensive attacks by gaining and maintaining possession of the ball.

The inside forwards combine with the halfbacks to gain control of the midfield area. Each forward is expected to go back to his own defense to help turn away the opponents' attacks on his goal. By moving back toward his defense when not in possession of the ball, he provides ready outlets for clearances out of his own defense in the initial stages of counterattack.

The inside forward has defensive responsibilities on defensive corner kicks when he comes back into his defense to guard any loose men around the goal area. An experienced inside forward generally has the freedom to roam the field in order to get into the positions that he knows will aid his team on attack and on defense.

The Outside Forwards (Wings)

The outside forwards must be fast and able to dribble well at top speed. The outsides patrol the touchlines on their respective sides. Each wing must constantly be working to get free of the fullback usually assigned to cover him so that his teammates will be able to get passes to him out on the wing. This is an invaluable function of the outside, since his presence on the outsides of the field requires the defense to spread out—not congregate centrally— thereby stretching their offensive forces across the field. This will then enable the attackers to use the spaces created in the defense to attack on a broad front.

Because the wing plays on the outside lines, he must be able to contend with the line on the one side and the opposing fullback on the other side. This therefore makes dribbling, and all of its related feinting techniques, a definite prerequisite for successful wing play.

By being able to bring the ball around or past the fullback, the defense has to move toward the wing in possession, thus overshifting to meet the threat he has established. At this instant, the outside can pass the ball over the defenders toward the goal to his attacking forwards, who are moving up on goal. The need for accurate passing is apparent here if he is to accomplish his objective. If the pass is too close to the goal, the goalkeeper will take it. If the pass is too deep and back toward midfield, the forwards will have to break stride and turn around to get the ball, which will take away from the speed and potential of the play.

Finally, the outside forward should be able to shoot since he will have the opportunity to come in on goal if he beats his fullback or to play a rebound that comes off the defense or the goalkeeper. His opportunities come a few times in each game and he should be ready and able to capitalize on them.

The outsides have their defensive responsibilities too. If a teammate loses possession of the ball, the outside should be able to challenge for its return. He should also be able to assist the halfback on his side of the field if the halfback is having a particularly hard time with his defensive responsibility.

The Halfbacks

The halfbacks are the liaison between the defense and the offense. Defense is the primary concern of the halfbacks. Most of the time the halfbacks will be charged with defending against the other team's center forward and inside forwards.

The halfbacks must be able to break up the opponent's attacks as they develop in midfield. All halfbacks should be aggressive, sure tacklers in order to fulfill their positional functions. The wing halfbacks team with the inside forwards to control midfield. They also can be counted on to move up behind the attackers.

In this attacking role, we find the other function of the halfbacks. They provide support for their forwards while the forwards are attacking the goal. This implies that the halfbacks must be good passers since they will very often gain possession of the ball and then must get the ball to forwards moving up.

Halfbacks moving up behind the attack provide depth for the offense. When a forward has moved up as far as possible, he should always know that he has a teammate coming up behind him. The forward can then pass back to the halfback, who will be facing the play and in a very good position to redistribute the ball to a forward in better position.

Halfback play in modern soccer is crucial to team success. The wing half in particular forms a good passing triangle with the outside and inside forward on his side of the field. This provides depth in the attack by creating combination possibilities for passing.

Through intelligent positional interchange, it is possible to get a halfback into the attack in such a way that his presence is undetected by the defense until it is too late to do much about it. The thing to remember in this sort of halfback attacking role is that when the halfback leaves the defense, he is leaving a space that the opponent can move into. It is at this point that the forward being replaced by the halfback should move back to cover for the halfback in case a counterattack develops.

The center halfback, because of his central defensive position, must be the quarterback and the brains behind the team's defensive play. His most apparent defensive responsibility will be to cover the opponent's center forward. However, with forward interchange being so important to the attack, the center halfback must not leave midfield with the center forward, since, invariably, another player will be moving into the center of the field position with the hope that the center halfback has vacated the area. This is the kind of strategy that has to be worked out between defensive players. Man-to-man coverage is important, but there are times and situations where a zone coverage must be kept so that the defense is not drawn out of its coverage easily.

As a defender, the center halfback must be a strong tackler, able to kick well under pressure, and sure of his head shots. He must be fast in order to go up against the best forwards the other team has opposing him. He must know how to exercise restraint so that he is not drawn into a foolish move by a cleverly designed feint or attack. In short, the center halfback has to be calm, decisive, and skilled in order to carry out this important midfield defensive function.

The center halfback also figures in his team's attack. From his central position he must be able to feed passes quickly and accurately to his wing halfbacks and his forwards. It is important that he be able to pass well since he often will be initiating attacks following his defensive work.

Enough cannot be said about the importance of the center halfback to his team. If he is a strong, skilled, and intelligent player, his control of midfield will have much to do with interfering with the opponent's plans. He will frustrate attacks up the middle, forcing the other team to the outside of the field for a route to the goal. This makes the job tougher on the opponent and more to the liking of the defense, which will be able to jockey the attackers to where they would prefer to have them—to the outside, away from the goal.

The Fullbacks

The primary function of the fullback is to defend against the opponent's wings. The fullbacks combine with the center halfback to form the next to last line of defense across the field. If the fullbacks are effectively covering the opponent's wings, and the center halfback is effectively covering the opponent's center forward, they have closed the tactical options of the opponent. The rest of the defensive responsibilities will be picked up by the wing halfbacks and the insides who come back to help on the defense.

The fullback plays between the wing and the goal, constantly striving to keep the outside forward from moving into the field. The fullback must be fast in order to keep up with speedy forwards he has to cover. By keeping the forward between the touchline and himself, the fullback can effectively shut off the wing as a threat. Naturally, he must be a sure tackler.

The fullbacks play in a tandem style. If one goes out to challenge the forward on his side, then the other slides into the middle of the field in front of the goal to assist his teammates in guarding against a pass from the man in possession.

As in all positions on the field, the fullback must also be attack oriented. Following a successful tackle, he will be in possession of the ball generally deep within his own territory. In order to get out of the defensive area, and away from opponents trying to regain control of the ball, the fullback must be able to dribble or pass accurately to a teammate. Ball control skills are definitely necessary to modern fullback play. It is not uncommon to see a fullback, if not challenged when in possession of the ball, continue upfield looking for a forward to pass to while his vacated position is covered by a halfback.

While his team is in possession of the ball, the fullback should move, supporting the attack with his eye on his defensive responsibility, as well as on the attack his team is making. His movement to upfield position allows him to play back balls cleared far out of the defense and to keep pressure on the opponents while sustaining his own team's attack. A further benefit of this movement upfield is to keep the opposing forwards up the field with him, since if they were to receive a pass behind him, it would most likely be offsides.

The Goalkeeper

The primary function of the goalkeeper is, of course, to prevent goals from being scored. He and his defensive teammates combine to meet this function and to control his own penalty area.

When he has made a save, or when he is putting a goal kick into play and he has full control of the ball, he is on the attack. His pass or kick to a teammate initiates the attack, so it must be accurate and easy to handle for the player who gets it. The goalkeeper must understand this aspect of the sport so that he will not waste his opportunity to start the attack.

TACTICAL CONCEPT BUILDING

The most innovative development in soccer in recent years has been the growth of concept, whole-team play, or total soccer. Simply stated, the concept is based on two principles that must be blended to provide success at soccer:

1. When any player on the team, regardless of position, has controlled possession of the ball, that entire team is on the offensive. This means that each player on the side must be thinking attack and moving aggressively to positions that will either aid in or support the offensive thrust.

2. When any member of the opposing team has possession of the ball, the entire team, regardless of position, is on defense. This means that each player on the defensive side must be actively contributing to the defensive effort, whether that means going for the ball or delaying the attack upfield so that the defense can gain the time it needs to position itself to meet the challenge.

Within this framework, theories of attack and defense become a working reality. A rationale is presented as to why players must be adept at all skills, regardless of designated position. Each player is able to see his responsibilities and functions in the broadest sense of team play. And, if total soccer concepts are understood, the objectives and goals of both offensive and defensive soccer become more meaningful to the individual player.

Offensive Objectives

The purpose of offensive soccer is to score goals. Attacking the goal successfully can be accomplished only by forcing the defense out of their planned defensive alignment and into weaker, less tenable positions. In order to accomplish this task, the offensive attack, regardless of the system employed, must carry out six prerequisites:

1. Possession of the ball and ball control. This requirement is easy to understand since it is obvious that in order to move the ball offensively, all team members must be able to pass, head, dribble, trap, and maintain possession of the ball. If possession cannot be maintained, the attack cannot be sustained.

2. Penetration into the defense. The team's objective, once in control of the ball, is to move through the opponent's defense—around, over, and even through defensive players in as controlled and accurate a manner as possible. Penetration refers to those moves, either with the ball or without the ball, that attackers make into the defense, thus moving closer to the objective—the opponent's goal.

Penetration can begin anywhere on the field. It should begin at the moment a player on the team gains control of the ball. Penetration is the result of the intelligent search for better field position from which to create the next move into the opponent's defensive areas.

Examples of penetrating tactics would be the movement of the wings down the sidelines with the ball, while the other forwards feint and maneuver into positions to receive a crossfield pass. A forward who is heavily guarded at midfield and is moving toward one of the touchlines, leaving a vacant spot into which a teammate can dash, creates another opportunity for penetration of the defense. All of the skills employed in passing and receiving passes that were discussed earlier are examples of this attack requirement—penetration.

3. Breadth of attack. In order to counter one of the basic principles of defense, that of the concentration of defenders in the high-scoring areas, the attack must be able to operate across the width of the field.

In order to penetrate the defense, the attacking team must be capable of mounting attacks on a broad front, from touchline to touchline. By being able to effectively get the ball out to the touchlines, the attackers are forcing the defense to go out and get the ball. Obviously, this would force some of the defenders away from the concentrated defensive areas.

If the opposing team is particularly defensive minded and uses many players to defend and congest the penalty area, the need for breadth in the attack becomes even more acute. Breadth in the attack is particularly useful while the opponent is retreating to set up his concentrated defense, in the instant following a turnover. It is in the initial stages of the defense formation that the defenders are vulnerable to attacks that emanate from the sidelines, since to avoid going out after the ball will assist the attackers in their penetration of the defense.

Breadth in the attack will also provide the opportunity to switch the attack from one side of the field to the other. When the defense shifts to one side to meet the posed threat, very often they will be giving up good striking positions on the side opposite the attack. It is at this point that a pass over the defense to the other side of the field can result in a successful attack on the goal. Both wings and both outside lanes along the touchlines should be used whenever possible.

4. Depth in the attack. Depth in the attack is accomplished through intelligent positioning and movement by players without the ball, in relationship to their teammate in possession of the ball.

    Players without the ball must move into the defense in a way that will provide options for the man with the ball should he get bogged down by the defense. Depth is accomplished in many ways, but all tactics are based on the idea of establishing options for the man in possession of the ball. A midfielder coming up behind a striker provides depth to the attack. Teammates on the right and left moving into good receiving positions provide for depth in the attack.

    The very idea of the whole-team attack provides for depth in the attack. See illustration 4-1. The fact that the midfielders and the full-backs move up the field as their attackers advance further illustrates the concept. The important thing, however, is that the depth is provided not only toward the rear but to the front and the sides.

An example of positioning for providing depth in the attack.

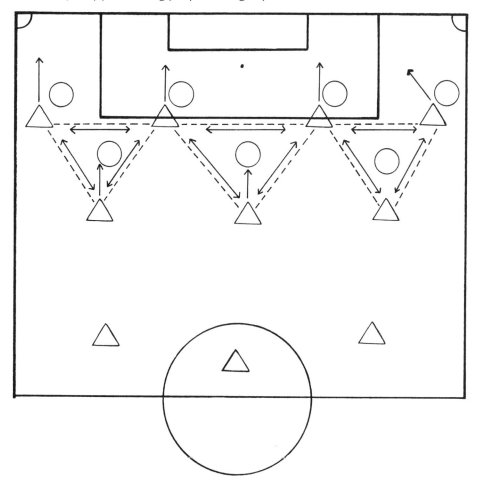

What is created are triangles of attacking players. These passing triangles assure the man in possession of the ball opportunities to move the ball in directions that will force the defenders out of their defensive posts.

The attackers, then, should never advance in a straight line across the field, but rather in front of or behind one another. This causes the defense to cover individually rather than being able to use one defender to get between the passer and the possible receiver and, therefore, cover two men with ease.

5. Versatility. This refers to the ability of players to interchange positions and their ability to be effective in their new position. These switches of position arise during games out of the necessity of moving the ball.

For example, an inside striker in possession of the ball may be forced to move toward the sidelines in order to be effective with the ball. At this point, the outside striker must be able to move inside and perform all of the functions of the inside striker on the attack, by virtue of his new position.

Another example of this positional interchange idea occurs when a forward moving into the defense is stopped around the penalty area, with no one to pass to in his striking force of forwards, turns and passes to a midfielder following up the play. The midfielder should be able to contribute to the attack with either a well-placed shot or an accurate pass to a free teammate.

Without this interchange of positions, the attack bogs down as each player becomes concerned with only his role in the team's overall plan. To allow a player to operate in this way is to divest the player of his opportunity to participate fully in the game of soccer.

6. Creativity in the attack. Although most teams strive to attack the opponent's goal through the attacking team's strengths, this is not always the way the defense will have it. Any good defense will be aware of and ready to cope with the opponent's strengths.

Therefore, it becomes necessary for teams to be able to change tactics and move into new ways of attack while the game is in progress. Just as we understand the need for individuals to be able to beat their opponent in many ways, so must a team be able to exercise many tactics to achieve its goal. To attack in the same way at all times is both unrealistic and nearly impossible. Each opponent provides new challenges to the team's strengths and weaknesses.

The team's tactics must be flexible. Flexibility is based on the creativity and ability of the attacking team to improvise on its basic theme. If, for example, the attacking team's strength lies in the great individual talents of a particularly strong, scoring striker, it is certain that the defense will counter by defending in a special way against this threat. The creative team will be able to use the attention given to a particular player to create opportunities for other strikers to succeed. The fact that a defense must respond to a strength makes it clear that they are giving priorities to certain phases of the attack. To cover one man with two defenders means that a sacrifice has been made in terms of another attacker. The good team will recognize this and move to capitalize on this weakness in the defense.

Defensive Objectives

Once the prerequisites for the attack have been established, it is necessary to understand the prerequisites necessary for coping with the offensive tactics. The defense, regardless of the system the team employs, must observe certain principles of attack.

1. Delay. Delaying tactics must be employed by the defense, immediately upon losing possession of the ball, to allow teammates to retreat to strong defensive positions on the field. The defensive forwards closest to the ball should be moving toward the man in possession of the ball while the other forwards move to shut off passing lanes between the man in possession of the ball and possible receivers.

    The slowing up of the attack is generally carried out in midfield while the midfielders and deep defenders are picking up their defensive responsibilities in front of the penalty area. It is in this area that the attack must be stopped.

    The forwards and midfielders carrying out this system of "fore-checking" must do so aggressively. Their positioning and challenges should be such that they force passes from the men in possession while at the same time they are closing off passing possibilities. Proper positioning and coverage will force the attackers to crossfield passes rather than allow them the kinds of penetration passes they will be looking for.

    The midfielders should be directly in the paths of the oncoming forwards, with the outside deep backs or fullbacks moving into positions that will guard against through passes to the wings moving up the touchlines.

    The defenders should be in front of the attacking team, between the forwards and the goal. This combination of challenges and proper defensive positioning will slow down the attack. Again, it is important to state that the entire team is participating in this defensive delay procedure. The whole-team defense concept is the only way of dealing with modern soccer offensive tactics.

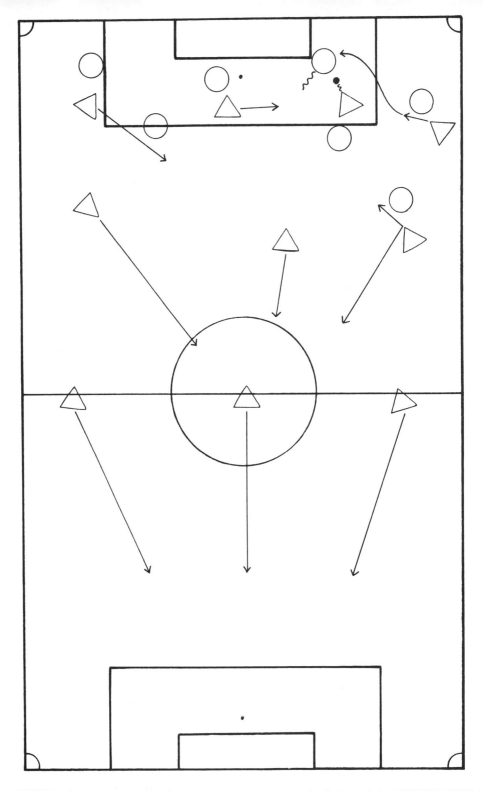

Delay. The defensive forwards closest to the ball should be moving toward the man in possession while the other forwards move to shut off passing lanes between the man in possession and possible receivers.

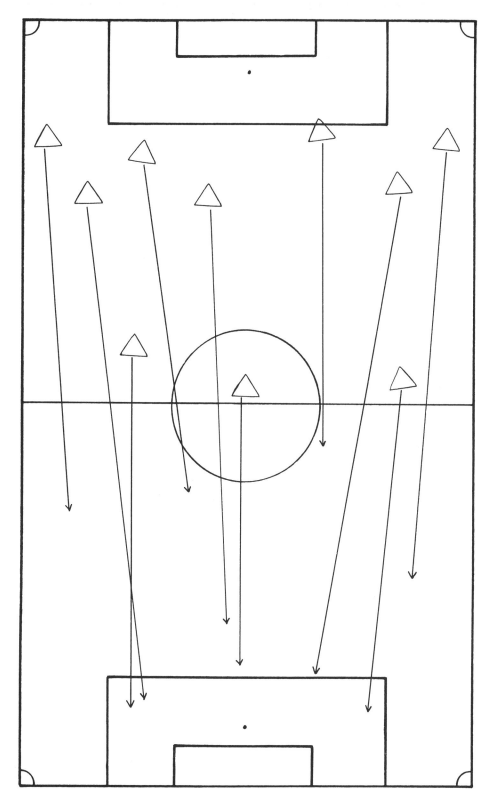

Funneling refers to the shape that emerges if the lines of retreat were drawn back toward the defensive areas.

2. Bunching the defense. Another objective of the defense is to clog the area just in front of the penalty area. It is here that the defense must effectively stop the attack and get the ball away from the attackers. Heavy defensive concentrations make passes and shots through the penalty area most difficult to carry off. Dribbling through a packed defense is also extremely difficult.

In order to accomplish the desired bunching and concentration the defense, retreating behind the delaying tactics of the forwards, move from their offensive wide supportive positions back toward midfield and the penalty area. This is often referred to as a funneling back on defense. Funneling refers to the shape of a funnel that would emerge if we were to draw the lines of retreat back toward the crucial defensive areas.

3. Compensation. Compensation in the defense refers to the need for teammates to fill vacant areas left by a defender who leaves his normal position to challenge an opponent for the ball.

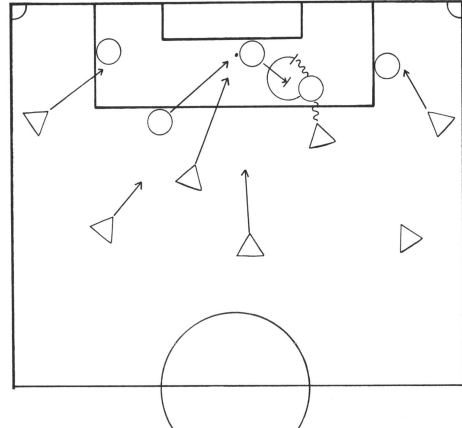

Compensation. Defenders in the goal area should move quickly to fill any spaces vacated by their teammates.

For example, if a fullback were to go out of the defense to challenge a forward at the sideline, he would naturally be leaving the defense one man short. Therefore, when one wide fullback moves out toward the touchline to mark a player, the other backs should move in toward the center of the field to cover the back who filled in for the departed fullback. This is reasonable since it is extremely difficult for the fullback who moved in toward midfield to be beaten by his defensive assignment, who is on the opposite side of the field, by a pass from the player in possession. If the back who went out to make the challenge at the touchline is beaten, then the back who covered for him is there to provide the support or depth to the defense. The back then must return as quickly as possible to a valid defensive role. He must get back into the play.

4. Depth. Defensive depth refers to defense men backing one another up in as many situations as possible. The example given previously reflects this kind of play. It is actually the setting up of obstacles to the attackers. If a tackle or interception misses, there should be another player coming up behind the play to try to take the ball away again. Defenders must take care to keep this depth and to cover for one another. If the defense allows itself to be strung out across the field, then it becomes easier for the attackers to penetrate the defense.

5. Self-control. This is perhaps the most difficult defensive requirement to teach. On the one hand we talk of aggressive soccer, and on the other we talk of self-control. Self-control refers to timing challenges for the ball in such ways that the defensive player does not over-commit himself or commit himself too soon, which would lead to his being beaten by the attacker.

    If a fullback or center back is the only man between the ball and the goal, the defender must make the attacker commit himself first, since to commit first and be beaten would leave the goalkeeper at the shooter's mercy. This phase of the game can come only from practice and drills and a sound understanding of defensive tactics.

OFFENSIVE AND DEFENSIVE PLAY FOR SPECIAL SITUATIONS

Kickoff: Offensive

At no time during a soccer match are there more defensive players between the ball and the goal as there are at the kickoff. It is for this reason that the

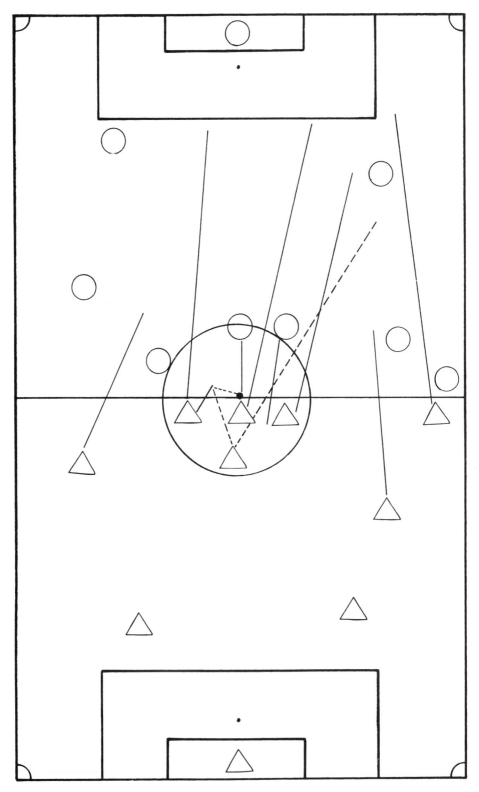

One example of a kickoff play.

kickoff plays are generally either overlooked completely or overplanned, with the result being wasted rather than constructive starts of the game.

The best plan of attack for the kickoff should be a direct, simple, and aggressive one. This is especially true at the beginning of the game, when most players are tense, waiting for the game to start and their first encounter. With beginning players, this is especially true and the tendency to make a mistake is great. The kickoff play should, therefore, try to capitalize on striking quickly into a tense defense.

The only rule to be concerned with on the kickoff is the one that states that the ball must roll in a forward direction for a distance of its own diameter.

The ball should be kicked the legal distance forward but on an angle to one of the inside forwards playing alongside the center forward. The inside then plays the ball back to one of the halfbacks (prearranged), and the other forwards take off as quickly as possible into the opponent's defense. The halfback in possession tries to place a long, hard kick into the defense, where the forwards go after it. In this way, a defensive player will be faced with the pressure of three or four forwards bearing down hard on him at the same time.

The reason for passing the ball back to a halfback is to get the opponent to send some of his players charging across the midfield line in an attempt to get the ball. This naturally results in cutting down the number of defenders on the defensive side of the field and is an important aid in penetrating the defense.

Variations of this kickoff play are easy to plan and carry off. The important thing to remember is that the play should be kept simple in design and the execution of it should be crisp and aggressive.

Defending Against Kickoffs

The best defense against kickoffs is alertness on the part of the defensive team. Players should be alert to the possibilities that are open to the opponents and move to shut off these possibilities.

Generally, the nonkicking team bunches its three forwards close together to cover the middle three on the kickoff team. This usually results in those players being bypassed easily. It is better to spread these defensive players so they can cut off direct running alleys down the field. They are then in a far better position to cut off passes or passing routes and, at the same time, are able to get in at the halfbacks should the opponent use a pass back.

The outside left and right should be brought into positions midway between the touchline and the ball. In this way they will assist in cutting off

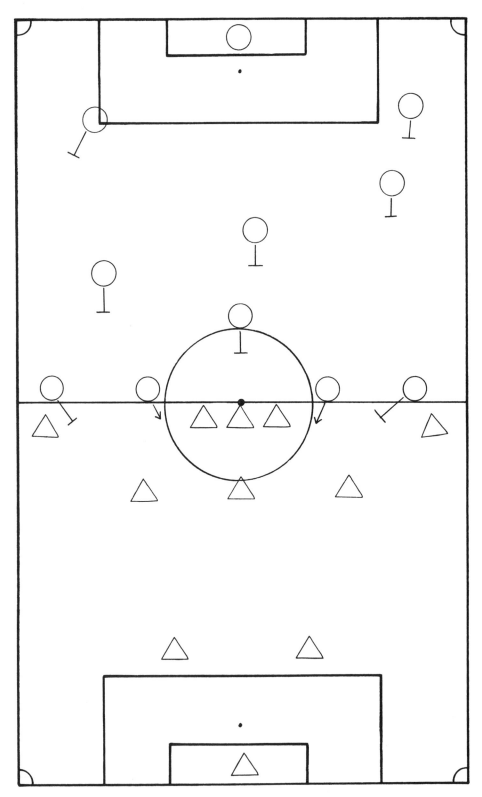

Basic defensive kickoff responsibilities.

running routes for wing halfbacks should they be moved into the play. The outsides are also in position to cover any passes to the opposing outside forwards should the kicker elect to hit one of them with a pass.

The rest of the defense should be alert to their defensive responsibilities, with the goalkeeper ready to move quickly into the penalty area should a ball come at him. He will have room to move if the pass is long and fast, thus enabling him to cut off the play at its start.

It is rare that a goal is scored on a kickoff play. This does not mean that the defense can afford to be complacent about the possibility of one being scored or that the attackers should forget to try.

It does mean, however, that the planning should be geared to an aggressive response to the kickoff, whether attacking or defending.

Corner Kicks: Offensive

There are many interesting ideas about how to play corner kicks. Much of the theory is good, but the realities of the kick demand that the strategy employed must be based on the players' ability and setting into motion those things that they can do to make a corner kick succeed. Goals resulting from corner kicks are difficult to come by, and generally when they are scored they are a surprise to all. This is because defensive guarding around the goal area is generally tight, and the shot has to be played quickly in order to be successful.

Rather than get involved in specific corner kick plays, it is far better to understand the elements that go into making a good attempt on goal from a corner kick.

The most important factor in attempting a corner kick is the kicker. He must be able to kick the ball in a consistently accurate way. Accuracy is necessary because he must keep the ball out of the reach of the goalkeeper, who would stop the play immediately if he were able to handle the ball safely. If the goalkeeper does gain control of the ball, he can, with a fast clearance, leave the opposing team with forwards out of position and unable to help the defense, which results in a strong fast break going the opposite way.

The kicker consistently must be able to make the ball cross the penalty area in front of the goal at head height. A ball that drops on the penalty area is of little use to the forwards since the congestion at that point would make a shot on goal very difficult.

The forwards should not be crowded in front of the goal, but should be stationed at the 18-yard line. This is important because the forwards can best attempt shots on goal if they are running to meet the ball rather than

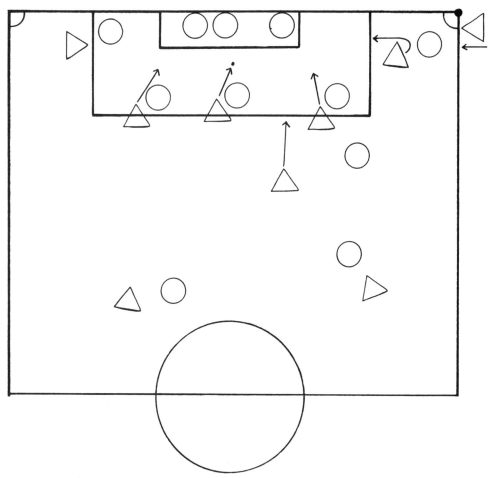

The basic offensive lineup for a corner kick.

standing still and waiting for the ball to come to them. (See Illustration 7-7.)

Another forward should be placed on the goalkeeper's box line on the side opposite the kicker. This forward is now in position to play the long kick that goes over the defense or the kick that very often slips by the forwards and the defenders, parallel to the goalmouth, thus giving him a shot on goal from "against the grain."

Most teams bring a halfback or two up to bolster the attack on goal by giving the attacking team extra men upfield to play the ball. By bringing halfbacks up to the goal the defense can be outmanned.

The remaining halfbacks and fullbacks should move upfield to the mid-field line to help contain the play, should the ball be kicked out of the defense. All players involved in the attempt on goal from the corner kick should immediately move back to their positions should the play be stopped. If they are slow in retreating to defense, they are apt to be caught in a fast break, with the defense being outnumbered.

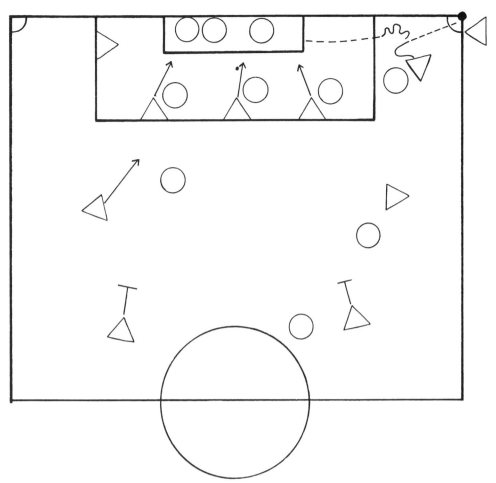

The basic offensive lineup for a short corner kick.

The Short Corner Kick

Rather than kick the ball directly into the penalty area, a team may elect to use a short corner kick. Though this may be used at any time, a short corner kick attempt is generally used to compensate for a weakness caused either by a lack of a good corner kick kicker or because weather conditions have dictated this approach.

Very windy days with the wind coming either straight at the kicker or across the intended line of flight make accuracy difficult and success at getting the ball into the goal even more difficult. Rain and mud, which make the ball heavier than usual, make lifting the ball into the penalty area difficult, too. In these cases the short corner kick can be used.

The objective of the short corner kick is to get the ball from the corner of the field to a forward waiting close to the ball. The forward then will attempt to finish the play from his position, which is nearer the penalty area. There are many plays that can be worked off this short corner, but the result is usually a return to a normal style of attack on goal since the advantages of the long kick have been lost. However, possession is maintained in an area close to the goal, thus giving some value to the play.

Defending Against Corner Kicks

As in most defensive responsibilities, defensive corner kick play involves cutting off the offensive possibilities. When a team understands what they are trying to do offensively to score, they will quickly realize what has to be done by the defense to prevent being scored on in the same situation.

Since the goalkeeper is the man the kicker must avoid in order to be successful, the defensive team must give the goalkeeper mobility and, at the same time, still protect the goal.

The basic lineup for defending against corner kicks.

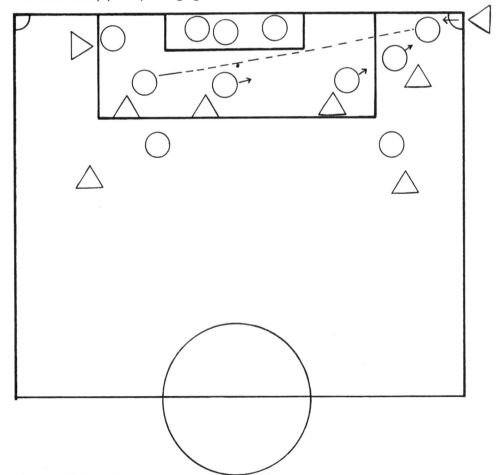

This can be accomplished by placing the two fullbacks on the goal line, inside of each upright. They remain there to protect the corners of the goal until the play is over. With these two men in proper position, the goalkeeper is able to make his move to cut off the ball as it comes into the penalty area.

All other defenders must guard their opponents in a tight man-to-man defense. Each defender must position himself in such a way that he can see his opponent and the ball, all the way into the goal area. The defender must follow his man regardless of where he goes on the play, alert and ready to challenge for the ball.

The inside forwards must be drawn back to help with the defensive responsibilities and to compensate for the fullbacks on the goal line who are not covering man to man but rather are protecting the goal in a zone defense. If extra attackers are brought up to help in the attack, the defensive team's forwards should be brought back to help cover—keeping the man-to-man relationship.

Once the play has been stopped, the defense must move quickly out of the penalty area to support their attack going the other way.

Against the short corner kick, the two defensive players responsible for the kicker and the man closest to him should move into position to stop the play as quickly as possible. These two defenders should move quickly in order to surround the pass receiver and challenge him for the ball immediately. One man on this defensive play will not be enough. All others cover as usual in the man-to-man defense.

Direct and Indirect Free Kicks

Both direct and indirect free kicks should be attempted and defended in the same manner. The strategy for attempting the kick and defending against it depend on the proximity to the goal.

If the free kick is awarded to an attacking team, near or in the danger area close to the goal, the defense will put a "wall" of players, varying from two to five, in front of the kick to cut down the angle the shooter will have while attempting to score.

Offensive Free Kicks

The basic premise in designing strategy for offensive free kicks is that the kick penalizes the opponent for a rule infraction. Therefore, it follows that there must be an advantage to this play. The advantage that the kicking team has is that it plays the ball first to wherever it wants to and without

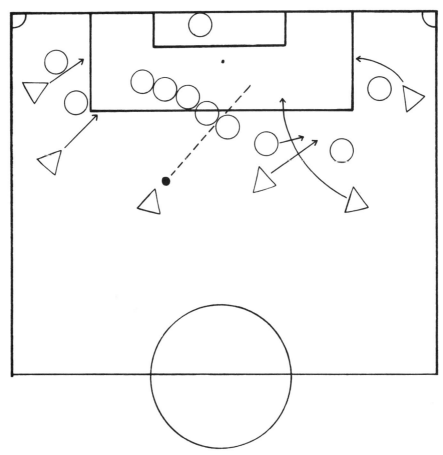

An example of attacking a defensive wall.

interference. This means that the first kick, following the whistle, should be an important one, one designed to set up the score.

When the official blows the whistle to stop play because of a rule infraction, most teams—especially inexperienced ones—tend to relax, if they are not trained to set up quickly. It is generally good procedure to put the ball in play as quickly as possible. This is especially true on free kicks awarded in midfield, where a wall would not be used by the defense.

The principles of attack from this point should be set up by the team to accomplish a quick, aggressive attack on goal. Though there are many ways to carry this off, the following principles should serve as guides to action.

1. The player nearest the ball comes up and kicks the ball quickly into play. He must scan the field looking for every possibility as he does so.
2. Teammates, generally forwards, take off into open spaces in the defense ready to take the kick.
3. The kick should be kept away from the goalkeeper, in order to give the forwards the opportunity to get the ball and get the shot off.

A free kick awarded near the goal will invariably be faced by a wall. Generally, it is futile to shoot at the players in the wall. A goal can be scored directly against a wall only if the men in the wall are in bad positions or if the kicker can lift the ball over or curve the ball around the wall. Needless to say, this is extremely difficult.

The best way to beat a wall is to quickly change the attack space from where the ball is to a place outside of the wall for a direct shot on goal.

The attacking players have the advantage of being able to set up at different spots outside of the wall, and being able to run into areas quickly to receive passes in open spaces. The defense, however, must stay committed to the wall until the threat of the first kick is over. Therefore, plays used to defeat the wall by getting the ball out to the side or chipped over the top of the wall involve general deception and spacing of players to produce openings.

Attackers should cut through and into the defense prior to the kick, and players should call for the ball from the kicker, with a lot of general, but planned, confusion taking place prior to the kick. Then the actual kick to beat the wall must be executed quickly and accurately to the intended receiver, for a quick strike at the goal.

Defending Against the Free Kick

On free kicks, well away from the goal, the best defense is to be alert and cover men in the same manner, using the same system. The defenders must hustle to their assignments to avoid being beaten by the quick free kick.

When the kick is to be taken near the goal, the wall must be used. Bearing in mind the purpose of the wall, the goalkeeper will call out quickly the number of men he wants in the wall. The goalkeeper should direct the positioning of the wall since the wall should reduce the danger of a direct shot into the goal. He will have to guard the rest.

Teammates must be brought back to help defend and match the number of attackers. The defenders should mark their men in a man-to-man defense, placing themselves so that they can see both the ball and the attacker they are guarding. They must seek to shut off the attackers' routes to the goal. Once the ball is played, the wall is disbanded and the closest men should be covered.

Throw-ins

The objective of a successful throw-in is possession. In the section about throw-in technique in Chapter 4, a number of possibilities for successful

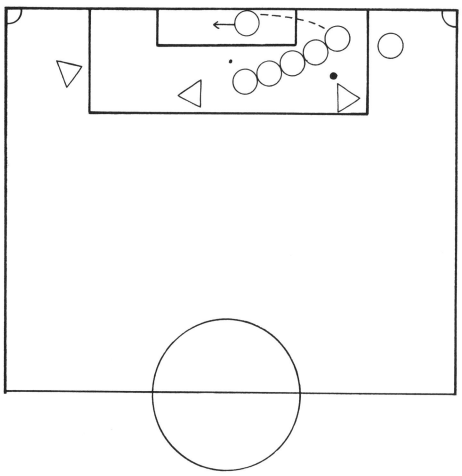

Setting up the wall.

throw-ins are given, but certain throw-in principles are worth further study.

All players on the field should and must be adept at throwing the ball in from outside the touchlines. Since throw-in rules prescribe throw-in technique, all players must be able to execute the throw-in legally and correctly. Quick throw-ins can sometimes be an advantage, especially when the defensive team has not had the opportunity to cover all its men. That is why it is so important that the player nearest the ball run for it, pick it up, and throw in quickly. If the team were to wait for a throw-in specialist, this opportunity would be lost.

Possible receivers must move into positions that will give them the opportunity to receive and control the ball. This can be accomplished in many ways.

1. A simple way to get a receiver free is to have the receivers line up at a good distance from the thrower. As the thrower gets to throw, the possible receivers break toward him, leaving their defensive cover behind. (See illustration 4-12.)
2. Positional interchange is another way to get receivers free. This involves a quick exchange of positions between players as the thrower gets set to make the throw. Defensive men can be caught in the interchange and forget to change defensive responsibilities, thus leaving a man open. (See illustration 4-13.)
3. Very often a throw-in that is thrown back toward the thrower's goal will find an unmarked fullback or even the goalkeeper. For some reason, teams often forget that possibility, and a fullback can end up with the ball, quite alone, able to play the ball constructively up to his forwards. (See illustration 4-14.)

Throw-in no. 1.

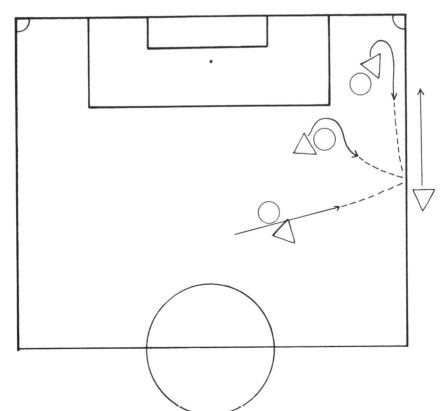

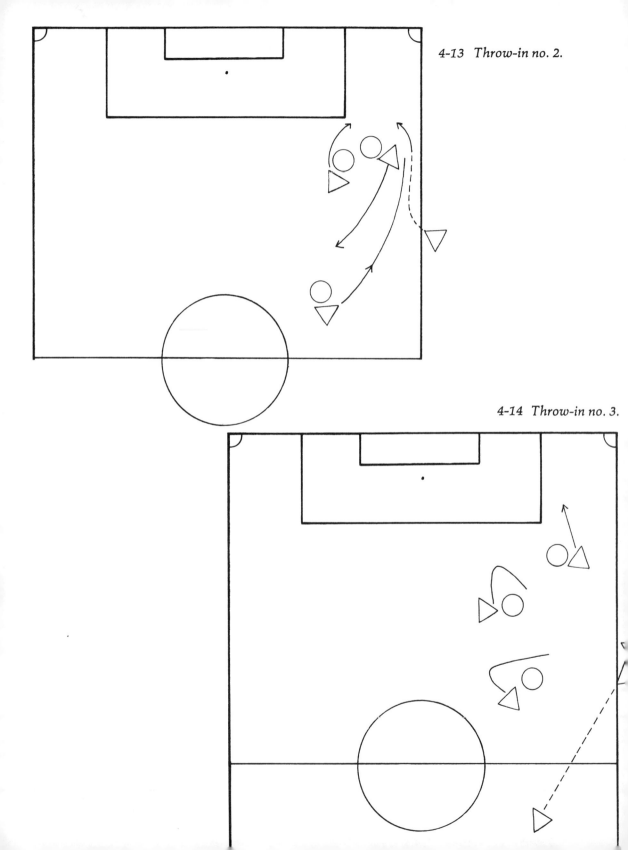

4-13   *Throw-in no. 2.*

4-14   *Throw-in no. 3.*

4. Individual feinting and faking movements, based on prearranged signals, can set a receiver free. For example, a player could take a few steps to his left, his defender would follow, then he suddenly pivots and takes off in the opposite direction, breaking free of his cover, open to receive the throw-in.

There are many exciting possibilities that can be employed to make the throw-in successful, but they all depend on the ability of all players to execute the throw-in correctly and intelligently.

Defending Against the Throw-in

The best defense against the throw-in is close man-to-man marking with all possible receivers covered. This is especially valuable with beginning players since their ball control after receiving the ball will be a little shaky.

By covering everybody in throwing distance and in all directions, the choices that the thrower has are limited. This, of course, is the objective—upset the thrower by limiting his choices and cover the receivers so that they must contend with a defensive play as they are trying to gain control of the ball.

The thrower should not be left out of the coverage plan since he is able to get onto the field immediately following his delivery and thus makes himself available as a free man for a return of the ball to him. If he is unmarked, this could prove dangerous to the defense. Cover them all.

Penalty Shots

The penalty shot has all of the advantage going to the man taking the shot. Therefore, it is important to have two men practice taking the penalty shots, with the better and more consistent of the two as the regular penalty shot taker. The reason for having two men practice taking the shot is that if the best shooter is injured or out of the game for some reason, a reliable substitute will be ready to assume the role.

The best penalty shots are those that are aimed for the upper or lower corners of the goal out of the reach of the goalkeeper. Good kicking technique should be used so as to ensure accuracy. The toe should not be used. This is mentioned because, for some reason, beginning players will want to kick hard at the ball and mistakenly will think that the toe will give them great power. Accuracy is more important than power in this case.

The rules state that the remaining players must take up positions outside of the penalty area until the kick is taken. The forwards should be dispersed

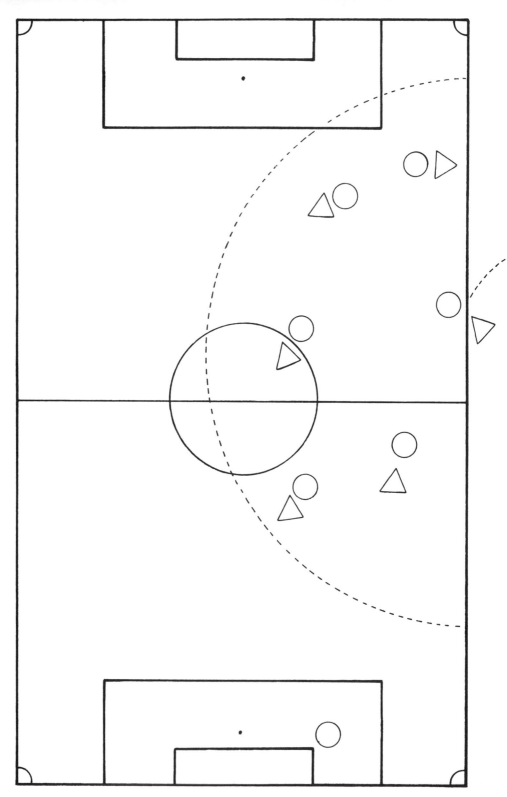

Defending against the throw-in.

around the penalty area, facing the goalkeeper, ready to charge into the penalty area should there be a rebound off the goalposts or off the goalkeeper.

But penalty shots should be automatic. Only practice, confidence, and proper kicking technique will make it so.

Defending the Penalty Kick

The rules state that the goalkeeper cannot move until the ball is kicked. Therefore, all he has to help him are his reflexes and, of course, the wish of all goalkeepers—that the kicker miskicks the ball.

The only way to plan for stopping penalty shots is to hope for a pattern that emerges in the kicker's preference as to where he generally kicks. This would be determined from scouting reports or from watching him in pregame warmups.

Defense men should line up around the penalty area, alert to the fact that the ball can be played on a rebound, and, therefore, be ready to go in quickly and clear the ball out of the area in any way possible.

TEAM SYSTEMS OF PLAY

Systems of play evolve in soccer, as in all team sports, from the need to structure the offense and defense to gain the maximum effectiveness of each phase of play. It is not enough to turn eleven players loose on a soccer field against eleven opponents. The result would be mayhem.

To develop a team system of play is to develop a pattern or style of play that gives order to the participants within the boundaries of objectives, individual functions, and rules and regulations of the sport.

The system of play chosen is dependent upon the utilization of the strengths and talents of the individual team members. The system must also realistically take into account any weaknesses present in particular areas. It also follows that because the opponent chooses its style or system of play in the same manner, the ability for each team to be flexible in its game plan should be built into the system.

The main factor that must be considered in the selection of the style of play to be adopted by the team is the soccer ability and talents of the individual players. The basic questions that must be asked are: Can these players carry out the fundamental skills of soccer in such a way that they can achieve the basic principles of offense and defense? Can they control the ball and move it consistently? Can they defend? If the answer to any of these questions is no, then the best style of play on paper becomes a disaster in use.

Many coaches and soccer theoreticians will choose a style of play by developing a philosophy of the kind of game they would like to play. For example, some like a free-wheeling attacking game; others prefer heavy defensive coverages, playing mainly to prevent being scored upon; still others ape a system being employed by some world class teams. Soccer theory and philosophy are important to the game, but the coach with inexperienced players or less than world class players begins with less esoteric problems.

To the average player and his coach, systems are really not as important as are passing, ball control, and the basic objectives of the game as defined by the individual and collective team members' abilities. It is by realistically studying individual and team capabilities that a system of play will evolve. Without being able to carry off fundamentals, no system can work. With mastery of fundamentals, all systems are possible.

The W-M System of Play

The W-M system of play became popular when the present offside rule came into effect in 1925. It was devised to allow the attack the opportunity of having players well upfield and in position to receive passes from out of the defense and to attack the goal quickly. The name is derived from the positioning assumed by the five forwards.

The center forward and the outside forwards are the upfield spearheads of the attack. Support and depth are provided for these attackers by the insides, who are dropped back toward midfield.

In order to cope with the attack, defensive alignments match defenders with attackers on a man-to-man basis. The center forward is marked by the center halfback, the wings are marked by the fullbacks, and the inside forwards are handled by the wing halfbacks, resulting in an inverted W or M.

The W system of play requires an exceptionally gifted center forward who is fast, able to shoot and pass with both feet, and able to head the ball well. The tight defensive coverage given this position makes it necessary for the center forward to be aggressive and physically tough.

The inside forwards are the quarterbacks of this attack. They must be talented in the skills of soccer and creative in their passing and ball handling. It is they who get the ball to the spearhead forwards. The insides must be able to feed passes and move intelligently to positions where they can receive return passes or shoot on goal.

The second major function of the inside forwards is to work with the wing halfbacks in effectively controlling the valuable midfield area. This is

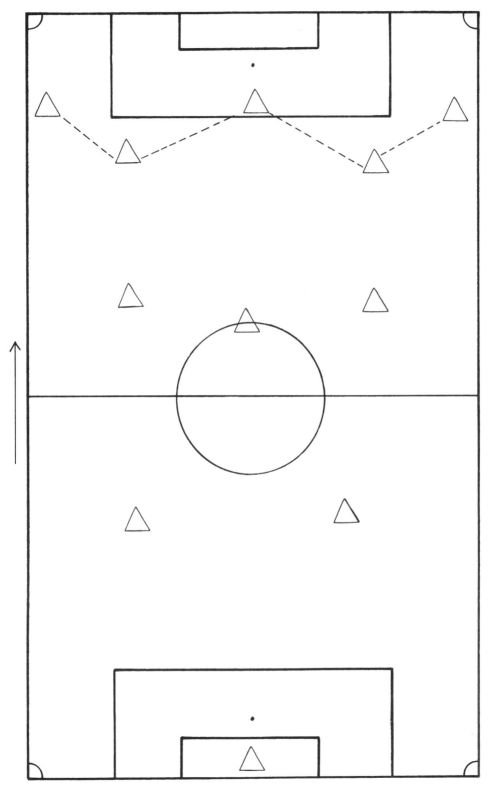

The W-M system of play.

crucial to their role since this is where attacks must begin and defense against the opponent's attacks must be initiated. Their multifaceted role demands that they be strong physically in order to carry out their duties to both the attack and the defense.

The wings, or outsides, must be fast, talented ball handlers. They must be able to take the ball down the sidelines and get by the opposing fullbacks who are intent on stopping them. They must be able to pass the ball accurately over the defense, while on the run, to their teammates attacking the goal. The wings are expected to be able to come inside when the situation presents itself and shoot on goal, as all forwards must.

The wing halfbacks provide the liaison between the deep defenders and the attacking forwards. Their first duty is defense, and that is a difficult job since they draw the inside forwards to defend against. The wing halfbacks operate in midfield where the opponent's attack is being built up. They must be sure tacklers and aggressive all-around defenders.

The wing halfbacks function offensively when they move up the field behind and in support of their forwards. In this role they must be able to feed clearances out of the defense back up to the forwards, thereby sustaining the attack on goal and maintaining the pressure.

The center halfback, by necessity, is concerned with staying close to his defensive assignment—the center forward. In many cases, this policeman's role divests him of the opportunities to take part in the attack for fear of leaving the center forward alone in a dangerous position. The most that could be expected of the center halfback in this system, in terms of attack, is that he would join with his wing halfbacks in trying to sustain the pressure of the attack on goal by moving up to midfield and trying to prevent clearances out of the defense.

Advantages of the W-M System

1. Because of the positioning of the forward line, the attack can be over a broad front, thereby keeping the defense spread and vulnerable to penetration.

2. Depth in the attack is provided for by the positioning and spacing of the forwards in the basic W pattern. This implies some forwards up and some forwards behind them to give basic depth.

3. Penetration is possible through passing alleys that develop from the halfbacks on up to the forwards.

4. Positional interchange is easily accomplished. Players can move into new positions that have been vacated by teammates in their effort to find attacking areas.

Disadvantages of the W-M System

1. A well-positioned and aggressive defense, played in a man-to-man style, will cut down the effectiveness of the through passes this system must employ. Receivers can be covered so that the passer will have very few options.
2. If the opponent utilizes an extra man in the defense, the attack is in trouble since each man will be marked closely, with this extra man in a position to cover should one of his teammates make an error or mistake.
3. The greatest disadvantage of this style of play concerns the development or lack of development of a fluid, improvised style of play. Halfbacks and fullbacks in particular become confined to the roles (defensive) of the game, thus losing the possibilities of helping in the attack without seriously impairing the function of the defense.

Some coaches believe that this style of play is the best to begin with for inexperienced players. It is commonly taught as the formation that must be mastered before anything else. This is not true. What has to be mastered is skill and ball control. The system then adopted will have more potential success regardless of the style of play chosen.

The form or style of play is dictated by the ability of the individual players to carry off the required fundamentals of the game. It should never be the other way around.

The M-W System of Play

The M pattern evolved naturally from the W system. When the defenses caught up to the tactics of the W, it became necessary to vary the attack. This was accomplished by utilizing the inside forwards as the spearheads of the attack, with the center forward dropping back toward the middle of the field to gather in balls and start the attack. The wings also dropped back, thus giving the shape of an M, or inverted W, to the attack. In this way, the wings were able to help in the crucial midfield area with the building up of the attack.

The idea of the M system of play is to put two talented forwards into the spaces created as the result of moving the wings and center forward back. This tactic results in having the fullbacks and the center halfback out of the penalty area, with the wing halfbacks covering the attacker's inside. This naturally provides more individual maneuvering room in the penalty area.

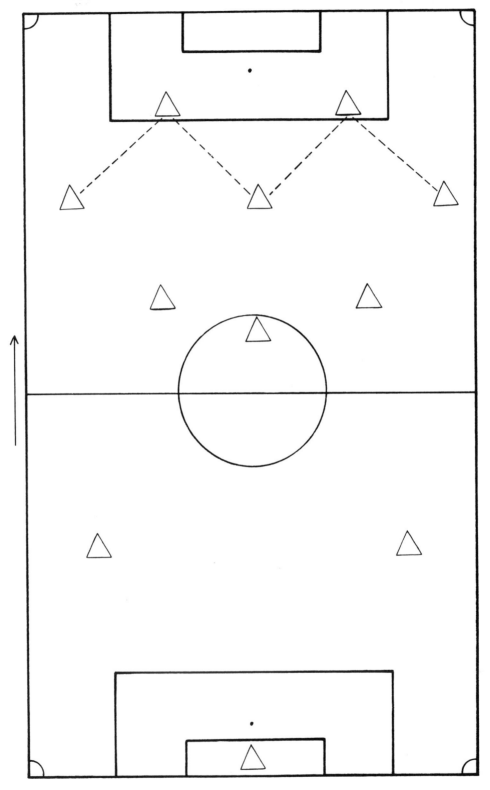

The M-W system of play.

Advantages of the M-W System

1. Greater control of midfield can be achieved now that the center forward and the outsides move into this area. Defense is thereby enhanced.
2. An inexperienced defense can be spread and moved out across the field, resulting in the highly desirable spaces to move into for attacks on goal.

The interesting thing to note at this point is that the team employing this style of play would probably be as inexperienced as the defense and would make few gains from this formation.

Disadvantages of the M-W System

1. The most serious disadvantage of the M system of play is the lack of attackers upfield in striking position. Scoring potential is cut down. If the defensive coverage is tight, the two forward attackers can easily be cut off from the support of the other forwards behind the play. This makes it extremely difficult to sustain the attack.
2. The two attackers are forced to rely on exceptional passing in order to get the ball. This is difficult under the best conditions and nearly impossible with beginning players. The defenders will definitely have the advantage in this system.
3. Teams utilizing this style become defense minded to the point where attacking becomes secondary rather than equal to the defense. This is not good soccer because the attacking force is diminished and players are divested of versatility by being confined to specific roles in rigidly adhering to a designated function.

The 4–2–4 System of Play

The 4–2–4 system of play is currently one of the most popular systems of play throughout the world. The system was devised primarily to provide greater defensive coverage, but, when used by teams with strong personnel, strength can also be added to the attack.

This system utilizes four forwards, two halfbacks, and four deep defenders. The extra defense man is acquired by dropping one of the forwards, generally an inside forward, from the forward line, resulting in a four-man forward line. This forward combines with one of the wing halfbacks to form

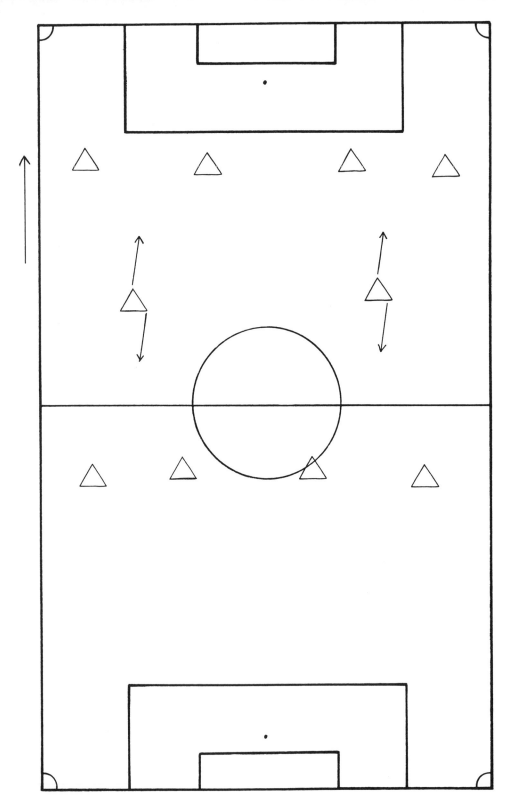

The 4–2–4 system of play.

the two-man link between the forward line and the four deep defenders. The center halfback and the remaining wing halfback join the two fullbacks to form the four-man defensive line in front of the goalkeeper.

The basic theory behind the 4–2–4 system is to allow a team to have a minimum of seven defenders covering the opponent's attack and, when they are on the attack, a minimum of six attackers moving toward the opponent's goal.

When the opposing team has possession of the ball, the two midfield players move quickly into the defense to become halfbacks. The defensive assignments are the same as in the previously described W-M formations. The fullbacks mark the opposing outside forwards, the halfbacks mark their opposing inside forwards, and the center halfback marks the opposing center forward, while the extra man that has been added to the defense from the forward line can perform several functions, depending upon the system of attack being employed by the opponent.

The extra defender can:

1. Play behind the four-man defensive line as a free man, with no particular defensive responsibility. In this way he can move to cover and back up any of his defensive teammates should an opponent be too much to handle alone or should a pass get through the defense. In short, he becomes a safety valve for the defense.
2. Play in front of the four-man defensive line, free to move where he is needed and to provide general harassment to the attacking team by going to the point of attack.
3. Mark any extra attacker that is put into the attack by the opponents, thus keeping the defensive matchup even at all times.
4. Be a luxury for the defense if the opponent does not attack at full strength or in numbers equal to the defense. This means that he is free to play in front or behind or move to wherever extra defensive help is required.

The attacking role of the two midfield players is very much the same as the attacking role of the inside forwards in any soccer system. These two players move up the field in support of their forwards, providing depth, penetration, and breadth to the attack. In short, these two midfield players must be versatile forwards as well as sure, strong defenders. They must be able to pass, shoot, think, and carry out all of the functions demanded of the forwards.

The advantage of this system of play lies both in the ability to get extra attackers into the offense and to get extra help for the defense, very often without a specific defensive responsibility.

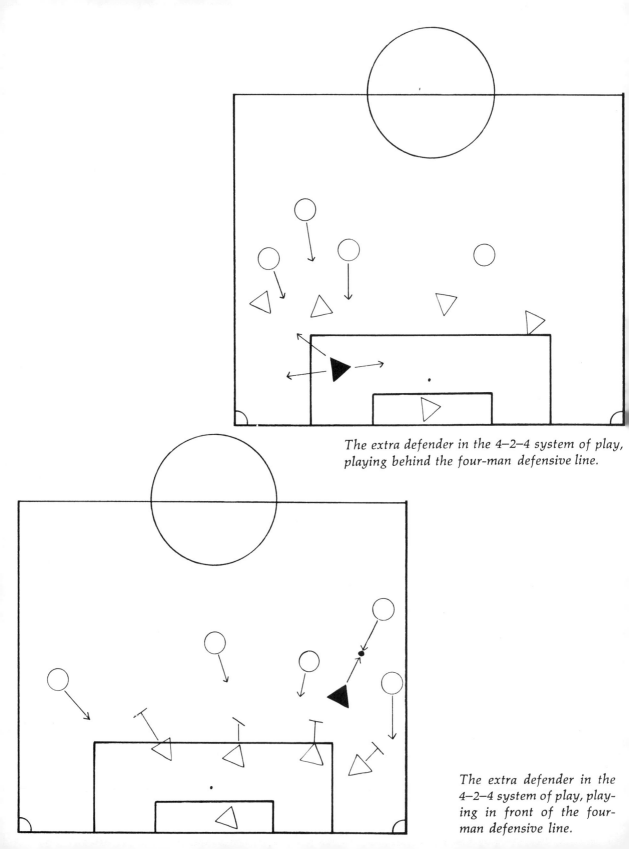

The extra defender in the 4–2–4 system of play, playing behind the four-man defensive line.

The extra defender in the 4–2–4 system of play, playing in front of the four-man defensive line.

However, it is obvious that the success of this system of play is contingent upon the talent, strength, and endurance of the two midfield players. This is also the possible disadvantage of the system. Unless these two midfield players are exceptionally gifted soccer players, the system will fail. If these men are weak, both the attack and the defense will suffer since both attack and defense depend on how well these two men join the two functions together. If these two cannot keep up with the fluidity of the game, gaps will develop at midfield and allow the opponent to utilize this valuable territory to build its attack. This will inevitably result in constant pressure on the defense, with the result being a loss of the ability to strike back at the opponent's goal.

It is for these reasons that a coach must truly evaluate his midfield personnel before going into this system. The two midfield players must be two of the best on the team, but even that will not ensure success with this system with beginning players.

The 4–3–3 System of Play

For a team that desires the defensive strength of the 4–2–4 system but is not blessed with the midfield personnel, there is an alternative to the 4–2–4 system that retains many of the basic qualities of the 4–2–4 but not the great dependency on the two key players. This is the 4–3–3 system.

The 4–3–3 system retains the strong defensive character of the four-man defensive line but further strengthens that line by putting another center halfback in front of these four, thus making a three-man liaison line between the deep defenders and the forward line. This is achieved by dropping still another inside from the forward line into what is called a semidefensive position. The center forward and the outside right and left remain upfield in the attacking role.

These three midfield players provide greater midfield coverage than does the two-man line, thus also providing an exceptionally strong defensive alignment. The individual defense assignments remain the same as the ones described in the 4–2–4 system, with the extra man becoming in reality an eighth defender.

This system of play is decidedly a defensive one and this is its greatest advantage. Teams that use this system are generally defense minded or up against powerful attacking teams. Therefore, they are content with playing defense and keeping the opponent from scoring, even if they don't score either. Another advantage to this system is that occasionally, a good team playing this system can get the extra defenders into the attack, but that is difficult. The only other time this system can be of value is late in a game

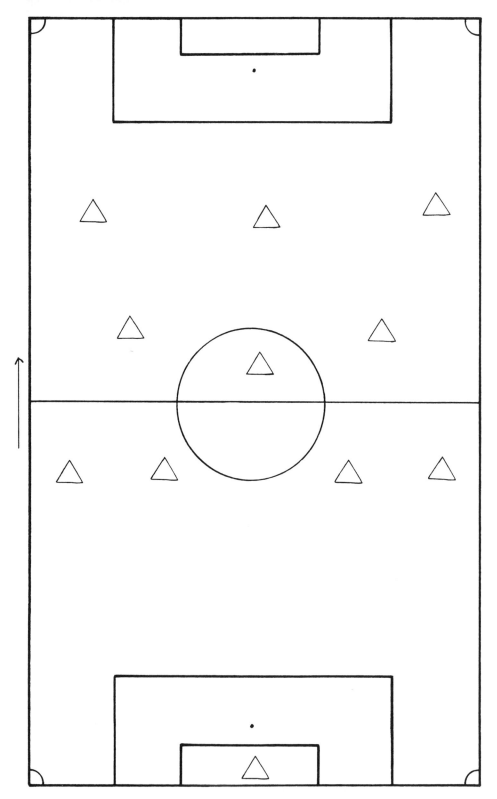

The 4–3–3 system of play.

when the team is trying to protect a lead. In this case, the team probably would have abandoned their scoring style of play and moved into this defensive alignment to protect their lead. However, this is doubtful strategy since a defense-minded team tends to stay around their own penalty area, and, with the crowd that will be attracted, anything can happen.

The disadvantage of this system is that players become overly defense conscious and tend to forget attack. By borrowing another forward from the forward line, attackers become scarce. The three attackers must have the support of the midfielders in order to overcome the defensive numbers against them. The three midfield players must move aggressively and quickly into good supporting positions for their forwards or the attack strength will be lost. It is for this reason that all defenders, including the four deep backs, must be encouraged to move out of the defense in support of the attack whenever the opportunity presents itself.

One more disadvantage of this system of play is that it can become boring to the players themselves. The style tends to divest the players of the creativity that can be part of good, balanced attacking and defensive soccer. Without this balance, the game can become dull.

The 3–3–4 System of Play

A further modification of both the 4–2–4 and the 4–3–3 systems of play is the 3–3–4 system, which employs four forwards, three midfield players, and three deep defenders.

This system is also based on the desire to get the extra defender into the defense but still retain the four forwards upfield and the midfield coverage that was lost in the 4–2–4 system. This system allows for the healthiest balance between offense and defense by retaining the midfield coverage that is needed by beginning soccer teams.

The 3–3–4 utilizes what can be called a double center halfback style of play. One center halfback plays between the two wing halfbacks and the other plays between the two fullbacks. The team's defensive marking of men is, always, based on the style of attack being used by the opponents.

If the opponent attacks with a similar style of play and the attackers equal the defenders, then the man-to-man system is still in effect with the same defensive responsibilities as stated earlier. The fullbacks defend against the outsides, the halfbacks defend against the inside forwards, and either one of the center halfbacks defends against the center forward—that chore generally going to the stronger defensive player, with the remaining center forward marking the extra man in the attack.

Should the opponent attack in lesser numbers, then one of the center half-

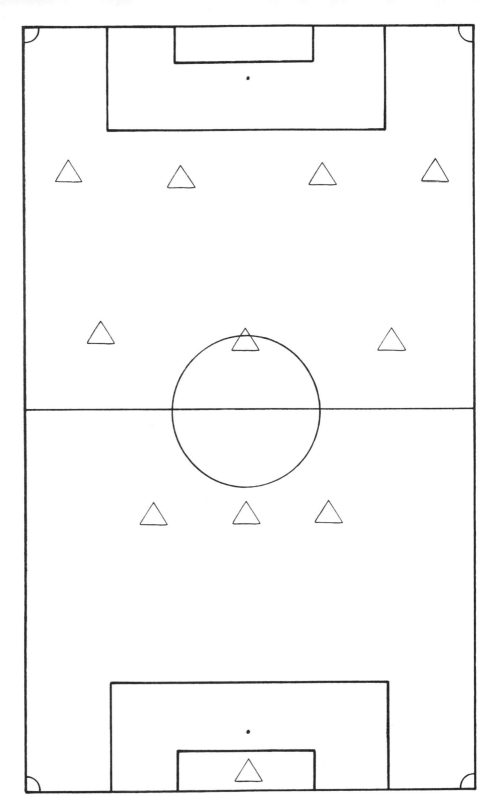

The 3–3–4 system of play.

backs is free to act as a "sweeper" back. This means that he plays in a free position, generally behind the other defenders, so that he can control the area in front of the goal and back up his defense in the area from which the attack is coming. In this case, the forward center halfback would be responsible for covering the opposing center forward.

The advantages of this system lie in the balance that can be established between the attack and the defense. Strength in the form of an extra man can add to both. This style of play also allows considerable coverage of the field in all areas, including midfield where attacks generally begin.

The disadvantage of this style of play can be found in the possible failure of the three midfield players to perform either their defensive or offensive responsibilities. Since they have important roles in both aspects of the game, they must deliver on both ends of the field.

This system of play is one of the most sensible to begin with since it lends itself to developing versatility in a team. A team can change easily from 4–3–3 to 3–3–4 and even 4–2–4 if they are good enough. The variations of this formation are many and limited only by the talents of the individual players. This system is one of the most popular in American college soccer and it also allows for modern, fluid, and exciting soccer to take place.

It must always be understood that the system of play is only secondary to the talents of the players. No system will work where ball control and individual skills have not been mastered. It is for this reason that the coach should tailor the system to the abilities of his players rather than try to force his players into a system that he likes because he saw a professional team use the system successfully. The system employed must be based on an honest appraisal of the team's strengths and weaknesses.

7

TRAINING AND
CONDITIONING
FOR SOCCER

One of the many reasons why soccer has so much appeal to both players and spectators is its constant flow and freedom of movement. No team sport rivals soccer's continuous, relatively uninterrupted fast pace. The run of the ball blends with the rapid and frequent transition from attack to defense, making great physical demands on players while providing exciting action for spectators.

As in all team sports, three basic factors must be attained in order to achieve success in soccer:

1. The acquisition and skillful execution of individual skills.
2. The development of a system of play based on the skill levels and capabilities of the players.
3. The physical fitness necessary to meet the physical demands of the game.

Of the three basic factors, the easiest to attain in a relatively short amount of time is fitness. Fitness is the prerequisite for acquiring soccer skills since fitness is needed for sustained practice of individual technique. And, of course, fitness is crucial for sustained participation in a skilled, safe manner in actual soccer matches.

Modern soccer coaching theory is built around the individual player's ability to carry out assignments as part of the tactical scheme over the entire course of a game. Regardless of designated position and the coaches' choice of tactical style, today's players are required to participate fully and actively in the team's total attacking and defensive strategy.

It is obvious that in order to achieve overall team objectives, each player must contribute his or her individual skills to the team effort. To accomplish individual and team objectives, each player must be brought to a high level of physical fitness. This can be achieved only through participation in a carefully planned training and conditioning program that is based on the recognition of the player's physical needs as determined by the demands of soccer.

To intelligently design a training and conditioning program for soccer, coaches and players must begin with an analysis and inventory of the physical demands made on each player in the course of a match. From this delineation of soccer-demand components, fitness needs and desired objectives will clearly emerge. With fitness needs understood, the design and implementation of specific training activities can be achieved on a sound, rational, and productive basis.

One more word before we analyze the physical demands made on soccer players. It has been my experience in teaching soccer to beginning players and in coaching on the university level that by allowing the players to share in the analysis of soccer's physical demands and by encouraging them to be active partners in the setting of fitness objectives and training activities, players approach training in a more highly motivated way. Motivated players who understand why they are working hard will achieve higher levels of training fitness because they are mentally stimulated to participate in training activities they helped design.

The following is a delineation of physical demands made on soccer players in the course of a match:

1. Soccer is basically a running game. Highly intensive sprinting is interspersed with lower level running or jogging. Most full or near-full sprints are performed without possession of the ball. Contact with the ball generally occurs at the start or finish of the sprint.
2. Sprints vary in distance covered from 5 to 45 yards, with most sprints falling into the 25- to 35-yard range. Most of these sprints tend to be run straight.
3. Soccer players must be able to perform quick changes of direction, accelerate, and stop quickly; accelerate, jump, or leap from stationary or near stationary starts; jump, feint, dodge, and run sideways and even backward.
4. While performing any of these movements, the player is expected to be able to receive, control, and redistribute the ball on the move, often while being challenged by an opponent.

As we review this inventory of soccer demands, it becomes apparent that the crucial areas of fitness for soccer are endurance, strength, and flexibility.

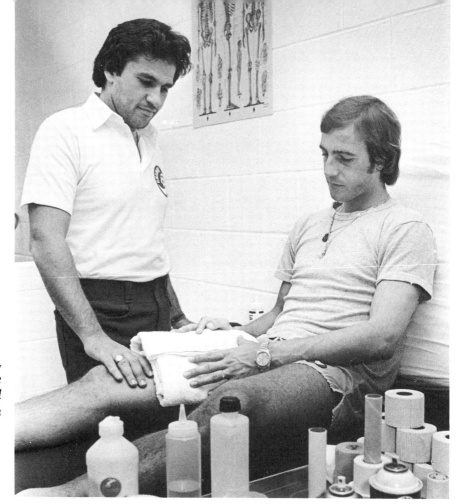

Arnold Trachtenberg, athletic trainer for the New York Cosmos, and player Jan Neeksens in the training room.

A word of caution at this point. Many coaches attempt to link skill training with conditioning activities. This is done in an attempt to save time by trying to reach skill goals and fitness goals at the same time. It has been my experience, particularly with beginning players, that for the most part it is far better to separate skill training from conditioning work. This is true because developing fitness demands all-out, intensive hard work. Skill development by its very nature is performed at a much lower work rate. If the objective of the particular activity is to control the ball, the physical work rate is cut because the player cannot control the ball while working and moving with full physical effort.

Conversely, when practicing individual ball control skills, the emphasis is placed on the correct, controlled acquisition and execution of the skill. While in the learning process, the application of intensive physical work will take away from the player's development of coordination, thereby negating the process.

BUILDING CARDIOVASCULAR AND MUSCULAR ENDURANCE

Endurance may be defined as the ability to take part in vigorous physical activity over an extended period of time. For our purposes, strength may be defined as the force with which the muscles contract. Building strength and muscular endurance are related, as will become clearer later on in this chapter.

Soccer specifically demands repeated short bursts of intensive activity interspersed with longer periods of low to moderate activity. The periods of low or moderate activity provide the soccer player with the time needed to recover from the frequent periods of intensive involvement.

There are two kinds of endurance that must be achieved for total fitness. The first is cardiovascular endurance, which involves the circulatory and respiratory systems and their function in sustaining total physical activity over long periods of time. The second is muscular endurance, which may be defined as the ability of specific muscle groups to perform their functions repeatedly over extended periods of time. The methods used to build muscular endurance are also employed in building muscular strength. Many of the principles of conditioning are common to both.

By looking at the specific nature of the two kinds of endurance, we will be able to understand better the rationale for training that must go into preparing soccer players for the physical demands of the sport.

Cardiovascular Endurance

The endurance needed to sustain general total physical effort for long periods of time is called cardiovascular endurance. A look at the basic physiological nature of the cardiovascular system will make clear how this system affects the soccer player.

Virtually every movement we make, as well as nearly every posture the body can assume, is caused by or supported by muscular contractions. Our muscles are constantly at work and, with their every contraction, from the smallest movement to large-scale running movements, they need fuel to provide their energy. The fuel necessary to provide energy to our muscles is oxygen, taken from the air and transported by the blood to the muscles.

As the oxygen is used up by the muscles, it must be replaced in the blood.

This function is performed by the respiratory system. The respiratory system involves the inhalation of air and is made up of those organs of the body especially equipped to take oxygen from the air and transfer it to the blood. The organs and body parts involved in this process are the nose and mouth, the lungs, and the passages for air that lead to the lungs.

The circulatory system carries the blood to the various parts of the body where the oxygen is needed and used. The circulatory system also carries the blood away from the muscles, taking with it the wastes that have accumulated as a result of the muscles using and burning the oxygen. The blood then returns to the lungs, where it exchanges the used air and accumulated wastes for freshly reoxygenated air.

The more strenuous the activity, the greater the need for oxygen will be to support the increased muscular contractions. At this point, the heart's function becomes even more crucial to the circulatory process. As the need for oxygen increases, the blood must be pumped faster to keep up with the demands for energy being made by the muscles. The heart is a muscular pump that pumps the oxygenated air in the blood, via the circulatory system, throughout the body. The harder the muscles work, the harder the heart must pump, to circulate the oxygenated blood and remove the wastes of respiration from the body. The signs of this physiological activity are quite clear. As the muscles work harder, the heart speeds up and breathing becomes more rapid, bringing more air into the lungs, all to keep pace with the body's demands brought on by intensive work.

The conditioning task, then, in training for cardiovascular endurance is aimed at giving the player the ability to inhale large amounts of oxygen from the air, exchange it in the lungs to the bloodstream, and circulate the oxygen efficiently through the entire body by way of the circulatory system.

This type of conditioning is based on providing the player with aerobic energy, meaning that the energy supplied to the muscles is formed with air or oxygen. Good overall physical fitness is built on having good aerobic energy formation capacity.

To achieve good aerobic capacity, continuous physical activity must be performed regularly. Jogging, cycling, and swimming are examples of cardiovascular endurance builders. The objective is to raise the heart and pulse rate generally above 140 beats per minute and keep the pace at that level for at least five minutes. The idea is to get the body, in its entirety, working beyond normal work levels, thus speeding up all the systems involved in general fitness. This kind of training program can be enjoyed by any healthy person, regardless of age, sex, or athletic ability. The one caution that applies to those beginning a fitness program, as well as to those undergoing intensive sports training programs, is that a proper medical checkup be taken before beginning work.

Muscular Endurance

While cardiovascular activity is vital to soccer training, it simply is not enough to meet soccer's vigorous demands. Therefore, the second kind of endurance and the one needed for soccer conditioning is muscular fitness.

Muscular endurance may be defined as the ability of the muscles to repeatedly apply force (strength and power) or to sustain muscular contractions over an extended period of time. Muscular endurance or the lack of it is easily measured by simply putting the muscles to work at a specific task or activity and then seeing how long the player can stay at it.

In soccer, muscular endurance is most necessary in the legs to sustain the varied and intense patterns of running. How many times a player can sprint 50 yards, for example, with a brief rest in between, would soon give the coach and the player a clue as to how capable the muscles are in terms of muscular endurance.

To further understand muscular endurance, we can look back at old-style soccer training techniques. In the early days of professional soccer, and indeed even into the 1950s in some American colleges, players were trained for endurance by endless running of laps on a track or on a soccer field. We all recognize this type of training since we see it daily on our streets and in our parks. It is the now popular conditioning program called jogging. This kind of lap running, just like jogging, did accomplish increased cardiovascular endurance through developing good aerobic capacity.

However, soccer is not played at a jogger's pace. Being required to run at near flat-out sprints repeatedly over the course of a match demands more than cardiovascular fitness. If muscular endurance has not been attained, cardiovascular fitness will not be enough to carry a soccer player through a match.

Coaches and players soon realized that the muscular endurance needed to play soccer had to come from activities specifically designed to make the muscles stronger and more efficient. It was obvious that low or moderate levels of running would not and could not provide the muscular strength and endurance called for in actual play.

The all-out sprints, leaping in the air to head a ball, the race with an opponent to gain possession of the ball—all demand intensive response to repeated situations. Muscle groups are called on over and over again to perform short-duration intense activities.

The short duration of the specific intensive activity precludes the demand for oxygen since the action is performed and over with rather quickly. The muscles are energized by the store of energy in them, energy stored in the form of carbohydrates, most notably glycogen. This kind of energy formation is called anaerobic, meaning without air or oxygen.

For a further example of how this energy is used, let us look at a 60-yard-dash sprinter. The sprinter completes the race so quickly that it is unnecessary to breathe at all during the event. Nearly all the energy needed to complete the short dash is stored energy. The cardiovascular endurance factor will come into play, as we shall see later, in the recovery period.

The energy stored in the muscles won't last for more than about two minutes under normal conditions. Muscular endurance training is aimed at conditioning the muscles to tolerate the conversion process of energy into muscular action and to handle more efficiently the wastes of that conversion. The muscles in turn become stronger and more efficient in response to intense demand. The more efficient the muscles become in working under anaerobic conditions, the greater their tolerance will become for intensive work.

With these basic understandings in mind, it becomes obvious that muscular strength and endurance and cardiovascular endurance are related. Muscular strength and endurance provide the player with the capability for performing repeated, intense vigorous activities. Cardiovascular endurance provides the overall fitness framework that allows efficient recovery to be made between heavy work demands.

Applying muscle therapy. Photo by George Bing, Audio-Visual Center, Brooklyn College. Photo courtesy of Professor William D. Chisholm, Director, Brooklyn College Sports Rehabilitation Center.

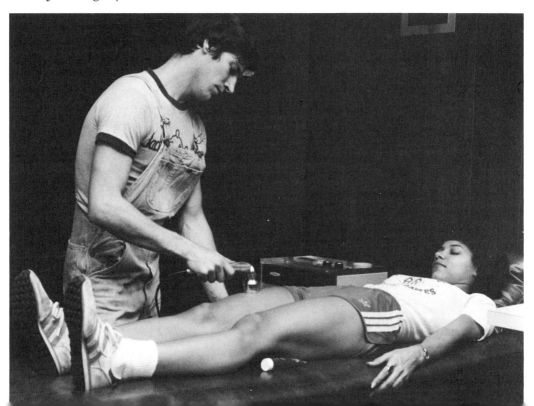

PRINCIPLES OF TRAINING

The human body is extremely adaptable in its ability to accommodate itself to the physical demands put upon it. Progressive adaptation to the specific demands of a physical activity will result in the increased ability to perform that specific physical activity. It must be stressed that the adaptation to or improvement in a specific activity will only increase the ability to meet that demand generally, not any other. This means, referring again to our earlier example, that if players jog to build cardiovascular fitness, then cardio-vascular fitness is what will result. They will not achieve muscular endurance or strength of the level needed to sustain repeated sprinting. Training specifically designed to sustain repeated sprints must involve repeated sprinting.

Therefore, because the body's tendency is to adapt specifically to demands, soccer training must be comprehensive and specific enough to provide the physical ability to meet the demands for strength, endurance, and flexibility that are made on the player in the course of a game.

The following are the four principles involved in specific training programs.

1. Overload. The basic principle involved in achieving specific physical improvement is called the overload principle. The overload principle states that the particular activity being performed, whether designed to improve cardiovascular endurance, muscular endurance, strength, or flexibility, must be such that it exceeds in intensity the demands normally made on the individual. It is obvious that an individual is not going to increase strength, for example, unless greater demand is put on his present strength capacity. This leads us to the next principle of training—progression.

2. Progression. The principle of progression works in concert with overload. As the individual begins applying overload, improvement will soon begin to be seen. As improvement is achieved, progressively greater demands must be made if improvement is to continue.

   This is how overload and progression can be attained in a soccer training program. In each specific demand area, overloading and progression remain the two underlying principles.

   Cardiovascular endurance training requires overloading of the large muscle groups of the body. When the large muscle groups become overloaded, they create a demand for more oxygen. When that demand is met, it is met by overloading specifically the respiratory and circulatory systems, resulting in the conditioning of these two vital systems.

Overloading for cardiovascular development can be achieved by increasing the rate of speed of the exercise or the distance covered or by combining the two options. This is precisely what jogging, cycling, and long-distance swimming aim at and accomplish.

Muscular endurance training requires the overloading of specific muscle groups. The purpose of the overloading is to strengthen the muscles and build tolerance to the strain of work and the resulting anaerobic metabolism taking place. Overloading for muscular endurance is achieved by increasing the work load on the muscles, increasing the repetitions of the specific activity, decreasing the rest intervals between repetitions, or by a combination of any of the three overload methods.

Overloading in flexibility training is accomplished by slowly increasing the range of motion through which the joint and specific muscle group are progressively stretching.

3. Regularity. In order to realize improvement in physiological and skill capacities, players must train regularly, and preferably on a daily basis. Even when satisfactory fitness levels have been reached, daily workouts are necessary to stay at high competitive levels.

4. Maintenance. The maintenance principle refers to the rather obvious fact that once high physical fitness and performance levels are reached, it is far easier to maintain that level than it was to achieve it. This principle has particular implications for the off season. The player will quickly get out of shape if strenuous, regular activity is not kept up. While the activity may not be soccer, it should be either a sport or training program that will constantly challenge the player's physical fitness.

CONDITIONING ACTIVITIES

Since muscular and cardiovascular endurance are necessary in order to sustain the practice of individual skills and team tactics, we will begin with and base our conditioning program on drills specifically aimed at these objectives.

Remember, the acquisition of endurance is the result of hard, intensive training. There is no easy way. The skilled coach is able to make the training demanding and, at the same time, varied enough so that players will remain interested and motivated. With some thought and imagination, what would have been boring repetitive drills can be transformed into exciting activities.

We base our endurance work training program on the following factors:

1. The age level of the players involved.
2. The physical condition the players are in at the start of training.
3. The individual differences the players bring to training (size, temperament, experience).
4. The objective of the drill in terms of its specific relationships to game conditions.

With these basic factors in mind, the coach must plan intensive running drills that progressively build to the amount of running a player, in his or her age group, will have to endure in a game. There is no set formula for arriving at maximum distances players will have to run in a game. Rather, this judgment must come from the coaches' experience with each age group to determine objectives.

Our endurance and speed training principles are based on the following:

1. Players should be trained to endure the maximum number of yards of intense running, as determined by the coach based on age level through intensive running drills.
2. Sprint distance should range between 40 and 50 yards.
3. Whenever possible, running patterns from actual play should be used. Change of direction, quick cuts, running with a partner in pursuit, hurdling over objects—all should be part of varied, demanding running activities.
4. Work toward improvement through progressive adaptation of training sprints. This can be done by increasing the number of sprints while maintaining recovery period time, by decreasing the recovery period, or by a combination of the two.

Specific Endurance Drills

Windsprints. Windsprints are invaluable in preparing players for repeated quick-start, full sprints over short distances and are a good example of a specific drill to meet a specific game demand. The all-out sprint from a near stationary position is required many times during play. Through the proper use of windsprints, muscular endurance can be achieved rather quickly and at the same time be made into a challenging, fun activity.

To do windsprints, the players begin at a starting line, sprint on command at top speed for 40 or 50 yards, jog back to the original starting line, and, on command, are off again at top speed.

The interval between windsprints should be used to jog to the next starting line or to perform some calisthenics. Twenty seconds between windsprints

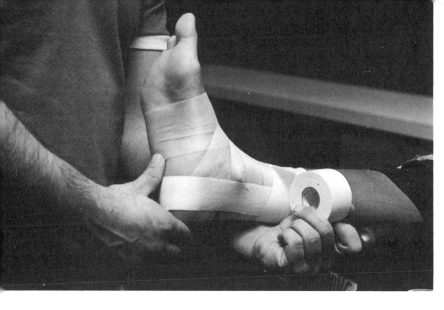

Protective strapping for an ankle prior to play. Photo by George Bing, Audio-Visual Center, Brooklyn College. Photo courtesy of Professor William D. Chisholm, Director, Brooklyn College Sports Rehabilitation Center.

should be the length of recovery. Windsprints should be done at the beginning and end of each practice session. An average goal of 500 yards at each windsprint session is a good objective.

Tag games and relay races can disguise windsprints, thus making them more palatable and interesting to players. This kind of pressure windsprint running approximates the competitive game situations.

In the course of a soccer match, players must make abrupt stops, sharp changes in direction, and bursts of acceleration. This all can be incorporated into windsprint drills by coaching commands, to be responded to while running.

Runs made sideways and backward are also called for in games. There should be ample opportunity to practice these movements. Since they are not as intensive in nature as all-out straight-ahead sprinting, they can be used during the recovery intervals between windsprints.

Interval Running. Interval running may be defined as intermittent intensive running in which a given distance is repeated several times with a recovery period in between each intensive run. The recovery period can be taken in the form of walking, jogging, or practicing ball control skills.

In my experience, I have found that when sprints are broken up into short, intensive runs, with recovery periods between them, players are able to perform greater work loads. This results in more running and better conditioning.

There are three ways of increasing the intensity of interval training for soccer:

1. Vary the distances to be run.
2. Progressively vary the number of times the distance run is to be repeated.
3. Vary the time and activity performed during the recovery period.

For example, an interval running drill for soccer might involve running six repetitions of 50 yards, each at full speed with a twenty-second rest interval between each sprint. The rest, in this case, would be an easy jog for the twenty-second interval. After the twenty seconds, the players are off again on the next 50-yard sprint.

By applying the three methods for intensifying interval training, we could progressively increase the work rate demand made on the players. This could be done by increasing the sprint distance to 60 yards, by increasing the number of repetitions of the sprint, or by cutting the recovery time.

It is always important to remember that the actual work load in interval training must be determined by the coach within the physiological levels of his players. The system of interval training is good at any level. Working out the demands to be placed on players requires the coach's understanding of objectives as they relate to the needs, level, and capabilities of the players.

A variation of the interval running program that I have found to be one of the best methods for building muscular and cardiovascular endurance is borrowed from track. This system is most effective in reaching objectives set for players and, equally important, one the players enjoyed participating in.

This training system was developed in Europe for the training of middle-distance runners. Middle-distance runners must maintain speed over relatively long periods of time and still have the muscular endurance to finish the race with a kick. The original system, called Fartlek, has been adopted and adapted by many professional and amateur teams because of its great value in building muscular and cardiac endurance and because of the many variations that can be put into its basic system.

In the adapted and modified Fartlek system, speed and pace vary from jogging to all-out sprints over a 2-mile course. The course run should go through parks or woods, on terrain that has hills, flat areas, and soft ground to run on. It is perfectly suitable for city teams, as most cities have parks that are ideal for intensive, cross-country style running. The variations in terrain provide interesting challenges for the runners, removing the tendency to boredom that comes from daily hard egort on the same track or field.

"Follow the leader" is the basic principle of this modified Fartlek running system. The leader sets the pace over the prescribed course. The leader operates within the following rules:

1. There is no walking.
2. The maximum sprint distance is 100 yards, with a return to a jogging pace following the sprint. As much of the sprinting as possible should be done at no less than 80 percent effort, with an all-out kick at the end of the run.
3. Sprint bursts of 30 to 50 yards should be liberally sprinkled through the runs, especially in going up hills.

Measuring athletes' cardiovascular capacities. Photo by George Bing, Audio-Visual Center, Brooklyn College. Photo courtesy of Professor William D. Chisholm, Director, Brooklyn College Sports Rehabilitation Center.

The overall course distance should be increased to meet the players' capabilities in terms of age, level of fitness, and ability.

This system can be used as often as every day in the preseason training period. Once the season begins, it can be used once or twice a week as a conditioning device and as a break from routine in-season practice sessions.

Developing Muscular Strength and Flexibility

Calisthenics play an important part in the training program because they loosen the muscles, warm up players before vigorous activity, and strengthen the muscles to withstand the rigors of soccer.

Calisthenics are divided into two parts for soccer purposes: exercises for stretching and loosening up, and exercises for building stronger, more powerful muscles.

Stretching and Loosening Up. These exercises are familiar to most people. They are easy to perform and can even be fun. Formations can be a circle or files, with room between the players to allow for easy and free movement. The following exercises involve the entire body. They should by no means be considered the only ones to be used. The choice of exercises should be varied so that players do not lose interest or get distracted easily. Walking or jogging is recommended between each exercise.

1. Neck Rotations. Feet in the straddle position, hands on hips. Rotate head and neck twenty times to the right, twenty times to the left.
2. Arm and Shoulder Rotations. Feet together, arms extended to sides and parallel to ground, palms facing up. Circle arms slowly forward twenty times, backward twenty times.
3. Trunk Twisting. Feet in straddle position, hands on hips, four-count exercise. Lean far to the right, front, left, back, return to upright position.
4. Toe Touch, or Windmill. Feet in straddle position, arms extended to sides and parallel to ground. Touch right hand to left toe, left hand to right toe in rhythm, thirty times.
5. Ground Touch. Same position as windmill. Touch ground with both hands between legs, moving hands farther toward rear, four times. (This will loosen back muscles.)
6. Leg Kicks. While walking, alternately kick each leg high into the air, ten times for each.
7. Leg Raises. While walking, alternately bring each knee straight up to the shoulder, twenty times for each leg.
8. Jumping Jack. From attention, jump to straddle position with arms directly over head and hands coming together in a clap, then return to starting position. Build to fifty Jumping Jacks per calisthenics drill.

Strengthening Calisthenics. These exercises are designed to toughen the player to withstand the physical contact and demands of competition. Other exercises may be used. Those given here form the core.

For these calisthenics, the player must lie or sit on the grass. He runs in place between each exercise. The player gets to his feet quickly from whatever ground position he has been in, runs in place, and then returns to the ground quickly for the next exercise.

1. Pushups. Standard pushup position. Weight in up position is on fingertips and toes. Body does not touch ground in down position. Build toward twenty pushups.
2. Situps. From flat on back, hands behind head. On up movement, legs are held rigid on ground and elbows are brought to knees, then return to down position. Twenty times.

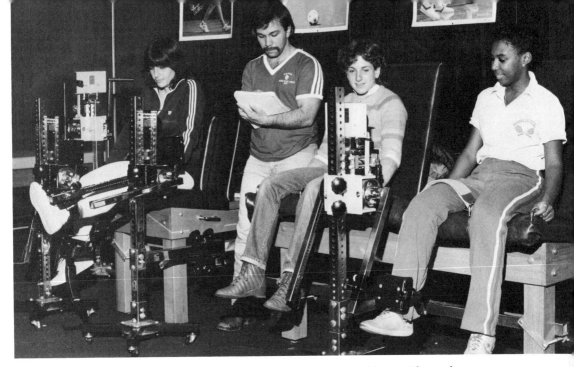

Strengthening thigh muscles on leg-lifting resistance machines. Photo by George Bing, Audio-Visual Center, Brooklyn College. Photo courtesy of Professor William D. Chisholm, Director, Brooklyn College Sports Rehabilitation Center.

3. Situp Variation. On up movement, twist body so that right elbow touches left knee, then return to starting position. On next up movement, left elbow touches right knee. Twenty times.
4. Neck Bridges. From flat on back, make a wrestler's bridge—body arched backward, with top of head and the feet supporting all weight —then roll back with weight of body on head. Ten times.
5. Rocking Horse. From flat on stomach, hands clasped behind back, legs raised from hip. Rock back and forth on chest and stomach. Ten times.

Scrimmage

The final conditioning program is the scrimmage. This is a practice game played between members of the team under all the conditions of a real game.

Scrimmage should become a large part of the conditioning process. It is the conditioning drill with the greatest motivation because of the natural fun of competition. Supervision must be rigid to prevent injuries and reinforce learning the rules. Players should dress properly, wearing shin guards and soccer shoes.

Practice sessions are carefully planned to ensure progressive development and individual skills and techniques, team tactics, and good physical conditioning. To accomplish these goals, athletes must work hard. They do not object if they see and feel intelligent direction and notice marked individual improvement and development in all areas of their game.

Therefore, the coach must recognize the individual strengths and weaknesses of each player and of his team. He must vary his approach to meet the needs of the group and to help keep up a high level of motivation.

The training program to achieve the difficult task of getting a team into playing condition and to work as a cohesive unit involves three phases:

1. The preseason phase, or the three to five weeks prior to the first game.
2. The in-season phase, or the training session conducted during the regular game-playing season.
3. The off-season phase, or the months between the end of the playing season and the beginning of the preseason phase.

Each practice phase has methods of reaching its own objectives.

Preseason Training. The emphasis during preseason training is on:

1. Physical fitness and conditioning.
2. Team tactics and play.
3. Refinement of individual skills and techniques.

Practice sessions are held daily, each session two to two and a half hours long. Following is a general outline of the activities in each session.

All sessions begin with a ten-to-fifteen-minute individual free-activity warmup. Soccer balls are available. The players report to the field and go through a light warmup, working on individual skills, jogging, passing with a teammate or two, and taking easy shots on goal.

This allows eager players the chance to limber up while waiting for slower teammates to dress and reach the field. This time is not counted as part of the whole training session. The actual practice session begins when all players have reached the field.

During the first ten to twenty minutes all players are involved in group loosening-up and stretching exercises, followed by body-strengthening calisthenics. Interest can be added if various players get the chance to conduct different sets of exercises. This also frees the coach to work with individual team members.

The next twenty minutes deal with speed and endurance.

One way to develop these qualities is to have the players form a double file on one of the touchlines with 5 yards between each pair. On the first whistle, the players begin a brisk trot around the field along the touchlines and goal lines. As the players are running, the coach gives commands. After each command is executed, the players return to the brisk trot and wait for the next command. Commands include sprinting, running sideways, both left and right, running backward, hopping on one foot and then the other, broad jumping or two-leg hopping, and walking whenever necessary. The commands are varied, and the coach keeps track of the number of all-out sprints to gauge conditioning progress.

Variation of this type of running and endurance drill should be included in the daily program along with the Fartlek drills. Relay races, with and without the ball, windsprints, 60- and 100-yard dash events, hurdles races, and obstacles races of all kinds provide speed and endurance training. The competitive aspect of the events masks the drudgery of hard work. This keeps practices lively, varied, and meaningful.

After this heavy endurance and training work, the players deserve a break. The best kind returns the players to a low level of activity but keeps them constructively busy.

The coach gives the players fifteen minutes to work on individual skills and techniques. He should maintain a checklist of basic skills that the individual players need. This is the period when the players have a chance to work on those deficiencies. They can do it individually, in pairs, or even in groups of more than two players. The coach uses this opportunity to correct individual problems, to teach new skills, or to polish those already learned.

The second phase of practice, which runs from forty-five minutes to an hour, is devoted to team tactics and play. The activities in this period are based on the needs of the team, offensively and defensvely.

The early practices of preseason training include games with five and six men to a side. These are played across the width of the field rather than on a full field. Two games can thus be played simultaneously, and all players get a chance to show what they can do under the pressure of competition. The demands of play on a small field are such that players must get rid of the ball quickly and accurately, defenders must cover closely, and off-the-ball movement becomes essential.

Under these conditions, the coach has ample opportunity to see the players under stress and to evaluate their reactions. He can then plan position play and overall tactics realistically.

Whether to use goalkeepers in these games depends on how far along in their training the players are and what the coach wants. For example, if the coach wants to impress collective responsibility on the defense to prevent goals, he dispenses with the goalkeeper, makes the goals smaller, and indicates the area in front of the goal from which a scoring shot may be taken. This rules out a long shot for goal, requires the attack to go in all the way to score, and forces the defense to make the stop at the designated area.

Regulation games with eleven to a side begin after the practice session has been in full swing for some time. At this point intensive tactical coaching concentrates on offensive and defensive play and special situations, such as corner kicks, free kicks, and throw-in tactics.

After the game situation, another break is necessary. This period is best used for polishing such skills as the throw-in, the goal kick, and work with the weak foot. All players should use the foot they favor less. Passing, trapping, and shooting with the weak foot are important to all-around development.

The practice sessions wind up with a series of 30- and 40-yard windsprints, the distance covered depending on weather, field condition, length of game period, and the level of the players' physical condition. This is followed by an easy jog around the field, which helps the players cool off and wind down slowly.

This is an outline of a typical two-to-three-hour preseason practice session. The coach may vary the activities in each session, depending on individual and team needs. As the coach becomes more familiar with his players, he adopts specific drills to meet those needs.

The amount of time given to team learning and physical development depends on the condition of the players and their attention span, the temperature, and field conditions. The coach must try to cram the greatest possible amount of learning and conditioning into each session.

From experience, coaches know when their players are physically and emotionally spent. That is the point at which practice should end.

In-Season Training. The in-season phase of training begins after drilling for and playing the first game. Integrating individual skills into the team system, developing team tactics, maintaining a high level of physical condition, and preparing for opponents become the important areas of activity during the season.

Scrimmage games accomplish all of these aims. They are self-motivating and give the coach the chance to call attention to specific moves. Scrimmages are also an opportunity to practice, under game conditions, the particular tactics needed against the next opponent.

If the playing schedule calls for one game a week—say, on Saturday—the team tries to reach game readiness by Thursday. The daily-practice pace builds as the week progresses. Sunday is a rest day. Monday's practice is generally given over to loosening up tired muscles, evaluating team play, and team-type drills.

A typical week's practice sessions follow:

Monday

20 to 30 minutes of team discussion concerning individual and team play in the preceding game. This is the time to go over mistakes and lapses in play and to present methods to correct and improve team play.

15 minutes of loosening-up exercises and calisthenics

20 minutes of individual skill and technique practice

30 minutes of team-skill practice; e.g., shooting drills for forwards and midfield players, passing drills, goalkeeping drills

5 to 10 minutes of running drills

Tuesday

15 minutes of loosening-up exercises and calisthenics

15 minutes of running drills

20 minutes of team-skill practice

45 minutes of team scrimmage with specific coaching for the next opponent

5 to 10 minutes of running drills

Wednesday

15 minutes of loosening-up exercises and calisthenics

20 minutes of team-skill practice

20 minutes of working on offensive and defensive special situations, e.g., corner kicks, free kicks

60 minutes of team scrimmage with coaching for opponent

Thursday

15 to 20 minutes of team-tactics discussion

15 minutes of loosening-up exercises and calisthenics

Regulation-time practice game under game conditions

Friday

15 to 20 minutes of review of game plan

15 minutes of loosening-up exercises and calisthenics

30 to 40 minutes of light team practice—shooting drills, passing, heading. Individual skills work, e.g., penalty shots, corner kicks, goal kicks, and throw-ins, for all.

This outline is a general guide to what can be accomplished during the week between games. The actual schedule for the week reflects the needs of a team and its members.

If the team schedule calls for an additional midweek game, much more work has to be crammed into the practice sessions. The demands on coach and team are heavy, and concentrated attention is required.

For example, if the game is on Wednesday, the following would be an outline of the activities planned for the practice days preceding and following the game:

Monday
20 to 30 minutes of team discussion of previous game
15 minutes of loosening-up exercises and calisthenics
40 minutes of light scrimmage working on game plan
10 minutes of running drills and team-skill practice
Tuesday
30 minutes of game-tactics discussion
40 to 60 minutes of light scrimmage practice with special attention on weak aspects of play

The practice sessions for Thursday and Friday are similar to those for Monday and Tuesday. The first priority goes to evaluating the previous game as it relates to the coming one. Of only slightly less importance is working on aspects of play that were shown to be weak under game conditions.

Off-Season Training. The ideal off-season training program allows players to practice skills and techniques individually or in groups. The coach plays an important role in stimulating and maintaining interest in the soccer program throughout the year by having facilities and equipment available. Players enjoy working out on their own, getting some personal off-season instruction from their coach, and feeling free to set their own limits.

Soccer players need little urging to get involved in six-on-a-side games, shooting contests, and variations of the game. The coach can help this tendency along by supplying balls, play areas, and encouragement.

Participation in other sports is also beneficial. Basketball, volleyball, gymnastics, handball, and track keep players in shape physically and mentally.

The danger period is the summer, when the players are out of school. Jobs and vacations away from school and the coach's watchful eye allow players to get out of shape.

This is why players need a training regimen for the summer. The program consists of calisthenics, running, ball-control work, and participation in athletic activities whenever possible.

The basic program is varied every three weeks, building toward hard work in the two weeks preceding the return to preseason training. Coaches also keep tabs on their men in the off season by having them send in replies to a questionnaire every three weeks. It inquires about the amount of running the player has been doing, his weight, and his time for running specific distances. The coach will be able to verify the results of the training program during the opening day's practice back at school.

Most players will return to school in good shape if they feel part of a team spirit and understand that each member of the team carries part of the responsibility for how well it performs.

8

GIRLS AND WOMEN IN SOCCER

Never before in the history of sports has there been an explosion to equal the repercussions felt by the surge of interest in and the participation of girls and women in individual and team sports, especially in North America. For far too long, girls and women had been denied the challenges, joys, sense of accomplishment, and physical well-being that can be attained through rigorous sports competition.

A variety of interacting forces had, prior to the 1960s, caused girls and women to turn away from athletics as a legitimate, wholesome method of self-expression. Sociologically, our culture imposed a stereotyped image of femininity on girls and women that excluded the athletically oriented, athletically skilled, and competitive girl or woman. Sadly, for years, most women accepted and believed that to be skilled in athletics and to openly express the desire to compete and want to win would create a threat to their self-concept as women.

To make matters worse for girls and women, medical experts were convinced and openly voiced their concern that physical harm would come to girls if they were to take part in strenuous physical activity. They were especially concerned with the physical harm that they believed would come to the structure and function of the reproductive system, particularly if athletics were performed during the menstrual cycle.

Folklore of this not so far distant past went even further by determining that women were supposed to be completely protected from any kind of emotional or physical trauma during menstruation. This theory, despite evidence to the contrary, lasted well into the 1950s, with even many women coaches and physical educators perpetuating and parroting it.

It is obvious that over the years most of the objections to girls and women participating in sports have been subjective in nature. These objections were often based on the charmingly sentimental but incorrect belief that girls and women are fragile, gentle in nature, dainty in appearance, and in constant need of protection from stress.

Fortunately, many of the reasons given in the past for keeping girls and women out of highly competitive athletics have been blown away. The physiological misinformation, used as a supportive rationale to prevent women from competing in athletics and directly attributable to the sociological and cultural, emotional, and physical factors establishing women's role in society, has been reexamined and mostly dismissed as fallacious.

Research into sports physiology is continually clearing the air of those fallacious arguments, which for far too long kept women out of sports. As more work is done on the questions of women in athletics, society in general will learn that vigorous physical activity is well within the capabilities of girls and women.

The purpose of this chapter is to assure those girls, women, parents, and coaches who are still not convinced that vigorous athletic competition, and soccer in particular, can provide girls and women with the same high levels of fitness, challenge, self-expression, and fun as for boys and men.

There is absolutely no reason—physical, emotional, or sociological—that should keep healthy girls and women from participating in a strenuous sport like soccer.

Soccer is a highly competitive team sport that demands skill, teamwork, and physical fitness from its participants. It does not require brute strength nor does it require large size. To play soccer well, the prerequisites one must bring to the game are speed, skill, endurance, and a willingness to play hard.

For these reasons, among others, soccer has undergone phenomenal growth in the United States and Canada. By simply requiring skill and fitness to compete, soccer provides nearly everyone the opportunity to play, regardless of size, age, or sex. The sheer bulk needed in football or height needed in basketball are not at all needed for soccer. And with violence not programmed into the game, soccer is relatively injury free, certainly adding to the game's appeal to players, parents, and coaches.

Soccer has spread to all parts of the United States and Canada, including states where football and basketball once reigned in splendid isolation. The main reason for this is that soccer provides a viable alternative to athletes either too small or unwilling to subject themselves to the brutality of football. As a matter of fact, well over 3 million youngsters are playing soccer in the United States. A fact that is astounding is that in 1980, the United States Soccer Federation reported that more than 1 million girls and women under the age of nineteen were playing soccer on teams all over the country. By now, the number of participants has increased further.

No longer are we surprised to see boys and girls playing on one team competing against boys and girls on an opposing team. But questions still remain in the minds of parents, players, and soccer fans as to whether or not soccer is a sport for girls and women. They express concern over whether girls' and women's bodies are strong enough to stand the pace of sustained soccer play. Are they tough enough to endure the inevitable knocks and falls that are a part of the game? Most of all, they want to know if boys and girls can safely compete against each other.

The answer to all three questions is a resounding "yes." The performances of women athletes in the full range of sports, from the demands of marathon running and competitive swimming through tennis and basketball to sports of all levels, attest to the fact that girls and women can play virtually any sport. Each Olympic Games sees women's records shattered as better prepared and conditioned women athletes come along. The performances of champions not only provide proof of women's skill, ability, and physical capabilities, but provide the model for girls and young women so necessary to maturation and cultural acceptance.

PREPARING GIRL AND WOMEN SOCCER PLAYERS

Girls and women are physically equipped to train for soccer using the same methods as boys and men, as outlined in Chapter 7 on training and conditioning. However, certain innate physical characteristics of females, such as less strength in the upper body, should receive greater emphasis, since increasing upper body strength would be an asset to any player. But all training programs should provide for individual differences and needs, so this specialized training poses no extraordinary demand on coaches or players. Cardiovascular endurance, muscular endurance, strength, and flexibility are the basic areas of concern in training soccer players. With this in mind, let us look at the similarities and differences between the sexes in soccer participation.

Boys and girls begin with similar physical capacities insofar as fitness for soccer or any other sport. Up until puberty, girls mature faster than boys, very often giving them the edge in size, strength, and sometimes even talent. It is not surprising in the prepubescent period to find many girls the outstanding players on sexually mixed soccer teams. In watching youth games, I was most impressed with one particular young lady who was one of the most physically intimidating defensive players I have ever seen. She was nondiscriminating as far as going after forwards attacking her area, and quite willing to take her opponent off the ball, regardless of his or her sex. But, with puberty, the physical situation changes abruptly.

In females, puberty finds the hormone estrogen building in the body, causing changes intended to prepare young females for their role as adult women. Girls grow faster at this time, reaching a growth spurt at around age thirteen that begins to taper off at about age sixteen. Along with this growth, secondary sex characteristics occur. The pelvic area broadens, the breasts grow, and the feminine pattern of fat distribution over the hips, thighs, and breasts takes place. During this time the menstrual cycle begins.

At male puberty, the hormone testosterone sets off the growth and developement of male secondary sex characteristics. Boys begin to mature sexually later than girls. They are generally anywhere from a year and a half to two years later than girls, but they keep on maturing and developing for a much longer period, sometimes as long as six to eight years more.

On the average, males will be about 10 percent bigger than females, and, in comparing age group standards of performance between top male and female athletes, the same 10 percent will stand up as the difference between the two sexes in terms of speed and performance.

Along with bigger size, men will develop longer bones, providing better leverage; wider shoulders, the basis from which to build a great advantage in upper body strength; and bigger hearts and lungs, which operate more powerfully and at a slower rate, to keep up with the demand of larger muscles.

While one of the secondary female characteristics is the growth of body fat, the male body is growing muscle. Testosterone adds bulk to the muscle fibers, making the muscles bigger and stronger, and this is a process that takes place regardless of whether or not the young man performs muscular exercise. This should lay to rest the idea that women will develope big muscles from athletic training. Testosterone must be present to form big muscles.

In summarizing the results of the maturation process, we see that in terms of sports, the anatomical differences between the sexes favor the male. Even though the maturation rate of females is accelerated, the longer, slower maturation period of the male results in a larger, heavier, and more rugged body structure that possesses mechanical and structural advantages, particularly in the upper body. The longer and heavier bones add to the body weight and, as longer levers, provide a much greater range to the moving ends—hands and feet—which are a decided advantage in throwing, kicking, and other explosive types of power movements. Conversely, the female athlete may be limited as far as achieving power equal to men, but she is certainly able to participate in these activities and, indeed, perform them well. Because of female body proportions, the female athlete enjoys the advantage over men in areas such as balance, stability, and flexibility.

Anthropometric differences indicate that mature female athletes should compete with athletes of their own sex in activities where strength and power are the principal factors, but that they can certainly hold their own against males in activities that demand high levels of endurance and dexterity.

Clearly, the changes that take place through maturation in women show nothing that precludes women from playing soccer. In fact, soccer is an ideal sport for girls and women since it demands and promotes physical fitness, afford benefits of team play, and is challenging to the need for competition in an active, wholesome way.

Let us look at some of the specific answers to the earlier questions concerning women's adaptability to and suitability for competitive sports. This will also provide further evidence as to why soccer, in particular, is as natural a sport for women as it is for men.

The fact that soccer demands overall endurance, both muscular and cardiovascular, makes women eminently suited to it. Some of the latest physiological research in the area of endurance was done in an effort to determine what made women so good at running long distances. The answers emerging from these studies show that women's endurance capacities may be equal to or perhaps even superior to men's in some ways because their metabolic system may be more efficient at turning stored fats into quickly usable energy.

This ability to draw on energy reserves for sustained running and longterm endurance seems less available to men. After about two hours of the intensive muscular endurance called for in marathon running, the last bits of glycogen stored in the muscles are burned up, leaving the anaerobic energy formation system low on fuel. At this point, many men are hit by sudden body pain and debilitating weakness. This happens rarely to women. Certainly they get tired, but they rarely go through what men do at this point of exertion. One popularly accepted theory is that when the glycogen is gone, the body then turns to fat for energy formation. Even well-trained and -conditioned women have more fat naturally on their bodies, and this reserve, plus the ability to call on them more easily, gives women greater endurance potential than men.

While soccer does not impose the demand of two hours plus staying time, we can draw some conclusions that are relevant to soccer based on the high work rate effect on women. The great number of women successfully training hard for long-distance running and the lack of any nontramatic physical damage as a result of training show that women certainly are capable of developing the endurance needed for soccer. And even more important, in terms of training for soccer, endurance training and endurance demands are no more damaging or overtaxing to women than they are to men. Women are capable of great endurance when properly trained.

Predisposal to injury is another major area of concern often used against girls and women playing soccer. In the early 1970s, when girls and women began to participate in sports in great numbers, many studies were done concerning the question of predisposal to injury. At that time, limited studies and surveys showed the greatest percentage of injuries to female athletes occurred in sports requiring sudden, precipitious efforts—sudden acceleration, rapid changes of direction, or quick stops. Obviously, these movements are all a part of soccer requirements.

The kinds of injuries that occurred commonly resulted from overstrain directly related to sudden movements. The feet, ankles, and knees took the greatest amount of physical abuse and strain, resulting in injury. The reason most often advanced as to why these injuries were so common to women was that the lighter bone density of the female, combined with weaker ligamentous support, makes women more susceptible and vulnerable to knee and ankle injury in particular.

In most recent studies on predisposal to injury, the injury rate seems to be holding at earlier levels despite the great increase in participants. This improvement is due to the fact that young girls are being encouraged to participate in sports that were not open to their older sisters. This head start in the years of early development provides far stronger bones and muscles and a better base from which to build fitness for later years. This is certainly as advantage in terms of preparing the body for sports stress.

A second and extremely vital factor contributing to lessening predisposal to injury is the increase in well-trained physical education teachers and coaches who intelligently work hard at developing well-trained, well-conditioned, and prepared women athletes. Training begins earlier in the child's school life with the emphasis on movement training, skill development, and conditioning, which all contribute to preparing girls for a lifetime of sports experiences. From these early experiences evolves the improvement in technique and physical endurance that provide the groundwork from which motivated youngsters can go on to more competitive levels.

When given this sort of proper groundwork in basic movement skills and fitness training, the female athlete is prepared to undergo specific training for soccer equal to the training given males. By following a well-regulated training program, the female soccer player is able to compete on a high level, with injury predispostion at no higher a rate than may be expected in males on an equal age level.

For many years one of the major arguments against female participation in strenuous physical activities has been that the demands and strain of athletic competition could permanently damage the reproductive system. Research shows that this is simply not true.

The female body is constructed so that the reproductive organs are well protected. The ovaries and uterus, for example, are located internally and float in the pelvic viscera, far better protected that the male external genitalia. The chances of painful injury to the male reproductive system are far greater.

The effect of menstruation on athletes is another area in which myths are being challenged. Most recent literature on the subject points to one basic fact—that the reaction of female athletes during menstruation is highly individualistic. A small percentage of athletes perform at a lower level when menstuating. For most women, there is litte effect other than the fact that it my be a nuisance.

The old theory that at "those certain times of the month" women do not operate at top form is not true for all women and is certainly not true for women athletes. It is a fact that women at all stages of their menstrual cycle have set world and Olympic records in every sport in which they have participated. The results of research on the menstrual cycle and its effects on athletes to date lead the coach and athlete to approach the matter on an individual basis. The individual woman's response to her menstrual cycle must govern practice and training participation. But the one thing that is certain is that the latest data refute the charge that intensive physical activity is harmful to the female reproductive system.

The final area of physical concern with regard to female athletes is the breasts. For years it was suspected that trauma, occurring through collision or by being struck by a ball, could lead to bruising that would predispose the athlete to breast cancer. Trauma to the breasts can lead to soreness and bruises, but there is no substantiatcd evidence linking breast cancer to such trauma.

Soccer has a specific rule, however, to prvent injury to the breasts. In the *National Association for Girls and Women in Sports Soccer Guide*, Rule 13, Section 55, states, "Legal chest protection shall be with the arms upon the chest with the palms flat against the body. The forearms must be in contact with the body."

This rule is put into the game to prevent injury to the breasts while performing the chest trap. It does nothing to interfere with play and does prevent injury to the breasts. It is the only rule variation and concession to specific female needs found between men's and women's rules.

Most women find that wearing a bra designed for athletics is sufficient to give them the protection, support, and confort needed while playing. There is no need to wear padded bras since the use of the arms, as stated in the rules, serves the purpose.

In terms of soccer equipment, women do not have any special needs. Soccer shoes are made in widths to accommodate all size feet, shin pads are made in standard sizes, and shorts and jerseys are made in enough variety to suit any taste or climate.

SOME SPECIFIC TRAINING FOR WOMEN

Crucial to the organization of training and practice sessions is the basic understanding of the athlete, in terms of the physical equipment he or she brings to the sport. Since we provide for individual differences among players on the same level, we ought to provide some specific training in areas needed to play soccer well where the differences are anatomical.

Because soccer is thought of primarily as a game of kicking and running, we tend to forget that the use of the upper body, from the waist up, is also very much a part of the game. Many coaches quite properly spend great amounts of time in strengthening and conditioning the legs and in developing overall endurance. Very often, upper body training is not given the attention it should, especially in working with women playing soccer.

Heading, throw-ins, goalkeeping, and even the incidental but inevitable body contact of soccer all require upper body strength. This is true in men's as well as women's soccer. But because the female athlete is weaker in the upper body than her male counterpart, because of anatomical structure, it is important to stress conditioning of this vital area.

Conditioning of the upper body begins with exercises specifically designed to strengthen the abdominal muscles, the muscles of the shoulder girdle, and the muscles of the arms and neck. All of these muscle groups perform the strenuous upper body action needed in soccer while the lower body, specifically the legs, provides the movement to the action and the base from which the work is done.

Heading requires well-conditioned neck, abdominal, shoulder, and back muscles to be able to provide impetus to the ball effectively and safely. Remember, the head strikes the ball—the ball never strikes the head. To head the ball properly requires body whip generated by the abdominal and back muscles finished off by the application of the head to the ball by strong muscles of the shoulders and neck.

The rules governing the throw-in require that the thrower must have a part of each foot touching the ground at the instant of release and that the throw must be taken from behind and over the head with equal use of both hands. In order to get pace and distance on the throw-in, the thrower must lean backward and then vigorously whip forward carrying the ball over her head to the release point. The whip or forward snap required is provided principally by the abdominal muscles.

Goalkeepers play much of their game with the upper body. Hands and arms must be strengthened in order to stop and control hard shots on goal. Clearances of the ball by throwing demand a strong arm and strong body follow-through if the ball is to get far from the penalty area. And strength in the upper body is crucial in terms of protecting goalkeepers when they dive for a tough shot to get bumped and jolted while in the air fielding a high cross.

And, finally, soccer is a contact sport. While contact is not necessary or even part of playing tactics, it inevitably occurs during the course of play.

It is for these reasons that coaches of women should pay particular attention to those exercises aimed specifically at strengthening the body from the waist up. In the chapter on training and conditioning for soccer, calisthenics are provided for strengthening the upper body.

These exercises should be performed by players at every training session while preparing for the season as outlined in the training schedules presented. They should also be performed as part of an off-season maintenance program, which will assure high levels of upper body fitness through the year.

The important thing to remember is that it is possible to compensate through training for areas that are weaker due to anatomical structure. The results of planned conditioning and strengthening of the upper body will soon be apparent in the execution of upper body skills and techniques.

9

NCAA SOCCER RULES

An approved Ruling (A.R.) is an official decision of the NCAA Soccer Committee regarding a specific rule or part of a rule. It serves to illustrate the spirit and application of the rules. Approved Rulings follow the rules they amplify.

Rule 1

THE FIELD AND EQUIPMENT

The Field of Play

Dimensions

Section 1. The field of play shall be rectangular, its length being not more than 120 yards [110.0m] nor less than 110 yards [100.0m] and its width not more than 75 yards [68.6m] nor less than 65 yards [64.0m]. The recommended size of the field is 120 yards [110.0m] by 75 yards [68.6m].

It is highly recommended that in constructing new fields that the size of the field be 120 yards [110.0m] by 75 yards [68.6m].

   A.R. 1. Prior to start of game, the field is found not to be in conformity with the rules. Team B insists that the field be brought up to required standards. Team A refuses to make any change. RULING: The game will not start and the referees will make a report to the proper authority.

   A.R. 2. If the field is of minimum dimension, 110 yards by 65 yards, can the inside dimensions be correspondingly smaller? RULING: No, the inside dimensions must always remain constant. Efforts must be made to change markings that are wrong.

   A.R. 3. Are the lines part of the areas they define? RULING: Yes.

Boundary Lines

Section 2. The field shall be marked with distinctive lines, in accordance with the plan, the longer boundary lines being called the touchlines and the shorter the goal lines. The home team is always responsible for the proper marking of the field.

The lines should meet at the corners; that is, the goal lines should extend completely across the field of play, including the goal, and the touchlines should extend the entire length of the field. They should be clearly marked but may not be made permanent by grooves in the ground because of danger to the players.

In the case of a field which is playable but on which during the course of the game the lines and markings have become invisible by reason of snow or other like reason, the lines and markings shall be assumed to be present and decisions rendered accordingly.

A.R. 4. The game is started with good weather but conditions rapidly deteriorate. Both teams insist on continuing the game. RULING: The referee has authority to terminate a game by reason of the elements.

Halfway Line, Center Circle

Section 3. A halfway line shall be marked out across the field of play. The center of the field shall be indicated by a suitable mark and a circle with a 10-yard [9.15m] radius shall be marked around it.

Goal Area

Section 4. At each end of the field of play two lines shall be drawn at right angles to the goal line, 6 yards [5.5m] from each goalpost. These shall extend into the field of play for a distance of 6 yards [5.5m] and shall be joined by a line drawn parallel with the goal line. Each of the spaces enclosed by these lines and the goal line shall be called a goal area.

Penalty Area

Section 5. At each end of the field of play two lines shall be drawn at right angles to the goal line, 18 yards [16.5m] from each goalpost. These shall extend into the field of play for a distance of 18 yards [16.5m] and shall be joined by a line drawn parallel with the goal line. Each of the spaces enclosed by these lines and the goal line shall be called a penalty area.

At each end of the field, a 2-foot [0.61m] line shall be placed at a point 12 yards [11.0m] from the midpoint of, and parallel to, the goal line. This line shall extend 1 foot [0.30m] on either side of the undrawn center line. The penalty kick may be taken from any position on this line.

Using the center of this penalty kick line, describe a 10-yard [9.15m] arc outside the penalty area and closing on the penalty area line. This is the restraining line for penalty kicks.

Photo courtesy of the New York Cosmos.

A.R. 5. The goalkeeper handles the ball on the 18-yard line. RULING: Legal play. The lines of the penalty area are within the penalty area.

Corner Area
Section 6. From each corner a quarter circle, having a radius of 1 yard [1.0m], shall be drawn inside the field of play.

Corner Flags
Section 7. A flag on a post not less than 5 feet [1.5m] high and having a nonpointed top shall be placed at each corner; a similar flagpost may be placed opposite the halfway line on each side of the field of play, not less than 1 yard [1.0m] outside the touchline.

The corner flag should be not less than 5 feet [1.5m] high from the surface of the ground. The staff or post should have a rounded top and should be about 1½ inches [3.81cm] thick, either round or square. The corner flag may not be removed for any purpose during the game. The flag should be of some bright color, easily distinguishable from the surroundings, and should be about 2 feet [0.61m] long by 1 foot [0.30m] wide and securely fastened to the post or staff.

For artificial turf surfaces, a flexible wire coil flag or soft cellulose pylon may be used.

> **A.R. 6.** On inspecting the field, the referee discovers the absence of corner flags on the corner-flag posts. RULING: Team A coach should find some flags. If unsuccessful, the game will begin; but the coach should be reminded that in the future, flags must be provided.

Goals

Section 8. The goals shall be placed in the center of each goal line and shall consist of two wooden or metal posts, equidistant from the corner flags and 8 yards [7.32m] apart (inside measurement), joined by a horizontal crossbar of similar material, the lower edge of which shall be 8 feet [2.44m] from the ground. The width and depth of the goalposts and the width and depth of the crossbar shall not be less than 4 inches [10.16cm] nor more than 5 inches [12.7cm] and shall be painted white.

> **A.R. 7.** The crossbar becomes displaced during the game. RULING: Play should stop and every effort made to repair the crossbar. If, in the referee's opinion, it cannot be repaired within a reasonable time, or in a manner so as not to present a danger, the match shall be terminated. A rope is not a satisfactory substitute for a crossbar. When the crossbar is replaced, the match shall restart by dropping the ball where it was when play was stopped; or if the ball was inside the penalty area, it shall be dropped at the nearest point outside the penalty area.

Goal Nets

Section 9. Nets shall be attached to the uprights, crossbar, and ground behind each goal.

The goal nets should be properly and firmly pegged down to the ground and put in order before every match, and care taken that there are no holes or possible openings for the escape of the ball. The nets should be properly supported so that the top of the net will extend backward on a level with the crossbar for a distance of about 2 feet [0.61m] from the crossbar to allow the goalkeeper ample room.

Team Benches, Timer's Tables, Spectator Area

Section 10. Team benches and timer's tables should be placed on the same side of the field and at least 10 feet [3.05m] (whenever possible) from the

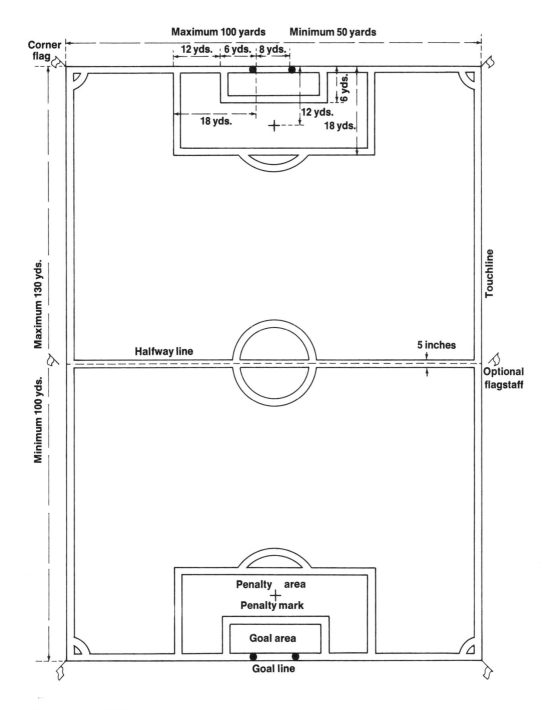

The playing field.

sidelines. It is recommended that a rope, fence, or some form of demarcation be utilized to keep spectators a minimum of 10 feet [3.05m] away from the field of play.

The Ball

Shape and Material
Section 11. The ball shall be spherical; the outer casing shall be of leather or approved synthetic and no material shall be used in its construction which might prove dangerous to the players. All balls used in a game shall be identical in size, make, grade, and color, and shall be furnished by the home team.

The home team has the responsibility for proper facilities and equipment as prescribed in the official NCAA Soccer Rules.

A.R. 8. Can the game start with a ball made of rubber? RULING: No. (See Rule 1-11).

Dimensions
Section 12. The circumference of the ball shall not be more than 28 inches [71.12cm] nor less than 27 inches [68.58cm]. The weight of the ball at the start of the game shall not be more than 16 ounces [454.4g] nor less than 14 ounces [397.6g], and the weight should not exceed 16.75 ounces [475g] even when wet and used. The ball shall be inflated to a pressure which will require the ball when dropped from a height of 100 inches [254cm] to a smooth cement floor to rebound between 60 and 65 inches [152.4 and 165.1cm]. (It is recommended that the manufacturer indicate on the ball the recommended air pressure to meet the above standards.)

Defective Ball
Section 13. If, during playing time, the ball becomes defective, it becomes dead where last played, and the game is restarted by a drop ball at that spot (see 4-9b).

If the ball becomes defective during a stoppage of the game, i.e., kickoff, goal kick, corner kick, penalty kick, free kick, or throw-in, the game shall be restarted accordingly.

A.R. 9. Is it a goal if, on a free kick from 25 yards, the ball strikes the crossbar, bursts, and falls over the goal line? RULING: No, if the ball bursts, it does not conform to Rule 1-11. The new ball should be dropped where last played.

A.R. 10. The ball bursts on a goal kick. RULING: If it bursts before it leaves the penalty area, the goal kick shall be retaken. However, if the ball became defective outside the penalty area, the ball shall be dropped at the point outside the penalty area where it entered play.

Player's Equipment

Uniform
Section 14. A player's uniform shall usually consist of a jersey or shirt, short trousers, stockings, shin pads, and shoes (see 1-17).

A.R. 11. May a player participate if he does not use footwear? RULING: No.

Contrasting Colors
Section 15. Players on the home team must wear white or some other light-colored jerseys and light-colored stockings, and the visiting team must wear dark-colored jerseys and dark-colored stockings.

Goalkeepers shall wear colors which distinguish them from all other players and referees.

Numbers Mandatory
Section 16. Numerals, at least 6 inches [15.24cm] in height, must be worn on the back of each player's jersey.

Numerals at least 4 inches [10.16cm] in height must be worn on the front of each player's jersey, effective with the first game of the 1982 season.

Shoes
Section 17. Shoes must conform to the following standards: all cleats, studs, or bars shall be not less than ½ inch [1.27cm] in diameter or width, and they shall not project from the sole or heel of the shoe more than ¾ inch [1.9cm]. Aluminum, leather, rubber, nylon, or plastic cleats with steel tips are legal if they conform to the width and length specifications.

EXCEPTION—A molded sole with multiple cleats less than ½ inch [1.27cm] in diameter which do not extend more than 5/16 inch [0.79cm] from the sole and are not of an extreme conical design is permissible.

Illegal Equipment
Section 18. A player may not wear anything which is dangerous to another player.

If the referee considers any article other than shoes liable to cause injury to another player, he must require the removal of that article; if the player fails to remove it, the referee must order the player off the field.

The use of any hard or dangerous head, face, or body protective equipment is illegal. Kneebraces with any metal parts are permissible provided no metal is exposed. Casts are permissible if they are covered with foam rubber and in the judgment of the officials are not dangerous.

It is mandatory that the referee in each game examine the equipment of each player to see that it complies with the foregoing standards. It is recommended that the shoes be inspected indoors whenever possible.

A player wearing any equipment not in compliance shall be sent off the field temporarily. He shall not return without first reporting to the referee, who shall satisfy himself that the player's equipment is in order. Then the player may reenter the game, only at a moment when the ball is not in play.

A.R. 12. May a player participate wearing protective covering such as knee-braces with a cover or cast? RULING: Yes, if not ruled dangerous by the referee.

A.R. 13. A player is wearing articles considered dangerous. The coach insists that the player in previous games had been allowed to wear these articles and refuses to make his player take off the articles. RULING: Player should be suspended until he conforms with Rule 1-18.

A.R. 14. Team B has two players wearing headbands. Team A demands that the headbands be removed. RULING: Headbands are legal unless they constitute a danger to other players.

A.R. 15. If a player was suspended for not conforming with Rule 1-18, may he return at any time after rectifying his equipment? RULING: If the player was not substituted for, he can enter the game when the ball is dead, after having equipment inspected by the referee.

A.R. 16. A player enters or reenters the field of play to join or rejoin his team without first reporting to the referee. RULING: The player shall be warned. If stoppage of play is necessary, the game shall be restarted by an indirect free kick, by a player of the opposing team, from the place where the ball was when the game was stopped.

A.R. 17. A player is wearing a cast. RULING: Casts should be inspected prior to the match. (See Rule 1-18.) All officials must agree that the cast is not dangerous, or the player shall not be allowed to participate. Both coaches should be informed of the officials' decision. If, during the match, the player is judged to be using a properly covered cast as an implement to gain an unfair advantage, or in a manner which might endanger or harm another participant, he shall not be allowed to take any further part in the match.

Rule 2

PLAYERS AND SUBSTITUTES

The Players

Number of Players

Section 1. The game shall be started by two teams of not more than eleven players each, one of which shall be the goalkeeper.

Only eighteen players may participate in any game or overtime. These may be substituted or resubstituted without limitations (see following sections, this Rule).

Teams may, by special arrangement, use more substitutes than are provided for in the rules, if they so desire.

NOTE—*It is suggested that when schools make their contracts with opponent schools, an agreement be reached concerning substitutes.*

A.R. 1. Is there a minimum number of players allowed to start and finish a game? RULING: No.

A.R. 2. Team A starts with ten players. May the eleventh player join his team during a stoppage of play? RULING: Yes, provided the player reports to the official scorer and is recognized by the referee.

A.R. 3. A player is ejected prior to the start of a match. Must his team play with only ten players? RULING: No, the team may begin the match with another player in place of the ejected player.

Substitutions

When Allowed

Section 2. Either team may substitute under the following conditions:

a. On a goal kick.
b. On a corner kick.
c. After a goal has been scored.
d. Between periods.
e. In the event of an injury.
f. When a player has been warned.

Penalty—Indirect free kick against the offending side from the location of the ball at the time the infraction is discovered.

In the event of an injury, only the injured player(s) may be replaced. The opponent may replace an equal number of players at the same time.

In case of player(s) being warned, the coach may substitute for the player(s) warned should he so desire. If such a substitution is made, the opponent shall have the opportunity to make a like number of substitutions at that time should he so desire.

A.R. 4. Team A player is injured and the coach sends in a substitute. At this point, Team B sends in two substitutes with the referees noticing it. RULING: After stoppage of play, the last Team B player to enter the game shall be sent off the field. Award an indirect free kick to Team A from the location of the ball at time the infraction was discovered.

A.R. 5. A player has been warned for misconduct. Before the kick is taken, may a player enter the game as a substitute for the warned player? RULING: Yes, and the opposing team may make a like number of substitutions.

Reporting into the Game

Section 3. A substitute must first report to the official scorer, remain at the scorer's table, and be recognized by the referee when he comes on the field. No player who has left the field of play with or without the permission of the referee after a game has started may return to the field or participate in play without first reporting to the referee.

Any player who leaves the field during the progress of the game, except through normal movement of play, without permission of the referee shall be guilty of ungentlemanly conduct.

Penalty—Indirect free kick from the location of the ball at the time of the infraction.

To facilitate the making of substitutions, it is required that a noise-producing instrument of quite different tone from the timekeeper's signaling device be used. A horn is suggested.

A.R. 6. If a player passes accidentally over one of the boundary lines, is he considered to have left the field of play? RULING: No.

A.R. 7. A player in possession of the ball passes over the touchline or goal line without the ball to beat an opponent. RULING: The player should not be penalized because going outside the field of play may be considered part of playing movement.

Changing Goalkeepers

Section 4. The referee must be given notice when any substitution for the goalkeeper is made, either by another player on the field changing places with the goalkeeper or by substitution from the team bench.

Penalty—Indirect free kick (see Section 3 above).

A.R. 8. On a penalty kick, the coach decides to substitute goalkeepers. RULING: Illegal substitution.

A.R. 9. May a teammate already on the field change positions with the goalkeeper for the taking of a penalty kick? RULING: Yes, provided the referee is notified.

A.R. 10. Team A changes its goalkeeper without notifying the referee, who only becomes aware of the situation when he sees the new goalkeeper handle the ball. RULING: An indirect free kick shall be awarded to Team B at the moment the goalkeeper handles the ball.

Rule 3

OFFICIALS AND THEIR DUTIES

Referees

Number of Referees
Section 1. Either the two- or three-man referee system is permitted. If the two-man system is employed, both officials shall have equal authority and responsibility in the calling of fouls and violations on any part of the field at any time.

Uniform
Section 2. It is mandatory that all officials dress in uniforms of the same type. The uniform should be either black and white striped shirt, with black shorts and black stockings with white tops; or black shirt with white collar and cuffs, black shorts, and black stockings with white tops.

Officials should wear shirts, the colors and styles of which are in contrast to the colors or styles worn by the competing teams.

Jurisdiction
Section 3. The jurisdiction of the referee shall begin when he enters the field of play for the pregame duties. Pregame duties should include inspecting the field markings, goals, nets, team benches, timer's table, corner flags, game balls, players' uniforms, and equipment. Any violation involving the above should be reported immediately to the home team administration and, if possible, necessary changes or repairs should be made before the contest.

The referee shall enforce the rules and decide any disputed point. His decision on points of fact connected with the play shall be final so far as the result of the game is concerned.

The referee's power of penalizing shall extend to offenses committed when play has been suspended temporarily or when the ball is out of play.

He shall, however, refrain from penalizing in cases where he is satisfied that by doing so he would be giving an advantage to the offending team. When the referee observes a foul which he is not to penalize, he shall call out the words "play on" and raise his hand (fist closed) over his head to indicate that he has seen the foul.

The referee must signal on all fouls. **This is mandatory.** He must also notify the timekeeper for all time outs, and confirm for the scorekeeper the players to be credited with goals and assists.

The referee shall allow no person other than the players and ball persons to enter the field of play without his permission. Trainers and coaches may enter the field only if called by the referee.

A.R. 1. Can a player be warned and/or ejected before a match begins, at halftime, or after it ends? RULING: Yes.

A.R. 2. A player is tripped at center field, but stays on his feet and the referee signals play to continue. The player goes a couple of more steps and falls down. He appeals for a foul. RULING: No foul, because the advantage clause has been invoked. The decision of the referee may not be changed in this case.

Discretionary Power
Section 4. The referee has discretionary power to:

a. Stop the game for any infringement of the rules and to suspend or terminate the game whenever, by reason of the elements, interference by spectators, or other cause, he deems such stoppage necessary.

b. Warn any player, coach, or team representative of misconduct or ungentlemanly behavior (persistent infringement of any of the rules of the game) and, if he persists, to suspend him from further participation in the game. When warning a player, coach, or team representative, the official shall display a yellow card and indicate the player concerned. The second card displayed shall be a red card. When suspending a player, coach, or team representative, a red card shall be displayed. A player receiving a red card shall be disqualified from the game and cannot be replaced. An ejected player, coach, or team representative shall leave the premises of the field of play to the point that the individual, in the opinion of the referee(s), shall not be a disruptive influence on the further progress of the game.

c. Forfeit the game to the opposing team if, in his judgment, a coach prolongs a discussion with an official or refuses to leave the field at the request that he do so.

d. Stop the game if, in his opinion, a player has been seriously injured. If, in the referee's opinion, the player is slightly injured, the game shall not be stopped until the ball has ceased to be in play. A player who is able to go to the touchline or goal line for attention of any kind shall not be treated on the field of play.

A.R. 3. What is the procedure for warning a player? RULING: The referee shall inquire of the player's name and jersey number and plainly state to the player that he is being warned and for what reason, and that any further acts of misconduct will result in suspension from the game. The yellow card should be displayed clearly, and the player should stand with his back to the scorekeeper. The coach may substitute immediately for a player so warned.

A.R. 4. Team A coach runs on the field protesting a decision and refuses to leave upon request of the referee. RULING: Team A forfeits game.

A.R. 5. A player from Team B deliberately kicks a player from Team A. RULING: The referee has absolute discretion on rough play.

A.R. 6. Team B coach complains that spectators behind the goal are bothering his goalkeeper. RULING: Remove all spectators behind and adjacent to the goals. Spectators must stay behind any ropes strung around the field.

A.R. 7. A player from Team B walks off the field, without permission, while the game is in progress, then walks back on the field. RULING: Any player who leaves the field without permission is guilty of ungentlemanly conduct.

A.R. 8. A player strikes the referee. RULING: If a player physically attacks the referee (strikes, pushes, kicks) in any manner, the player will be ejected from the game immediately and no substitution allowed.

A.R. 9. May a referee reverse his decision? RULING: Yes, if the game has not been restarted.

A.R. 10. A player commits two infringements of a different nature at the same time. RULING: The more serious offense should be administered.

A.R. 11. If a match is terminated by the referee because of the elements, interference by spectators, grave disorders, or other causes, can a forfeit be declared? RULING: No, the referee has no authority to decide that either team is disqualified, unless specifically stated in a rule.

A.R. 12. During a match, one of the referees becomes unable to continue. RULING: The other referee will continue and complete the match.

A.R. 13. What is meant by the premises of the field of play? RULING: When a player or coach is ejected from the game for misconduct, he shall be required to go to the team's dressing area and remain there until the game has ended. If there is no team dressing area, the ejected player or coach shall be required to go to the team's bus, car, or the area where parked, provided the area is far enough away to satisfy the referee. In the event neither of these is possible, the player or coach shall retire to a distance far enough away from the field of play to not be a disruptive influence on the progress of the game. That distance usually means out of sight and sound of the field of play.

Ball Persons

Number, Duties

Section 5. At least two ball persons shall be provided by the home team, whose duties shall be to carry an extra game ball and to act as ball retrievers, to avoid delay of the game. All ball persons shall be instructed by and are under the direct supervision of the game referees.

The referees shall decide all touchline outs.

A.R. 14. As the ball goes out of bounds, the ball person indicates the direction of the throw-in. RULING: Illegal. Ball persons should be informed that their duties are limited to supplying the teams with the ball when it goes out of bounds.

Timekeeper

Number, Duties

Section 6. There shall be one official timekeeper designated by the home team. It is recommended that faculty members or managers perform this function.

Before the game the referee should instruct the timer as to his or her duties. He should arrange with the timekeeper an understandable series of signals, covering time outs, substitutions, termination of playing periods, and out of bounds.

The timer shall use one stop clock or stop watch that shall be visible at all times. An extra clock and signaling device should be available for immediate use if necessary.

The timer shall:

a. Keep track of playing time;
b. Stop the clock:
    (1) When signaled by the referee to do so,
    (2) When a goal is scored,
    (3) When a penalty kick is awarded,
    (4) When a player is carded;
c. Start the clock when the ball is put into play;
d. Signal the referee when a substitution is to be made in accordance with Rule 2-2, signaling only when the ball is not in play, using a noise-producing instrument or quite different tone from the signaling device, a horn being suggested;
e. Keep track of the halftime interval and notify the referees and teams two minutes in advance of the start of the second half;
f. Call off audibly to the nearest official the last ten seconds of playing time in any period, and signal for the termination of the period;
g. Signal with gun or horn (not whistle) when time has expired.

NOTE—*The expiration of time is the moment when the timekeeper's signal starts, regardless of the position of the ball.*

A.R. 15. Is the timekeeper subject to jurisdiction of the referee? RULING: Yes.

A.R. 16. May the referee dispense with using the timekeeper and keep time on the field, in the event of a discrepancy? RULING: Yes.

Rule 4

TIME FACTORS, PLAY, AND SCORING

Time Factors

Length of Game

Section 1. The duration of the game shall be two equal periods of forty-five minutes, unless otherwise mutually agreed upon. In the case of a tie, two extra periods of ten minutes each are to be played. The score of the game shall then stand as official, with the following exception: time shall be extended beyond the expiration of any period only to permit a penalty kick to be taken.

> **AR. 1.** The ball is in flight as the signal sounds denoting the end of the game, and the ball continues into the goal. RULING: No goal. As soon as the signal sounds, the game is over.
>
> **A.R. 2.** The ball is in flight and the signal denoting the end of the game malfunctions. The ball goes into the goal. RULING: Disallow the goal. The countdown by the timekeeper (Rule 3-6) will suffice for the game's end.
>
> **A.R. 3.** A penalty kick is awarded, but before the clock is stopped the signal sounds denoting the end of the game. RULING: The game shall be extended, and the extension shall last until the moment the penalty kick is completed.
>
> **A.R. 4.** What is the forfeiture time for lateness of a team? RULING: Discretion of home team.
>
> **A.R. 5.** Can time be extended for a corner kick? RULING: No.

Halftime Interval

Section 2. The halftime interval shall not exceed ten minutes except by consent of the referee and both coaches.

> **A.R. 6.** Because of inclement weather, both teams wish to turn around immediately at halftime. RULING: Legal.

Start of Play

Coin Toss

Section 3. At the beginning of a game, choice of ends and the kickoff shall be decided by the toss of a coin. The team winning the toss shall have the choice of ends or the kickoff.

> **A.R. 7.** What statement should the referee make to both captains during the toss of the coin? RULING: Goalkeepers must not be interfered with while in possession of the ball, and players guilty of intentionally fouling the goalkeeper will be ejected without warning.
>
> **A.R. 8.** The team that wins coin toss chooses end of field. Does the other team have a choice? RULING: No, it must kick off.

Kickoff

Section 4. At the referee's signal (whistle), the game shall be started by a player taking a place kick (i.e., a kick at the ball while it is stationary on the ground in the center of the field of play) into his opponents' half of the field of play. Every player shall be in his half of the field and every player of the team opposing that of the kicker shall remain at least 10 yards [9.15m] from the ball until it is kicked off. A goal may not be scored direct from the kickoff.

The kicker may not play the ball again after he has kicked off until it has been touched or played by another player.

Penalty—Indirect free kick.

The game is started only when the ball is properly kicked off; that is, kicked forward at least the distance of its own circumference (27 inches, or 0.68m). If the ball is not properly kicked forward, the ball will again be placed on the kickoff mark and properly kicked forward.

After the ball has been properly kicked off, it may be kicked in any direction.

Any player who repeatedly kicks off improperly, willfully encroaches on the 10-yard [9.15m] distance, or willfully moves beyond his own halfway line will be warned and, on repetition, ordered off the field.

A.R. 9. On the kickoff, a player from Team A kicks the ball forward, but realizing that a man from his team will not get it, he kicks the ball a second time. RULING: Illegal play. Team B receives indirect free kick.

A.R. 10. On the kickoff, the person kicking off kicks the ball directly into his opponents' goal. RULING: No goal, because a goal cannot be scored from a place kick. Award goal kick.

A.R. 11. On the kickoff, the ball is passed back to a defensive player, who moves forward with the ball. RULING: Illegal play. A place kick must be kicked forward.

A.R. 12. When does the game actually start? RULING: When the ball is kicked forward its circumference.

After a Goal

Section 5. After a goal is scored, the ball shall be taken to the center of the field and kicked off under precisely the same conditions as when the game is started (Sec. 4), by the side against which the goal was scored.

Change of Ends

Section 6. Teams shall change ends of the field at the start of the second half, and play shall then start with a kickoff by a member of the team opposite to that of the team taking the kickoff at the start of the game. If overtime is necessary, a toss of the coin will determine choice of ends of the field or the kickoff and teams shall change ends to start each overtime period.

Ball In and Out of Play

Out of Play

Section 7. The ball is out of play in the following circumstances:

a. When it has completely crossed a boundary line, whether on the ground or in the air. Even if the ball has landed within the field after being beyond the line in midair, it is still out of bounds;

b. When the game has been stopped by the referee.

The referee shall blow his whistle when the ball is out of play.

A.R. 13. The ball rolls along the line, then outside the line, and finally back into play. RULING: If the whole of the ball passed over the line, the ball is out of play.

In Play

Section 8. The ball is in play at all other times from the start of the match to the finish, including rebounds from a goalpost, crossbar, or corner flag-post into the field of play. If the ball rebounds from either referee when he is in the field of play, it is still in play.

A.R. 14. The ball, in flight, strikes the referee and goes directly into the goal. RULING: Legal goal. The referee is part of the field of play.

A.R. 15. Is the ball in play if it strikes the referee? RULING: Yes.

A.R. 16. The ball strikes the corner flag and rebounds into play. RULING: The ball is playable. The corner flags are part of the field of play.

Restarts

Section 9. A ball out of play is put back into play in the following methods:

a. **After crossing a boundary line**—When the ball crosses a touchline or goal line, a throw-in, goal kick, or corner kick is used to put it in play.

b. **Drop ball**—When restarting the game after a temporary suspension of play, except on a free kick or throw-in, the referee shall drop the ball at the place where it was when play was suspended; and the ball is in play when it touches the ground. If the ball is played before it touches the ground, the ball shall be dropped again. If play was stopped with the ball in the penalty area, the ball is dropped at the nearest point outside the penalty area.

c. **Kickoff**—(See Sec. 5).

A.R. 17. The referee drops the ball and it goes out of bounds before a player from either side touches it. RULING: The ball must be dropped again at the point where it crossed the line.

A.R. 18. The goalkeeper, in possession of ball, has been hurt in a goalmouth scramble, but no foul has been committed. RULING: If play was stopped in the penalty area, the ball must be brought out to the nearest point outside the penalty area and dropped.

A.R. 19. The ball is about to be dropped and a defending player in the penalty area strikes an opponent before it touches the ground. RULING: If the misconduct took place inside the penalty area, a penalty kick must not be awarded because the ball was not in play at the time the offense was committed. The game should be restarted by dropping the ball.

A.R. 20. How should the referee drop the ball when restarting play? RULING: The ball should be held at waist level and dropped to the ground, but not thrown down in any way.

A.R. 21. The ball becomes lodged between two players, causing possible injury. RULING: Stop play, then restart by dropping the ball.

Scoring

Method of Scoring

Section 10. A goal is scored when the whole of the ball has passed over the goal line, between the goalposts and under the crossbar, provided it has not been thrown, carried, or propelled by hand or arm, by a player of the attacking side, except as otherwise provided by these rules.

NOTE—*The ball must pass* **completely** *over and be clear of the goal line between the posts and under the crossbar. On the line is not over the line. The ball may roll all along the goal line and even be partly over the line and yet not pass through the goal. The goalkeeper may even be behind the goal line and yet prevent a goal. It is the position of the ball which counts, so it is not impossible for the goalkeeper to have his feet on or in front of the goal line with the ball in his possession and yet have a goal scored on him by reason of swinging his body and arms around to clear an opponent or to get room to throw or otherwise thrust the ball from him. The referee, however, must under no circumstances give a goal unless he is sure that the ball is completely over the line and he is in position to so decide. This applies also if the crossbar has been displaced.*

If the defending team deliberately stops or deflects the ball with hands or arm to stop a goal, it should be scored a goal if it goes in.

A.R. 22. Standing on his own goal line, the goalkeeper catches the ball and, in attempting to throw the ball, carries the ball over the goal line. RULING: Legal goal, if the whole of the ball passed over the goal line, between the goalposts and under the crossbar.

A.R. 23. On a shot at goal, the defensive player touches the ball with his hand and deflects the ball into the goal. RULING: Legal goal.

A.R. 24. On a shot at goal with the goalkeeper beaten, the ball strikes a dog that has run on the field. The dog deflects the ball away from the goal. RULING: No goal can be awarded. The ball has been stopped by an outside agency.

A.R. 25. Team A goalkeeper saves a shot and throws the ball down the field. Without anyone else touching it, the ball goes directly into Team B's goal. RULING: Legal goal. His throw is equal to a shot.

A.R. 26. The ball goes halfway across the goal line. RULING: No goal. The ball must be all the way over the goal line.

A.R. 27. The goalkeeper is standing behind the goal line when he catches the ball. RULING: It is the position of the ball that counts in determining if the ball is out or not out, or over or not over.

A.R. 28. Shall a goal be allowed if a defensive player, while in his own penalty area, handles the ball intentionally and propels it into his own goal? RULING: Yes.

A.R. 29. The referee whistles to signal a goal before the ball has passed completely over the goal line and the goal, and he immediately realizes his error. RULING: No goal. The game should be restarted by dropping the ball at the nearest point outside the penalty area.

A.R. 30. A player kicks the ball directly into the net from a corner kick. RULING: Legal goal.

A.R. 31. A player kicks the ball into the opponent's goal from a kickoff. RULING: No goal.

A.R. 32. A player kicks the ball into the goal from a free kick for offside. RULING: No goal.

A.R. 33. A player takes a shot and puts the ball into the net after getting rebound from his own penalty kick shot which caromed off crossbar. No other player touched the ball. RULING: No goal.

Displaced Crossbar

Section 11. Should the crossbar become displaced for any reason during the game, and the ball crosses the goal line at a point which, in the opinion of the referee, is below where the crossbar should have been, he shall award a goal.

Winning the Game

Section 12. The team scoring the greater number of goals during a game shall be the winner. If no goals or an equal number of goals are scored, the game shall be termed a "draw."

If tournament committees or athletic conferences employ tie-breaker systems other than Rule 4-1, the game still shall be considered a draw for NCAA records and selection committee purposes.

Forfeited Game

Section 13. The score of a forfeited game shall be 1–0.

Rule 5

OFFSIDE

Section 1. The fundamental point of offside is the position of the ball with respect to the player.

When Offside

Section 2. A player is offside if he is nearer his opponents' goal line than the ball is at the moment the ball is played unless:

a. He is in his own half of the field of play;
b. Two of his opponents are **nearer** to their own goal line than he is;
c. The ball last touched an opponent or was last played by him;
d. He receives the ball direct from a goal kick, a corner kick, a throw-in, or when it is dropped by the referee.

Penalty—Indirect free kick from point of infraction.

When a player is in an offside position, he has no right to interfere with an opponent or with the play; that is, to station himself so near the goalkeeper or any other opponent as to hamper his movements or obstruct his sight of the ball.

Penalty—Indirect free kick from point of infraction.

A.R. 1. Can a player be offside when the ball hits one of the uprights or cross-bar and rebounds into the field of play? RULING: Yes, if the ball kicked by an attacking player is received by a member of his team, who was in an offside position at the moment the ball was first kicked.

When Not Offside

Section 3. In the following situations, a player cannot be offside:

a. If he is not ahead of the ball when it is last played;
b. If he is ahead of the ball when it is last played by one of his own side, he must have two opponents between him and the opposing goal line;
c. If he receives the ball from an opponent;
d. When an opponent last plays the ball;
e. On a corner kick, goal kick, drop ball, or throw-in.

A.R. 2. Should a player be called offside when a defensive player deliberately steps off the field of play? RULING: No, the defensive player should be warned for ungentlemanly conduct.

A.R. 3. A player receives the ball from a throw-in, clearly in an offside position, but he shoots the ball and scores. RULING: Legal goal. A player cannot be offside on a throw-in.

A.R. 4. Is a teammate allowed to stand in an offside position at the taking of a penalty kick? RULING: Yes, but he would be charged with offside if the kicker failed to score directly and the player attempted to interfere with the game.

A.R. 5. Can a player be offside when a free kick is taken? RULING: Yes, in accordance with Rule 5-2.

Getting Back Onside

Section 4. A player once offside cannot put himself onside. This can only be done for him in three ways:

a.   If an opponent next plays the ball;
b.   If he is behind the ball when it is next played by one of his own side;
c.   If he has two opponents between him and their goal line when the ball is played by one of his own side farther from the opponents' goal line than himself.

NOTE—*The ball rebounding off a goalpost or the crossbar does not put a player onside who was offside when the ball was last played.*

Offside Not Penalized

Section 5. A player in an offside position shall not be penalized unless, in the opinion of the referee, he is interfering with the play or with an opponent, or is seeking to gain advantage by being in an offside position.

A.R. 6. Is it an offense to be in an offside position? RULING: No, it only becomes an offense at the moment the ball is played, as stated in Rule 5-5.

A.R. 7. A player steps off the field to avoid being offside. RULING: No penalty if the player left the field for the sole purpose of not being offside. If, upon leaving the field, the player distracts an opponent or assists a teammate, he is guilty of an infraction.

Rule 6

VIOLATIONS AND MISCONDUCT

Violations

Kicking, Striking, Jumping, or Tripping

Section 1. A player shall be penalized if he **intentionally** kicks, strikes, attempts to kick or strike, or jumps at an opponent.

He also shall be penalized if he trips, or attempts to trip, including throwing or attempting to throw, an opponent by the use of the legs, or by stooping in front of or behind him.

Penalty—Direct free kick.

NOTE—*Jumping at an opponent is quite different from jumping to play the ball.*

Deliberate tripping, kicking, striking, or jumping at an opponent or attempting to do same is dangerous and liable to cause injury, which compels the referee to warn the offending player that a repetition will necessitate the player's being ordered off the field.

A.R. 1. An offensive player is struck by an opponent in the penalty area, but the ball is in the center of the field at the time. RULING: A penalty kick will be awarded if the foul is deliberate. The offending player will be suspended from the game for violent conduct.

A.R. 2. On a goal kick, the ball is kicked forward and an offensive player runs into the penalty area and is tripped. RULING: Kick must be retaken because the ball did not leave the penalty area.

A.R. 3. An offensive player trips the goalkeeper. RULING: If the foul constituted misconduct, the offender shall be warned, and a direct free kick awarded from the point of the foul.

A.R. 4. A player jumps at an opponent to prevent him from playing the ball. RULING: Award a direct free kick.

A.R. 5. What is the difference between a sliding tackle and tripping? RULING: For a sliding tackle to be permissible, the foot or feet should be at or near the ground, the tackle should be for the ball and not the opponent, the ball should be played first, and it should be judged as not dangerous or violent.

A.R. 6. Is a tackle from behind permissible? RULING: Yes, if it meets qualifications of A.R. 5, above.

A.R. 7. A defender in his own penalty area strikes an opponent while the ball is in play in the opponent's penalty area. RULING: Penalty kick.

A.R. 8. May a player bait an opponent into an unfair tackle? RULING: If a player deliberately turns his back to an opponent when he is about to be tackled, he may be charged but not in a dangerous or violent manner.

Handling

Section 2. A player shall be penalized if he **intentionally** handles the ball; that is, carries, strikes, or propels it with his hands or arms. (This does not apply to the goalkeeper within his own penalty area.)

Penalty—Direct free kick.

Unintentional handling (the ball touching the hands or arms) shall not be penalized even though the offending player or his team gain an advantage by such unintentional handling. It is suggested that the referee call out the words "play on" and raise his hand (fist closed) over his head to indicate that he has seen the incident.

A.R. 9. The ball strikes a player on the arm below the elbow. RULING: Hand ball if the move is intentional.

A.R. 10. May a goalkeeper handle the ball outside the penalty area? RULING: No. Direct free kick shall be awarded.

A.R. 11. A fullback takes a goal kick and the wind blows the ball back into the area. The same fullback deflects the ball to stop it from entering the net. RULING: Penalty kick.

A.R. 12. May a player put his hands in front of his face or groin to protect himself before a kick? RULING: Yes, as long as the player does not move his hands.

Holding and Pushing

Section 3. A player shall be penalized if he holds or pushes an opponent with his hand or hands, or with his arms extended from his body.

Holding includes the obstruction of a player by the hand or any part of the arm extended from the body. Under no circumstances is a player permitted to push an opponent with his hands or arms.

Penalty—Direct free kick.

> **A.R. 13.** A player, upon being fairly charged, falls down outside the field of play, but immediately grabs his opponent's ankle, causing him to trip. The opponent was in the field of play. RULING: Direct free kick and a warning to the offending player.

Violent or Dangerous Charging

Section 4. A player shall be penalized if he charges in a violent or dangerous manner.

A fair charge consists of a nudge or a contact with the near shoulder, when both players are in an upright position, within playing distance of the ball, and have at least one foot on the ground and their arms held close to the body.

Penalty—Direct free kick.

> **A.R. 14.** Two players are chasing a ball when one player charges the other player shoulder to shoulder. RULING: Indirect free kick.

Charging Goalkeeper

Section 5. The referee will remove without warning any player who intentionally charges the goalkeeper in possession of the ball.

Penalty—Direct free kick.

A.R. 15. Should a player be ejected for any type of charge upon an opposing goalkeeper who is in possession of the ball? RULING: No. In a case where the charge is intentionally unfair, and is judged violent, serious, or dangerous, then the player is to be ejected without warning. In all other cases, the referee is to penalize appropriately.

Kicking Ball Held by Goalkeeper

Section 6. A player shall be penalized if he kicks or attempts to kick the ball when it is in possession of the goalkeeper.

Penalty—Indirect free kick.

Obstruction

Section 7. A player shall be penalized if he obstructs an opponent when not playing the ball; that is, runs between an opponent and the ball or interposes his body as to form an obstacle to an opponent.

Penalty—Indirect free kick.

A.R. 16. What is tactical or legal obstruction? RULING: When a player places himself between an opponent and the ball, keeping the ball within his playing distance, and covers up the ball in an attempt not to have it played by his opponent.

A.R. 17. May a player be charged from behind during tactical obstruction? RULING: Yes; however, this must be a charge in the region of the shoulder, not the back itself.

A.R. 18. How do you define playing distance when judging obstruction? RULING: By whether the player can play the ball at any given moment, if the ball is beyond his control in terms of distance and if he is preventing his opponent from playing it.

Dangerous Play

Section 8. A player shall be penalized if he engages in play which is of a dangerous nature or likely to cause injury. Some examples of dangerous play are:

a. Raising the foot to the level which may endanger an opponent when the opponent is in a normal stance;
b. "Hitching" or double kicking, which may endanger an opponent;
c. Lowering the head to a position level with or below the waist in an effort to head the ball in the presence of an oncoming player (this is likely to cause injury to the player heading the ball in such a manner);
d. A player other than the goalkeeper covering the ball while sitting, kneeling, or lying on the ground.

Penalty—Indirect free kick.

Usually when dangerous or potentially dangerous play is observed by the referee, he will warn the offender against a repetition. But dangerous play may likely be of such a character as to warrant the referee's sending the offender off the field without a warning.

A.R. 19. Is the scissors kick permitted? RULING: Yes, if the act does not endanger an opponent.

Goalkeeper Privileges and Violations

Privileges
Section 9. Within his own penalty area, the goalkeeper has certain privileges which are not given to any other player. These privileges include:

a. **Handling**—The goalkeeper may carry, strike, or propel the ball with his hands or arms;

b. **Immunity**—The goalkeeper may not be charged, interfered with, or impeded in any manner by an opponent while he is in possession of the ball. Possession includes the act of dribbling the ball with the hand and also the dropping of the ball for the kick, but does not include rolling the ball along the ground.

Outside the penalty area, the goalkeeper has no more privilege than any other player.

A.R. 20. A player stands in front of the goalkeeper during a corner kick without trying to play the ball but merely trying to stop the goalkeeper from playing it. RULING: Indirect free kick.

A.R. 21. A player raises his foot as the goalkeeper kicks the ball from his hands. RULING: Indirect free kick.

A.R. 22. When can the goalkeeper be legally charged? RULING: When the ball is not in his possession, that is, being rolled on the ground or dribbled with his feet, but within playing distance of the goalkeeper.

A.R. 23. The goalkeeper receives the ball and an opponent takes a position directly in front of him. RULING: Violation, if the player is interfering or impeding the goalkeeper.

Violations
Section 10. With the goalkeeper's special privileges comes the capability for certain violations of these privileges which could not be applied to any other player. These violations are:

a. **Steps by goalkeeper**—The goalkeeper, when in possession of the ball, may not carry the ball more than four steps while holding, bouncing, or throwing the ball in the air and catching it again, without releasing it so that it is played by another player.

Penalty—Indirect free kick from point of infraction.

b. The goalkeeper must not deliberately delay getting rid of the ball when it is in his possession.

Penalty—Indirect free kick from point of infraction.

c. The goalkeeper may not intentionally strike an opponent by throwing the ball vigorously at him, or push him with the ball while holding it.

Penalty (if offense occurred in penalty area)—Penalty kick.

A.R. 24. What are some examples of the goalkeeper being limited to four steps while in possession of the ball? RULING: (1) The goalkeeper has possession of the ball and takes two steps, then rolls ball on ground. He picks up the ball and has two more steps. He must then make the ball playable to another player. (2) The goalkeeper takes four steps. He must then make ball playable to another player at once. (3) The goalkeeper takes one step, then rolls ball on ground. He picks up the ball and takes three more steps. He must then make ball playable to another player. (4) The goalkeeper has possession and throws ball in the air and takes four steps before catching it. He must then make ball playable to another player.
A.R. 25. Can the four steps allowed to the goalkeeper be taken at different times? RULING: Yes.
A.R. 26. If the goalkeeper takes four steps while in possession of the ball, how may he get four more steps? RULING: He may play the ball to another player, teammate or opponent, and regain possession and the right to four more steps.
A.R. 27. May the goalkeeper throw the ball in the air over the head of an opponent and catch it after taking more than four steps? RULING: No, the ball must be released after four steps.
A.R. 28. Is it permissible for the goalkeeper to take more than four steps while holding the ball and only touching the ground with it, but without releasing it? RULING: No.
A.R. 29. Is the "air dribble" considered possession for the purpose of counting goalkeeper steps? RULING: Yes, and his steps are counted during the "air dribble."
A.R. 30. May the ball be played by an opponent while the goalkeeper makes an "air dribble?" RULING: Yes.

Misconduct

Ungentlemanly Behavior

Section 11. Persistent infringement of any of the rules of the game constitutes misconduct or ungentlemanly behavior. A player and/or coach who is guilty of misconduct or ungentlemanly behavior shall first be warned by the referee, and, if he persists, shall be suspended from further participation in the game.

Penalty—Indirect free kick.

A.R. 31. Players of the winning team are wasting time in the waning minutes on throw-ins and goal kicks. RULING: The referee has the authority to stop the clock and warn the offending players for ungentlemanly conduct.

A.R. 32. If a referee warns a player, who in turn apologizes for his misconduct, can the referee forget the incident? RULING: No, all misconduct must be reported.

A.R. 33. A player intentionally lies on the ball for an unreasonable length of time. RULING: Warn the player for ungentlemanly conduct and award indirect free kick to the opposing team.

A.R. 34. A defensive player strikes an offensive player in the penalty area before a free kick is taken. RULING: Do not award a penalty kick. The infringement occurred when the ball was dead, and the game can only be started with the original free kick.

A.R. 35. Must a match be stopped immediately to warn or eject? RULING: No, if the referee applies the advantage, he shall warn or eject when play stops.

A.R. 36. Can certain types of obstruction be considered misconduct? RULING: Yes, such as a player intentionally stretching his arms, moving them up and down to delay his opponent and forcing him to change course, without making bodily contact. Award indirect free kick for ungentlemanly conduct.

A.R. 37. Whom can the referee warn and eject? RULING: Any player, coach, team official, or participant, whether he is within or outside the field of play, whose conduct is ungentlemanly or violent.

A.R. 38. Is encroachment a form of misconduct? RULING: Yes. The referee has the authority to warn, and eject on recurrence. Also, he has the disciplinary option of employing a team warning.

A.R. 39. Two players of the same team commit ungentlemanly or violent conduct toward each other on the field of play. RULING: The players should be warned or dismissed from the game and the game restarted by an indirect free kick.

A.R. 40. What is violent conduct? RULING: Acts of brutality such as striking or attempting to strike an opponent, kicking or attempting to kick an opponent, insulting or striking the referee, or the use of foul and abusive language.

A.R. 41. May a player be sent off the field without having been previously warned? RULING: Yes, when the player is guilty of violent conduct.

A.R. 42. Is spitting a form of misconduct? RULING: Yes.

A.R. 43. A player complains vigorously about the referee's decision. RULING: The offending player will be warned that any further showing of dissent will result in suspension.

A.R. 44. A player has been sent off in accordance with Rule 1-18 but returns to the field without getting permission from the referee, and handles the ball while play is in progress. RULING: Direct free kick for handling the ball. The referee still may warn the player for entering the field without permission.

A.R. 45. A player enters or returns to the field of play without receiving a signal from the referee, and, apart from this, commits another more serious infringement. RULING: The player shall be warned for entering or returning to the field without a signal and punished for the more serious infringement.

A.R. 46. A team persistently kicks the ball out of play to waste time. RULING: Stop clock and give a team warning. Eject the player on next offense.

A.R. 47. Defensive players are catching the ball to keep an attack from developing. RULING: Offending player will be warned and further misconduct will result in suspension. If the act is becoming widespread by different players, a team warning will be given to the captain with expulsion for the next offense.

A.R. 48. The defensive team tries delaying tactics by not getting the required 10 yards. RULING: Stop clock and warn the offending player that a repeat violation will result in immediate expulsion for the offender.

A.R. 49. A player, who has received approval to leave the field of play, places himself near the touchline and puts his foot into the field of play causing an opponent to fall. RULING: Player should be warned and game restarted by direct free kick.

A.R. 50. A player asks to leave the field and, as he is walking off the field, the ball comes toward him and he shoots a goal. RULING: Player shall be warned and game restarted by indirect free kick by opposing team from place where infringement occurred.

A.R. 51. What is the proper way to issue a second yellow card to a player? RULING: There is no second yellow card, or warning. The second card displayed shall be a red card, to denote ejection for persistent misconduct.

Violent Conduct

Section 12. The referee has the discretionary power to suspend from further participation in the game, without previous warning, a player or coach guilty of violent conduct or abusive language to a referee or a player.

Penalty—Indirect free kick.

Nonparticipants on Field

Section 13. No person other than the players and the ball persons are allowed on the field of play without permission from the referee. Trainers and coaches may enter the field only if called to do so by the referee.

Penalty—Indirect free kick from location of ball at the time of infraction.

Coaching from Sidelines
Section 14. Coaching from the sidelines is restricted to verbal communication, without the use of aids, with one's own team, and is confined to the immediate bench area.

If an infraction occurs, the referee will advise the offending coach that on a recurrence he will award an indirect free kick against his team given from the point where the ball was when the infraction occurred.

It is permissible for a player to call instructions to a player on his own team during the game. Referees should penalize such calling only when it is done to intentionally distract an opponent.

Warning
Section 15. A player shall be warned by the referee if he:

a. Joins his team after the kickoff or returns to the field of play without first reporting to the referee;
b. Demonstrates ungentlemanly conduct by persistently infringing any of the rules of the game;
c. Shows dissent by word of mouth or action to decisions given by the referee.

Penalty—Indirect free kick.

NOTE—*If a nonparticipant player is warned, the game shall be resumed by an indirect free kick, against his team, given from the point where the ball was when the infraction occurred.*

Expulsion
Section 16. A player shall be ordered off the field by the referee if he:

a. Persists in misconduct after having received a warning;
b. Is guilty of violent conduct, i.e., using foul or abusive language; or in the opinion of the referee is guilty of persistent infringement of the rules of the game (Sec. 11);
c. Wears illegal or dangerous equipment.

Penalty—Indirect free kick from the point of infraction.

A player who has been ordered off shall not return to the field of play. EXCEPTION—A player who has been sent off to replace or repair illegal equipment may return to the field when he has complied with the rules.

A.R. 52. Is a player permitted to swear in a game? RULING: The referee is judge as to the severity of the action. Any player who swears at or threatens a referee must be removed from the game and no substitution may be per-mitted.

A.R. 53. A player is ejected for violent conduct when kicking or striking an opponent within the penalty area. RULING: Award a penalty kick, provided the ball was in play at the moment the offense was committed.

A.R. 54. A referee is about to warn a player and before he has done so, the player commits another offense which merits a warning. RULING: Eject the player.

A.R. 55. May the referee eject a player who dissents? RULING: While dissent as a form of misconduct is penalized by a warning, the referee has authority to eject without prior warning any dissent that is judged as violent, abusive, or persistent after a warning.

Rule 7

AWARDED KICKS AND THE THROW-IN

Free Kicks

Types, When Taken

Section 1. A free kick is taken to resume play after the play has been stopped by the referee for any of the offenses listed in Sections 3 and 4 of this Rule. The kick is taken by a member of the team against which the offense is committed, and is taken from the point where the infraction occurred.

Free kicks are classified either as "direct" or "indirect":

a. **Direct free kick**—A direct free kick is one on which a goal can be scored directly from the kick against the offending team;

b. **Indirect free kick**—An indirect free kick is one from which a goal cannot be scored unless the ball has been played or touched by a player other than the kicker before passing through the goal.

How Taken

Section 2. When a free kick is being taken, a player of the opposite team shall not approach within 10 yards [9.15m] of the ball until it is in play, unless he is standing on his own goal line, between the goalposts. The kick shall be retaken if a player is within 10 yards [9.15m] of the ball and intentionally interferes with the kick. If a player tries to slow the game by not getting 10 yards [9.15m] from the ball, he shall be warned, and if any member of the team repeats the infraction, that player may be removed from the game.

As soon as the ball is in position to be played, the referee must give a signal, which may be a whistle. The ball may be kicked in any direction. The ball must be stationary when the kick is taken, and is not in play until it has traveled the distance of its own circumference (27 inches, or 0.68m). The kicker may not play the ball a second time until it has been touched or played by another player.

Penalty—Indirect free kick from point of infraction.

When a free kick is awarded to the defending team in the penalty area, the ball must be kicked out of the penalty area. The goalkeeper may not receive the ball into his hand from a free kick in order to thereafter kick the ball into play, or the kick must be retaken. All opponents must be outside the penalty area and at least 10 yards [9.15m] from the ball, or the kick must be retaken.

A.R. 1. On a free kick, does the attacking team also have to stand 10 yards from the ball? RULING: No, the attacking team may stand as close as it wishes but may not touch the ball until it has traveled a distance equal to its circumference.

A.R. 2. A player takes a direct free kick from 20 yards. He passes the ball back to his goalkeeper, who does not touch it, and the ball goes into the goal. RULING: No goal. Free kicks can only be scored directly against the offending team. It is a corner kick.

A.R. 3. A player taking a free kick inside his own penalty area inadvertently kicks the ball into his own goal. RULING: Because the ball did not leave the penalty area, it must be retaken. If the ball had left the penalty area and then gone into the goal, a corner kick would be awarded.

A.R. 4. On a direct free kick from 20 yards, a player takes the kick without waiting for the referee's whistle and scores a goal. RULING: Legal goal. A second whistle is only required for the kickoff, penalty kick, and whenever the referee indicates the players must await the whistle to restart play.

A.R. 5. Can a direct or indirect free kick be kicked in any direction? RULING: Yes.

A.R. 6. The ball from an indirect free kick touches an opponent and enters the net. RULING: Legal goal.

A.R. 7. Is the free kick lifted with one foot allowed? RULING: Yes, provided that in all other respect its execution does not violate the rules.

Direct Free Kick Offense

Section 3. Offenses for which a direct free kick will be awarded are (see Rule 6):

a. Handling the ball;
b. Holding an opponent;
c. Pushing an opponent;
d. Striking or attempting to strike an opponent;
e. Jumping at an opponent;

f. Kicking or attempting to kick an opponent;

g. Tripping or attempting to trip an opponent;

h. Using the knee on an opponent;

i. Charging an opponent violently or dangerously;

j. Handling by the goalkeeper outside the penalty area;

k. Illegally charging the goalkeeper in the penalty area;

l. Goalkeeper intentionally striking or attempting to strike an opponent with the ball;

m. Charging from the rear unless being obstructed.

All direct kicks awarded to the offensive team in the penalty area are **penalty kicks** (see Sections 5 and 6, this Rule).

A.R. 8. A direct free kick is awarded 6 yards inside the penalty area and a player from the opposing team stands 1 yard outside the penalty area. RULING: All players opposite to the team taking the kick must be 10 yards from the ball.

A.R. 9. A player takes a free kick and then intentionally handles the ball before it has been played by another player. RULING: Punish with the more serious offense, by a direct free kick, or by a penalty kick if the offense took place in the penalty area.

Indirect Free Kick Offenses

Section 4. Offenses for which an indirect free kick will be awarded are:

a. A player playing the ball a second time before it has been played by another player at the kickoff, on a throw-in, on a free kick, on a corner kick, or on a goal kick (if the ball has passed outside the penalty area);

b. A goalkeeper carrying the ball more than four steps;

c. The goalkeeper delays getting rid of the ball;

d. A substitution or resubstitution being made at an improper time;

e. A substitution or resubstitution being made without reporting to the referee;

f. Persons other than the players and ball persons entering the field of play without the referee's permission;

g. Illegal coaching from the sidelines after previously being advised by the referee against a recurrence;

h. Dissenting by word or action with a referee's decision;

i. Ungentlemanly behavior;

j. Dangerous play;

k. To resume play after a player has been ordered off the field;

l. Offside;

m. Charging illegally (not violent or dangerous);

n. Interfering with the goalkeeper or impeding him in any manner until he releases the ball, or kicking or attempting to kick the ball when it is in his possession;

o. Obstruction other than holding;

p. Player leaving the field of play during the progress of the game without the consent of the referee.

A.R. 10. What is the penalty for persistent coaching from the sideline? RULING: Indirect free kick from the place the ball was when the infraction was called, after a warning from the referee.

A.R. 11. A player scores a goal directly on the award of a foul for dangerous play. RULING: The penalty for dangerous play is an indirect free kick, and if the ball goes directly into the opponent's goal, a goal cannot be given. A goal kick is awarded to the defensive team.

A.R. 12. What is meant by charging illegally (not violently or dangerously)? RULING: An illegal charge is one that involves a nudge or contact with the near shoulder, against an opponent, while the ball is in play; which is made when both players are not in an upright position, not within playing distance of the ball, and do not have at least one foot on the ground and their arms held close to the body.

Penalty Kick

When Taken

Section 5. A penalty kick is awarded for any infringement of the rules by the defending team within the penalty area which is penalized by a direct free kick.

A penalty kick can be awarded irrespective of the position of the ball, if the offense by the defending team is committed within the penalty area. A goal may be scored direct from a penalty kick.

A penalty kick is **not** awarded for offenses which call for an indirect free kick, regardless of where or by whom the offense is committed.

How Taken

Section 6. The penalty kick is taken from any place on the penalty mark line.

When it is being taken, all players (except for the kicker and the opposing goalkeeper) shall be within the field of play, but outside the penalty area and at least 10 yards [9.15m] from the penalty mark.

The opposing goalkeeper must stand, without moving his feet, on his own goal line between the goalposts, until the ball is kicked.

The player taking the kick must kick the ball forward the length of its own circumference in order for it to be in play. If the ball is not put into play properly, the kick must be retaken.

The kicker may not play the ball a second time until it has been touched by another player. If the ball hits the goalposts or the crossbar and rebounds into play, the kicker still may not play the ball until it has been played by another player.

A.R. 13. At the taking of a penalty kick, a player of the defensive team wishes to stand off the field. RULING: All players, with the exception of the goalkeeper and the player taking the kick, must stand on the field of play outside the penalty area.

A.R. 14. On taking a penalty kick, the kicker passes the ball back to a teammate who shoots and scores. RULING: No goal. The kick must be retaken because the ball must go forward on a penalty kick.

A.R. 15. On a penalty kick, the kicker kicks the ball against the crossbar; it rebounds to him and he shoots and scores. RULING: No goal. Award an indirect free kick for kicking the ball twice.

A.R. 16. On the taking of a penalty kick, the ball bursts on contact with the kicker's foot. RULING: Kick will be retaken.

A.R. 17. Does the referee have to blow the whistle as the signal for taking the penalty kick? RULING: Yes.

A.R. 18. Do all players have to be behind the ball on the taking of a penalty kick? RULING: No, but if they stand in front of the ball and outside the penalty area, they would be offside if the ball rebounds from the goalpost and they participate in the play.

A.R. 19. Can a player taking a penalty kick push the ball forward for a teammate to run to it and score? RULING: Yes, provided (1) all of the players, except the player taking the kick and the opposing goalkeeper, are outside the penalty area and not within 10 yards of the penalty mark at the time the kick is taken, (2) the teammate to whom the ball is passed is not in an offside position when the ball is kicked and does not enter the penalty area until the ball has traveled the length of it own circumference, (3) the penalty kick is taken in normal time.

A.R. 20. At the taking of a penalty kick, the ball strikes the goalpost or crossbar and bursts. RULING: Restart the game by dropping the ball at the nearest point outside the penalty area. If the penalty kick is being taken in extended time, the game ends.

A.R. 21. If a penalty kick is being retaken for any reason, may another player of the same team take it? RULING: Yes, provided he was on the field at the time the penalty kick was awarded.

A.R. 22. Is a player taking a penalty kick allowed to place the ball elsewhere than on the penalty line owing to the waterlogged state of the pitch? RULING: No.

A.R. 23. Can a substitute be allowed to take a penalty kick, in a game in which time has been extended? RULING: No, only a player who was on the field when time expired may take the kick.

A.R. 24. May the player taking the penalty kick go outside the penalty area? RULING: Yes, after the signal he may go outside the penalty area to take a longer run at the ball, though he cannot demand that the opponents give him a clear path.

Infringements
Section 7.

a. On a penalty kick, for any infringement by the defending team, the kick shall be retaken if a goal **has not** resulted.
b. On a penalty kick, for an infringement by the attacking team other than the player taking the kick, the kick shall be retaken if a goal **has** resulted.
c. On a penalty kick, for any infringement by the player taking the kick, a goal may not be scored and a player of the opposite team shall take an indirect free kick from the spot where the infringement occurred.

A.R. 25. The whistle has blown for the taking of a penalty kick and before the actual kick the goalkeeper moves his feet. RULING: Do not stop play until after the penalty kick. If a goal is scored, the infraction will be ignored, but if a goal is not scored the kick will be retaken.

A.R. 26. On a penalty kick, the defending team infringes upon the rule. RULING: If a goal was scored, the goal will stand. If a goal was not scored, the kick will be retaken.

A.R. 27. On a penalty kick, the offensive team infringes upon the rule. RULING: The kick will be retaken if a goal is scored. If a goal is not scored and the ball rebounds into play, an indirect free kick will be awarded against the offending team. If the ball goes out of play over the goal line, a goal kick will be given.

A.R. 28. The player taking a penalty kick commits ungentlemanly conduct before the kick is taken. RULING: The kicker shall be warned and if a goal is scored, the kick shall be retaken.

A.R. 29. A player intentionally goes beyond the boundary of the field of play at the taking of a penalty kick. RULING: Player should be warned and sent off if he repeats the offense.

End of Time Variations
Section 8. If the ball touches the goalkeeper before passing between the posts when a penalty kick is being taken at or after the expiration of time, it does not nullify a goal.

If necessary, time of play shall be extended at halftime or full time to allow a penalty kick to be taken.

If a penalty kick is taken after the expiration of time, only the kicker may play the ball.

A.R. 30. A penalty kick has been awarded at the close of a period without any time remaining. When shall the period end? RULING: The extension shall last until the moment the kick has been completed, when one of the following happens: (1) The moment the whole of the ball crosses the goal line it is a goal. (2) The ball rebounds into the goal from the goalposts. (3) The ball passes over the goal line outside the goalposts. (4) The ball rebounds back into play from the goalposts, crossbar, or goalkeeper. (5) The ball touches the goalkeeper and enters the goal. (6) The ball is clearly saved by the goalkeeper. (7) The game should be further extended if the ball is stopped by an outside agency. (8) The game should be further extended if a defending player encroaches and a goal is not scored. (9) Forward movement of the ball has ceased after traveling its own circumference. (10) Kick should be retaken if a goal is scored after encroachment by a teammate.

Goal Kick

When Taken
Section 9. A goal kick is taken by a member of the defending team when the ball passes completely over the goal line (excluding that portion between the goalposts), either in the air or on the ground, having last been played by a member of the **attacking** team.

How Taken
Section 10. The ball is placed on the ground at a point within that half of the goal area nearest to where it crossed the goal line, and is kicked in any direction from that point. The ball must be kicked beyond the penalty area, or the kick shall be retaken. A goal may not be scored from a goal kick. The goal kick is an indirect kick.

Players of the team opposing that of the player taking the goal kick shall remain outside the penalty area until the ball goes over the penalty area line after the kick has been taken, or the kick shall be retaken.

The goalkeeper shall not receive the ball into his hand from a goal kick in order that he may thereafter kick it into play. The goalkeeper cannot pick up the ball and kick it—the ball must be placed on the ground and kicked from there.

The kicker may not play the ball a second time after it has passed beyond the penalty area and before it has touched or been played by another player.

Penalty—Indirect free kick from point of infraction.

A.R. 31. A goalkeeper takes a goal kick on a muddy field and the ball goes only 6 yards. He then picks up the ball and punts it. RULING: Illegal play.

The ball must leave the penalty area. The goal kick will be retaken.

A.R. 32. The ball is kicked out over the goal line to the right of the goal. Can the goal kick be taken any place on the 6-yard line? RULING: No, it must be kicked from the side of the goal corresponding to the side of the field it went out.

A.R. 33. A player is clearly in an offside position when a ball is kicked to him from a goal kick, and he receives the ball and scores a goal. RULING: Legal goal. A player cannot be offside directly from a goal kick.

A.R. 34. Rules 7-10 and 7-2 seem to be in conflict. What is the difference? RULING: There is no conflict. In both instances the ball is not in play until it has left the penalty area. On goal kicks, opponents may not enter the penalty area until the ball leaves the area. On free kicks taken from within the penalty area, opponents may not enter the area and may not come within 10 yards of the ball until it is in play.

Corner Kick

When Taken
Section 11. A corner kick is taken by a member of the attacking team when the ball passes completely over the goal line (excluding that portion between the goalposts), either in the air or on the ground, having last been played by a member of the **defending** team.

How Taken
Section 12. A member of the attacking team shall take a kick from within the quarter circle at the nearest corner flagpost, which must not be removed. A goal may be scored direct from a corner kick.

Players of the team opposing that of the player taking a corner kick shall not approach within 10 yards [9.15m] of the ball until the ball is in play, that is, has traveled the distance of its own circumference, or the kick shall be retaken.

The kicker may not play the ball a second time after the ball is in play until it has been touched or played by another player. If the ball hits the goalpost and rebounds toward him, he still may not play the ball until it has been played by another player.

Penalty—Indirect free kick from point of infraction.

A.R. 35. A ball is kicked directly into the opponent's goal from a corner kick. RULING: Legal goal.

A.R. 36. A player from Team A takes a corner kick. The ball hits the goalpost and rebounds to the same player, who kicks it into the goal. RULING: No goal. Award indirect free kick from the point he played the ball the second time.

A.R. 37. Can a player remove the corner flag taking a corner kick? RULING: No.

A.R. 38. An offensive player, clearly in an offside position, receives the ball directly from a corner kick and scores. RULING: Legal goal. An offensive player cannot be offside on a corner kick.

A.R. 39. A defensive player places himself less than 10 yards from the ball on a corner kick. RULING: Player should be instructed to move 10 yards from the ball. Continued infringement would result in a warning and possible suspension from the game.

A.R. 40. Before a corner kick is taken, the defensive fullback strikes an offensive player in the penalty area. RULING: Do not award a penalty kick because the ball is dead. However, this does not preclude the offending player from being penalized for misconduct.

Throw-in

When Taken

Section 13. A throw-in is taken to put the ball back into play after it has passed **completely** over a touchline, either on the ground or in the air (4-8a), from the point where it crossed the line, being thrown in any direction by a player of the team opposite to that of the player who last touched the ball.

How Taken

Section 14. The thrower, at the moment of delivering the ball, must face the field of play and part of each foot shall be either on the touchline or on the ground outside the touchline. The thrower shall use both hands equally and shall deliver the ball from behind and over his head. The ball shall be in play from the throw as soon as it enters the field of play. A goal may not be scored direct from a throw-in.

If the ball is improperly thrown in, the throw-in shall be taken by a player of the opposing team.

The thrower may not play the ball a second time before it has been touched or played by another player.

Penalty—Indirect free kick from point of infraction.

A.R. 41. A player taking a throw-in throws the ball so that it does not enter the field of play, but passes outside the touchline or hits the ground before entering the field of play. RULING: The throw-in should be retaken.

A.R. 42. A player throws the ball in, and upon seeing that one of his teammates will not reach it, handles the ball and knocks it out of bounds. RULING: Award a direct free kick for the more serious offense.

A.R. 43. An opponent stands in front of the thrower and jumps up and down waving his arms. RULING: Warn the player for ungentlemanly conduct.

A.R. 44. May a thrower take a long run before releasing the ball? RULING: Yes, provided the player is facing the field of play, has part of either foot on or behind the line, delivers the ball from behind his head and throws the ball in from the point it crossed the touchline.

A.R. 45. On a throw-in the ball is thrown directly into the opponent's goal. RULING: No goal. Award a goal kick.

A.R. 46. On a throw-in the ball is thrown directly into his own goal. RULING: No goal. Award a corner kick.

A.R. 47. On a throw-in the ball lands on the line. RULING: Legal play, the ball is in play.

A.R. 48. On a throw-in, the ball crosses the touchline in the air, but is blown out of the field of play by the wind and lands outside the field of play. RULING: Throw-in for the opposing team.

A.R. 49. A player throws the ball against an opponent's back and plays the rebound. RULING: Legal play, unless done in a violent or ungentlemanly manner.

A.R. 50. Is it permissible for a goalkeeper to take a throw-in? RULING: Yes, since he may play anywhere on the field.

A.R. 51. When shall the ball be considered in play from a throw-in? RULING: As soon as any part of the ball touches or covers any part of the touchline, either on the ground or in the air.

A.R. 52. During a throw-in, may any part of either foot or both feet extend past the touchline into the field of play? RULING: No.

Official Soccer Signals

10

MISL CONDENSED LAWS

From The Official Indoor Soccer Rules, United States Soccer Federation

LAW 1—Field of Play: Approx. 200 ft. long by 85 ft. wide
Perimeter wall: 3 ft. 6 in. to 4 ft. 6 in. high, fully enclosing area topped by Plexiglas
Goal: 6 ft. 6 in. high by 12 ft. wide
Goal area: 16 ft. wide by 5 ft. from the goal line
Penalty area: 30 ft. wide by 25 ft. from the goal line
Corner spot: 9-in. diameter
Center spot: 9-in. diameter
Center circle: 10-ft. radius
Red lines: 30 ft. from center line across field width, each half
Markings: Minimum 3 in., maximum 5 in. wide
Center line: Indicated by a white line across field
Touch line: Broken line from corner spot to corner spot on both sides of the field at a distance of 3 ft. from the perimeter wall
LAW 2—The Ball: Special MISL Rocket Red; circumference (27–28 in.) and weight (14–16 oz.) same as in outdoor soccer
LAW 3—Number of Players: Maximum of 16 may dress; Maximum of 6 per team on field at any time and minimum of 4; Time penalty is delayed if it would reduce a team below 4; Substitutions may occur on an unlimited basis and "on the fly" provided a player leaving the field arrives at the bench before his replacement enters the field. Play will be held up to allow substitutions after a stoppage for a goal, time penalty, injury or after the ball has left the field.
LAW 4—Player Equipment: Consists of a long-sleeved shirt, shorts, socks, and flat-soled or indoor shoes except that goalkeeper must wear long pants. Goalkeeper must wear colors which will distinguish him from all other players and referee.
LAW 5—Referees: One referee on the field, responsible for control of the

game; an assistant referee stationed at the timekeeper's bench to assist the referee and call three-line and substitution violations.

LAW 6—Assistant Referee & Other Game Officials: Timekeepers operate the time and scoreboard details and the time penalties under the referee's jurisdiction. One attendant in each penalty box. Goal Judges indicate whether the whole ball has crossed the goal line for a goal.

LAW 7—Duration of the Game: Four quarters of 15 minutes each, with one 15-minute halftime interval and two 3-minute quarter intervals. The clock stops on every referee's whistle and starts upon a signal. Each team is allowed 1 timeout per half. If the game ends in a tie, sudden death play begins at the flip of a coin and proceeds to the maximum of one 15-minute quarter. If no one scores, an MISL shootout will decide the winner.

LAW 8—Start of Play: The visiting team has first possession in the first and third quarter; the home team in the second and fourth quarter. The home team has decided in advance the direction to attack in the first quarter. Teams change direction at each quarter interval.

LAW 9—Ball in and out of Play: The ball is out of play when it passes over the perimeter wall, when a goal is scored, or when the referee stops play. The ball is in play at all other times, even if it rebounds from the referee, perimeter wall, goalpost, surrounding plexiglas, etc.

LAW 10—Method of Scoring: A goal is scored when the whole of the ball passes completely over the goal line, provided no infraction has been committed by the attacking team.

LAW 11—Red Line Violation: The outdoor offside rule does not apply to indoor soccer; instead, there are red line violations. It is a violation if the ball is passed forward by any member of the attacking team so that it passes over two red lines in the air without being touched by any other player (of either team). If this happens, the referee will award an indirect free kick to the opposing team, to be taken at the point where the ball crossed the red line nearest to the goal being defended by the player committing the violation.

LAW 12—Fouls and Misconduct: A player who intentionally kicks, trips, strikes, boards, jumps at, pushes, holds, violently charges, or charges in the back of an opponent, or who intentionally handles the ball (except the goalkeeper), shall be penalized by a direct free kick. Any one of these offenses committed in the penalty area by a defender will result in a penalty kick for the offensive team and a two-minute penalty to the offender. Any of these offenses judged to be very serious by the referee regardless of their location shall be penalized by a two-minute penalty against the offender. A player guilty of a second penal offense in any game shall receive a mandatory caution. The third such penalty shall result in a mandatory ejection. A player guilty of intentionally causing the ball to leave the field of play shall be awarded a two-minute penalty. However, this is not a penal offense.

If a player or coach is guilty of misconduct, ungentlemanly conduct, or conduct likely to bring the game into dispute, he (or a selected player if the misconduct is by a coach) shall serve a two-minute time penalty and may be issued a caution (yellow card).

If a player is guilty of violent conduct (or serious foul play) he shall be ejected (red card) permanently and must retire to the dressing room. He may be replaced by a substitute but the substitute must go into the penalty box and serve a five-minute penalty before entering the game. Players will be released after one goal in cases of ejection for an accumulation of yellow cards or third penal offense.

Delay of Game Penalty: If the goalkeeper delays action by holding the ball for five seconds; if a defender passes back to the goalkeeper from another zone and the goalkeeper plays the ball with his hands, then an indirect free kick is awarded to the opposing team.

Delayed Time Penalties: A time penalty can be suspended temporarily only if the penalty would reduce a team below four active players on the field.

Penalty Against Goalkeeper: When a two-minute penalty is awarded against a goalkeeper, it can be served by one of the other players on the field.

Power Play Return: If one team is reduced by penalties to fewer players on the field than its opponents and the team having more players scores a goal, then the player who has served the most of his penalty time can return to the game. Only one penalized player may return on each goal.

LAW 13—Free Kicks: Classified into two categories—direct, from which a goal can be scored directly against the offending team, and indirect, from which a goal cannot be scored unless the ball has been touched by a second player before entering the goal.

LAW 14—Penalty Kicks: Awarded for offenses committed by defenders against an attacker in the penalty area. The kick is taken from the penalty spot (24 feet from goal line) by any player on the offended team. The goalkeeper must stand on the goal line and between the posts. All players except the kicker and goalkeeper must be outside the penalty area. The ball is in play as soon as it is kicked forward one-half rotation.

LAW 15—Kick In: In place of the throw as used in outdoor soccer, the ball is put back into play with an indirect free kick, with the ball being placed on the touchline at the point nearest where it went out of play.

LAW 16—Goal Kick: When the ball completely crosses the perimeter wall at the goal line between the two corner flags after being last touched by a player from the attacking team, it is put back into play by a kick from the goal area by the defending team.

LAW 17—Corner Kick: When the ball completely crosses the perimeter wall at the goal line between the two corner flags after being last touched by a player from the defending team, it is put back into play by a kick from the corner spot on the side of the field the ball had left. The corner kick is a direct free kick for the attacking team.

GLOSSARY

Attack

A team is on the attack when any player on that team has possession and control of the ball, regardless of field position.

Backs

The general name given to defenders.

Corner Kick

A corner kick is awarded to the attacking team if a defender was last to touch the ball before it went out of bounds over the goal line. The kick is taken from the corner of the field closest to where the ball went out of bounds. (See rule governing Corner Kick.)

Cover

A player who is positioned behind a teammate challenging an opponent for the ball and who is standing by should the challenge be unsuccessful.

Cross

A cross is a pass in the air crossing from one side of the field to the other.

Dangerous Play

Dangerous play is ruled by the referee when a player does something that is likely to cause or result in injury. Bringing the foot above shoulder level or putting the head down to head a low ball while closely surrounded by other players are examples of dangerous play. The offending team loses possession of the ball and the opponent is awarded a free kick from the point of infraction.

Defense

A team is on defense when any member of the opposing team has possession and control of the ball, regardless of field position.

Direct Free Kick

A direct free kick is awarded as a result of a personal foul, such as kicking, tripping, pushing, or holding, and is taken from the point of infraction. The player taking the kick may score directly without any other player having to touch the ball.

Drop Ball

A drop ball is called when a referee is not sure who last touched the ball before it went out of bounds, also on a restart if the referee stopped play for an other than normal reason. The referee holds the ball between two opposing players and then drops it between them; neither player may touch the ball until it has contacted the ground.

Goal

A goal is scored when the ball passes completely over the goal line, under and between the uprights and crossbar. A goal counts as 1 point.

Goal Lines

The shorter boundary lines on each end of the field where goals are situated.

Indirect Free Kick

An indirect free kick is awarded for infractions generally in violation of playing rules, such as offside, delay of the game, and ungentlemanly conduct. For a goal to be scored as a result of an indirect kick, it is necessary that another player other than the kicker touch the ball before it can be scored. The kick is awarded from the point of the infraction.

Man-to-Man Defense

A man-to-man defense is a defensive system in which each defending player is assigned a specific attacker to defend against.

Marking

Marking is the soccer term for guarding an opponent. It is generally applied in relation to man-to-man defending.

Midfielders

The modern term applied to midfield players who are responsible for linking the forwards and defenders.

Offside

A player is ruled offside if he is nearer than the ball to his opponents' goal line at the moment the ball is played, unless he is in his own half of the field; if there are two opponents nearer to the goal line than he is, one of whom may be the goalkeeper; or if the ball last touched an opponent or was played by him. There are no offsides on a corner kick, goal kick, throw-in, or drop ball.

Penalty Area

The penalty area is the area in front of the goal, 18 yards long and 44 yards wide, in which the goalkeeper may use his hands.

Penalty Kick

A penalty kick is awarded for any personal fouls or for intentional handling of the ball by a defensive player within his own penalty area. The direct penalty kick is taken from the designated spot 12 yards from the goal line in the center of the penalty area, with only the goalkeeper defending against it.

Pitch

The English term for a soccer field.

Save

The term used when referring to a goalkeeper's successful prevention of a scoring attempt.

Strikers

The modern term for forwards or attackers.

Sweeper

A defender who generally roams behind the deep backs with no specific marking assignment. The sweeper's assignment is to provide cover at the point of attack and to collect passes that penetrate the defense.

Tackling

Taking the ball away from an opponent by using the feet.

Throw-in

The throw-in is the method of returning the ball to play after the ball has gone out of bounds over the touchlines. The throw-in is awarded to the team opposing the player who last touched the ball before it went out of touch. The thrower must use a two-handed, over-the-head throw, with both feet remaining in contact with the ground at release. The throw-in is taken from the point where the ball went out over the line.

Touchlines

The touchlines are the longer side boundaries of the field.

Volley

A volley is kicking the ball while it is in flight before it touches the ground.

Zone Defense

A zone defense is a defensive system in which defenders are given specific areas to cover rather than a specific opponent to mark.

INDEX